ROGUE WOLF

DAVID ARCHER

& VINCE VOGEL

ROGUE WOLF

*A
NOAH WOLF
THRILLER*

NOAH WOLF SERIES

Code Name Camelot

Lone Wolf

In Sheep's Clothing

Hit for Hire

The Wolf's Bite

Black Sheep

Balance of Power

Time to Hunt

Red Square

Highest Order

Edge of Anarchy

Unknown Evil

Black Harvest

World Order

Caged Animal

Deep Allegiance

Pack Leader

High Treason

A Wolf Among Men

Rogue Intelligence

Alpha

Rogue Wolf

PROLOGUE

The assassin moved with a purposeful grace, a shadow flitting through the night. Wearing a marvel of modern espionage technology known as a quantum cloak, he was almost invisible to the cameras that watched over Kirtland's main gatehouse. To those watching the footage, he was nothing but a faint ripple on the screen, a trick of the light easily dismissed.

He kept low, his movements fluid and silent as he approached the gatehouse. Inside, two guards sat unaware of the phantom that was now on the verge of breaching their perimeter. The assassin's hand moved to a small, wand-like device clipped to his belt—a parametric speaker. With a subtle adjustment, he directed a sound, a faint whisper of someone calling out, to the far side of the gatehouse. The guards, intrigued and confused by the phantom sound, stepped outside to investigate, their attention drawn away from the very real threat sauntering past behind them.

Slipping under the barrier with the ease of a practiced intruder, the assassin made his way onto the site. In the security hub, guards watched their monitors, oblivious to the intruder among them. On the screens, everything seemed normal, save for the occasional, almost imperceptible distortion—a ghost moving unseen, unheard.

The offices of E & E loomed ahead for the assassin. He retrieved another tool from his belt, a compact air-launched grapple. Coming around the rear of the building, he fired it expertly up at an open third-floor window, the hook catching securely on the brickwork of the fourth floor. With practiced ease, he began to ascend, the rope barely making a sound as it uncoiled.

Reaching the window, he slipped through it into a storeroom, his movements as fluid as water. The moment his feet touched the floor, a voice crackled through the comms unit in his ear. "Okay. So you're in," a man's voice said with a hint of relief mixed with urgency. "From what I see, you haven't alerted anyone—their security system is still on amber. Now move."

The assassin nodded to himself, the message clear. Time was of the essence. With every passing second, the cloak's power dwindled, bringing him closer to visibility, to vulnerability.

At the storeroom door, the assassin paused, his hand reaching down to his belt for a rectangular device that resembled a small, rugged carry case with thick handles on both sides for grip: a Through-Wall Radar Imaging (TWRI) unit. He activated it, and the device hummed to life, sending out waves of sonar that penetrated the office walls. The screen on the device flickered, then displayed a real-time layout of the building on the other side—walls, furniture, and most importantly, the people moving around. His eyes scanned the images, looking for the right moment to strike.

When a clear path presented itself, he didn't hesitate. The assassin stepped through the door and moved swiftly along the corridors. The security cameras, blind to his quantum-shrouded presence, captured nothing but the slightest distortion in the footage—a ghostly presence that defied detection.

The assassin's steps were measured, calculated. He made his way to a particular office, its significance marked by the nameplate on the door: *Allison Peterson*.

Without a moment's delay, he burst inside.

Allison Peterson, her graying blond hair swept back to reveal the stern features of a powerful woman in her fifties, was seated behind her desk. She stood up sharply, her face a mask of surprise and confusion. "What is this?" she demanded in a voice edged with authority and disbelief.

The assassin, a silhouette of death, uttered just three words, his voice tinged with an emotion that didn't fit the scene: "I'm so sorry." Then with a practiced motion, he lifted a silenced pistol and fired. A single bullet found its mark in the center of her forehead.

As Allison Peterson, the head of E & E, slumped in her chair, a movement caught the assassin's attention —a sharp intake of breath from behind him. He spun around, the pistol ready in his hand. In the corner of the office, one side of the door through which he had entered, stood another figure.

Molly Hanson, her eyes wide behind her glasses, stared in horror at the assassin—at the eyes that peered out from behind the black ski mask. "Noah?" she whispered, disbelief etching her voice.

The assassin hesitated for just a fraction of a second, a flicker of emotion crossing his obscured face. "I'm so sorry, Molly," he said, and the room echoed with another gunshot.

As Molly crumpled to the floor, the voice in his earpiece crackled to life, cold and detached. "Good work, Mr. Wolf. Now it's time to get out of there so you can terminate the remaining names on the list."

The words were a cruel reminder of the path he had chosen, of the decisions that had led him to this moment. Noah Wolf, the ghost in the machine, moved on, the weight of his actions heavy in the fog of his mind.

CHAPTER ONE

One week earlier.

Only a week earlier, Noah's life had been so very different.

The first light of dawn filtered through the curtains of the Florida Keys mansion he shared with his family. It cast a soft glow across the room. Noah lay in the tranquil embrace of sleep, his mind adrift in the quiet sea of restfulness. Suddenly, the gentle calm was broken by a small, energetic force that bounded into the room and leaped onto the bed.

"Daddy! Mommy!" exclaimed a tiny voice, full of excitement and joy.

Noah's eyes fluttered open, meeting the bright, cheerful gaze of his four-year-old daughter, Norah. Her cheeks flushed with the enthusiasm of youth, her small hands reached out to him with uncontainable happiness. Beside Noah, Sarah stirred, her eyes opening to the sight of their daughter's radiant smile.

"Good morning, Monkey," Noah said, his voice thick with sleep but filled with warmth as he reached out, pulling Norah into a gentle embrace.

"Morning, Monkey," Sarah echoed, her arms joining the cuddle, enveloping their daughter in a loving family embrace.

For the next thirty minutes, the bed became an island of comfort and affection, the trio nestled together in a cocoon of familial love as they watched cartoons on a laptop.

As the morning progressed, the family readied themselves for a day out on the water. As they drove to the marina, the Florida sun shone brightly, its rays sparkling off the gentle waves of the Keys. They boarded their boat, a sturdy Lowe SS210 pontoon, and soon the family was joining the countless other Florida Key residents who were out on their boats today.

Noah took the helm, steering the boat with practiced ease, the salt air tangy and invigorating against his skin. Sarah sat beside him, her blond hair fluttering in the breeze. Norah, safe in her life jacket, clapped her hands in delight as the boat cut through the water, her eyes wide with wonder and excitement.

As the day wore on, they made their way to their favorite beachside restaurant, mooring at a nearby jetty. Hand in hand, the trio made their way toward Keyside Kookout Café & Grill, the scent of the sea mingling with the aroma of freshly cooked seafood and spices. They picked a table on the terrace with a view of the ocean, the sound of the waves a soothing backdrop to their meal.

"This is perfect," Sarah said, her eyes reflecting the sky.

Noah looked at his wife, then at his daughter, a sense of contentment washing over him. "It doesn't get better than this," he agreed, his hand finding Sarah's across the table, their fingers intertwining.

For a moment, the world outside their family bubble ceased to exist. There was only the sun, the sea, and the unbreakable bond of a family united in love and happiness.

But even the most serene moments aren't meant to last.

A hooded figure had just jumped the rope barrier. Noah had caught it in the corner of his eye. The figure was now darting between the tables, and before Noah could react, he had snatched an old man's wallet with the swiftness of a practiced thief. The peaceful atmosphere of the terrace erupted into chaos as the startled diners reacted to the sudden intrusion.

Noah's instincts kicked in. His senses sharpened. The tranquility of moments ago was replaced by the adrenaline rush of action. Without hesitation, he sprang from his chair. In one fluid motion, he kicked a vacant chair out from the table, sending it skidding across the tiled floor. The shot was perfect. The chair collided with the fleeing robber, tripping him as he made a beeline for his accomplice waiting on a getaway scooter at the edge of the terrace.

The thief stumbled and went down. Noah was on him in an instant, grabbing the would-be robber as he tried to scramble back to his feet. "Hey!" the kid on the moped cried out, his voice laced with panic.

The second thief dismounted the scooter, rushing to aid his partner in crime. But Noah was already one step ahead. He ripped a strand of bunting from a nearby restaurant display, moving with a precision and speed that belied his seemingly relaxed demeanor just moments before. With deft movements, he secured the first thief's hands behind his back just as the second thief lunged at him, aiming a kick at his face.

Noah's reflexes were sharp, his movements fluid.

He ducked back, evading the attack with ease. The foot whooshed past his head, missing its target.

Noah rose, facing his assailant. The thief swung wildly, haymakers that were all force and no finesse. Not the types of punches fighters throw but the type used by street thugs with no training. Noah avoided each blow with a dancer's grace, his body moving in perfect harmony with his trained instincts.

Sarah's voice broke through the commotion. "Noah, just let him go."

"I'm trying," Noah called back over his shoulder.

As the guy squared up to him, already panting, Noah issued a final warning. "I'm highly trained. You're not. If you leave now, it's just your pal in the slammer."

But the thief was beyond listening. "Let him go," he demanded for his fallen comrade.

"Just leave," Noah eased out of his mouth.

"Fuck you!" the guy cried, lunging at him.

In a heartbeat, Noah executed a precise sweep kick, toppling the second thief to the ground. In mere seconds, he had the man hogtied on the pavement next to his accomplice.

The terrace, which had erupted into chaos only moments ago, now burst into applause. Noah, the reluctant hero, tried to play it down as he returned to his family, his heart still racing from the encounter. On his way to his table, he handed the wallet back to the old man, who was overcome with gratitude. "Your meal is on me," the old man insisted, his voice shaking with emotion. "This country needs more men like you, son."

Noah, returning to his table, felt a surge of satisfaction mixed with a secret longing for the life he had left behind. The rush of action had awakened a part of him that he thought he had put to rest. But as he looked at Sarah and Norah, he was reminded of why he had chosen the peaceful existence of retirement, a life far removed from the danger and shadows of his past.

***

The drive home from the marina was serene, the Florida landscape a blur of green and blue as they made their way along the Overseas Highway. Inside the car, the atmosphere was a mix of contentment and unspoken thoughts.

Like always, Sarah broke the silence first, her voice soft but probing.

"How do you feel?" she asked Noah, glancing sideways at her husband from the passenger seat.

Noah looked momentarily puzzled. "What do you mean?"

"I mean, I know you better than anyone else, right?" Sarah persisted, her eyes searching his.

"Yes," Noah replied, his gaze returning to the road ahead.

"Well..." Sarah began, but her words were interrupted by a small voice from the backseat.

"Please, Mommy. Can you put on Dora?"

Norah's request cut through the tension, and Sarah quickly obliged, playing the show on her phone before handing it over to Norah as the four-year-old sat in her car seat.

With Dora's voice filling the back of the vehicle, Sarah returned her attention to Noah. "So I saw that look in your eye back there. There was an excitement

I haven't seen in over a year. Not since E & E got disbanded."

A faint smile flickered across Noah's usually stoic face. "Yeah. Okay. It was nice to put my skills to use again. Don't get me wrong. I love our life here. The sun, the sea, you and Norah. Our friends. It's perfect."

"But...?" Sarah prompted, sensing there was more he wanted to say.

"But I'm hardly doing what I do best out here. Taking out the garbage and mowing the lawn isn't exactly the same as bursting into a room full of armed men and neutralizing them all before they get a single shot off." Again, that slight smile, a glimpse of the man he used to be.

"Then maybe it'll be a good thing," Sarah mused as they turned onto their street.

"What will be a good thing?"

"The rumors. That the new president wants to bring E & E back. Renée and I were talking the other night about it. It's probably not true—or at least not possible."

"I don't know," Noah replied thoughtfully as they pulled into their driveway. "Looks like there might be something in it."

"Why'd you say that?" Sarah asked.

Bringing the car to a stop, Noah nodded at the front of their six-bedroom Florida Keys mansion. Sarah turned to see what he meant. Standing in the shade provided by the porch were Allison Peterson and Molly Hanson. Noah's expression shifted subtly as he stepped out of his black Dodge Durango.

"Molly," he said, greeting his oldest childhood

friend and former colleague at E & E with a polite nod. "Hello, Dragon Lady," he added with another nod aimed at Allison.

"Hello, Noah," Allison replied, her tone carrying a hint of annoyance as her gaze flickered to Molly, who was struggling to suppress a smirk.

"What brings you both here?" Noah asked, his tone casual but guarded.

"I wanted to do this in person," Allison began.

"Do what in person?" Noah's question hung in the air.

Before Allison could respond, Norah's excited voice burst out, cutting through the tension. "Aunt Ali! Aunt Molly!" She ran toward them, arms open wide. Allison scooped her up, holding her close.

"My, you've grown," she remarked.

"Yes. I'm forty-three and a half inches tall now," Norah declared proudly, having memorized every measurement since her mother began measuring her a year and half ago.

"My, that is big," Allison replied with a smile.

Sarah approached the group, her expression one of polite neutrality. "Allison. Molly."

The women exchanged nods. "Sarah."

"Can we do this inside?" Allison suggested, her tone indicating that the matter at hand was both serious and urgent.

A moment later, they were all inside the lavish mansion. The shadowy atmosphere was in stark contrast to the bright Florida sun outside. The sitting room, adorned with plush furnishings and a few Banksy prints, exuded an air of comfort and luxury.

They all settled in, with Norah perched contentedly on Allison's lap.

The Dragon Lady, a figure renowned and feared in espionage circles across the globe, made a strange picture sitting there with the little girl. It was an image akin to a ferocious lioness gently cradling a kitten.

"I take it you've both heard the rumors?" Allison said, her gaze shifting from Norah to Noah and Sarah, who sat opposite.

"Yes. We have," Sarah answered, her voice a mix of caution and curiosity.

Allison shifted slightly, her expression becoming more businesslike. "Well, it's true. I've spent the last week getting Kirtland back up and running."

The statement hung in the air, heavy with unspoken implications. The room fell silent, the only sound the faint rustling of Norah shifting in Allison's lap.

"I need my best assassin," Allison continued, her tone resolute. "E & E isn't E & E without Noah Wolf."

The words reverberated in the room, a clear and direct call to arms. It was a reminder of a past filled with danger, intrigue, and the weight of responsibility. Noah's face remained impassive, but his eyes betrayed a flicker of the old fire, a spark reignited by the prospect of returning to the life he knew so well.

But then his eyes dropped from the face of Allison, and he looked at his daughter.

"No, I can't," he said.

Both Allison and Molly looked disappointed. It was obvious they'd put a lot of faith into coming out here.

"I'm not asking you for an answer right now,"

Allison stated.

"But you're getting one anyway," Noah countered.

"It's a no. All those years spent living in the shadows, constantly looking over my shoulder, never knowing who to trust. It does something to a guy's mind, you know? When every conversation could be a trap, every ally a potential enemy, it's hard to find solid ground. And now, I have more than just myself to consider. I have a daughter, a little girl who waits for me to come through that door every evening, whose world revolves around our small, simple routines. She relies on me, not just for care, but for stability, for a sense of safety that I never had. How can I plunge back into that world, knowing it could mean not being there for her? The answer has to be no."

The two, Allison and Noah, Dragon and Wolf, stared at each other, their steel-eyed gazes locked.

"Like I said," Allison told him, "think on it. This is something for all of you to discuss."

The words hung in the air like a challenge, a turning point that beckoned Noah back to a world he had left but perhaps never truly escaped.

***

Later that evening, the warm glow of the setting sun cast a serene ambiance over the quaint outdoor restaurant. Noah and Sarah were seated at a rustic table with Marco and Renée, their fellow retiree assassins and long-time friends. The air was filled with the sounds of clinking glasses and subdued conversations from nearby tables.

Marco, always the more outspoken of the two, leaned forward, his curiosity evident. "So tell us about

Allison and Molly's visit. What did they want?"

Sarah exchanged a glance with Noah before replying, "They came to talk about reviving E & E. Apparently, the new president Jackson T. Whitmore is behind it."

Renée chimed in, "And what did you say?"

"We told them we'd think about it," Noah said, his voice even but with a hint of the internal conflict he felt.

Marco raised his eyebrows, surprised. "Think about it? Man, I thought you'd jump at the chance to get back into action."

Noah took a sip of his drink, considering his words. "It's not that simple anymore. We have Norah, our life here… it's a lot to consider."

Renée nodded in understanding. "It's a big decision. Life has changed for all of us."

As they ate, the conversation drifted to other topics, but the undercurrent of the earlier discussion lingered. Every now and then, their eyes would meet, an unspoken understanding passing between the four. They were a team, bound by shared experiences and a history that was hard to leave behind.

With the evening wearing on, the conversation turned to a loosely related topic. "You know, Noah stopped a robbery earlier today," Sarah revealed, her eyes on Noah as she spoke.

The others looked at Noah with a mix of surprise and curiosity.

"Do tell," Renée said, the warmth of the wine evident in her tone.

As Noah relayed the story, glossing over the details but capturing the essence of the action, Marco's interest was piqued. "Did you feel a rush?" he asked, his eyes locked on Noah's.

Noah paused, then nodded. "Yeah, I guess I did," he admitted, a trace of the old adrenaline-fueled energy surfacing in his voice.

The revelation seemed to open a door to further confessions, because it was at that moment that Marco and Renée exchanged a glance and her hand found his under the table, a gesture of unity and support.

Lifting their hands out from the table, Marco brought hers to his lips in a tender kiss. Then, turning back to Noah and Sarah, the couple shared their own news. "Allison visited us as well," Marco began, his voice steady.

"And did you take the deal?" Sarah asked, her eyes moving between the two.

With the ocean breeze gently stirring the air, Marco and Renée faced their friends, a mix of resolve and nostalgia in their expressions. "We're moving back into our old place in Kirtland tomorrow," Renée announced, her voice holding a note of finality.

The revelation hung in the air, a testament to the ever-present pull of their past lives. As they sat there, the four of them bonded by years of shared experiences, the decision to return to E & E seemed not just about duty, but also about returning to a part of themselves that they had never truly left behind.

***

That night, after the lively dinner and the weighty conversations, the quiet of their home felt like a sanctuary. Noah, ever the doting father, sat by Norah's bedside, reading her favorite story, *Charlotte's Web*, with gentle enthusiasm. Norah's eyes, filled with wonder and sleepiness, followed each word until they slowly drifted shut. With a soft kiss on her forehead, Noah whispered good night and tiptoed out of her room, leaving the door ajar with a sliver of light from the hallway casting a comforting glow.

In the master bedroom, the world outside seemed to fade away. Noah slipped into bed, spooning Sarah in the comforting silence of their room. The darkness enveloped them, a blanket of intimacy and unspoken thoughts cradling them.

It was Sarah who broke the silence, her voice soft but certain. "We're going back to Kirtland, aren't we?"

Noah let out a long, contemplative sigh. The decision, though unspoken until now, hung heavily in the air. "Yeah," he finally replied, his voice tinged with a mix of resignation and resolve. "We're going back to Kirtland."

In the darkness, their shared understanding was a tangible thing. They were stepping back into a world they had left behind, a world of danger and excitement but also of purpose. As they lay there, wrapped in each other's arms, the quiet of the night seemed to hold their decision. It certainly was a significant turning point in their lives. Yet in that moment, there was also a sense of coming home, of returning to a part of themselves that had been waiting, silently, to be awakened once again.

***

The tranquility of the Florida Keys neighborhood, usually undisturbed at this hour, was subtly and unknowingly breached. Parked at the end of the street, blending seamlessly into the night, sat a nondescript black van. To any casual observer, it was just another vehicle, perhaps belonging to a resident working late or a visitor. But this van was far from ordinary.

Inside, the dim glow of electronic equipment illuminated the interior, casting eerie shadows on the face of the man seated within. He wore headphones, his expression one of intense concentration as he listened to the conversation unfolding in Noah and Sarah's bedroom. Every word, every pause, every sigh was captured, analyzed, and stored away in his memory.

The man was more than just an eavesdropper; he was a predator waiting in the shadows. As he listened to the couple discussing their imminent return to Kirtland, a cold smile played on his lips.

Once the conversation ended and the room fell silent, the man removed his headphones. He reached for a secure phone, its screen casting a blue light on his focused face. With a few deft taps, he dialed a number, waiting for the call to connect.

"I have good news, Henrik." He spoke quietly but with an edge of triumph in his voice. "They've agreed to come back. Looks like the next phase is a go."

His words were met with a brief pause on the other end, then a response, equally sinister and expectant. "Good. I'll begin getting everything in order."

The plan, it seemed, was larger than just a simple eavesdrop; it was a cog in a much bigger machine, one that was now set into motion with Noah and Sarah's decision.

As the man in the van ended the call, he sat back in his seat, a shadowy figure in a world of covert schemes and hidden agendas. The quiet street outside belied the dark undercurrents now in play, and as the night deepened, so too did the intrigue surrounding Noah and Sarah's impending return to Kirtland.

CHAPTER TWO

In the enclosed valleys of the Rocky Mountains, tucked away from the prying eyes of the world, lay Kirtland. This clandestine haven, sprawling over thirty-six meticulously planned city blocks, was the operational heart of E & E, an organization shrouded in as much mystery as the location itself.

Kirtland, with its six-block by six-block grid, resembled a miniature city, self-contained and self-sufficient, designed to cater to every need of its residents. The gray January skyline was punctuated by imposing office buildings, the nerve centers of E & E's covert operations. Banks stood at strategic points, facilitating the financial transactions necessary for the organization's shadowy dealings. Residential areas contained neatly lined houses and apartment buildings, offering solace and a semblance of normal life to those who lived on the edge of espionage.

The large hotel in Kirtland served as a temporary abode for visiting agents and dignitaries, a reminder of the organization's far-reaching influence. The bustling shopping center, theaters, and a variety of restaurants added a layer of normalcy, masking the extraordinary nature of the town's inhabitants and their work. The comprehensive school complex ensured that education and normalcy prevailed for the children of those who led double lives.

At the heart of this concealed community stood an advanced hospital, a symbol of Kirtland's readiness for any eventuality, be it mundane medical needs or emergency situations arising from their covert operations.

Two days after their pivotal meeting with Allison, Noah, Sarah, and their daughter Norah arrived at Kirtland. The journey, shrouded in the same secrecy as their lives, brought them to the gates of this hidden bastion. As their car navigated through the snow-covered streets, the familiar yet always awe-inspiring sight of Kirtland unfolded before them.

At the edge of town, a winding road took them away from the picturesque buildings and into the surrounding hillsides, their journey concluding at a farmhouse that sat on a bank of the vast Temple Lake. This idyllic retreat, nestled on sixty acres of lush land with an expansive eight hundred feet of lakeshore, stood as a testament to their life of contrasts—serene yet always on the brink of action.

As they stepped out of the Durango, the chill mountain air greeted them, a distinct contrast to the warm tropical air of the Florida Keys they'd left behind.

The farmhouse was a haven of tranquility. Its four bedrooms echoed with the silent stories of their past. The heart of the home was the kitchen, where the couple had once shared meals and conversations with their friends and colleagues, now waiting to be revived with warmth and laughter. The living room with its large windows offered panoramic views of the serene Temple Lake, inviting the calmness of nature into the internal spaces.

Outside, the property extended to a private dock and a boat, symbols of leisurely days spent on the water. The two-car attached garage had once housed more than just vehicles. It had concealed tools and gear essential for their clandestine operations. It looked like it would again.

Scattered across the property were other structures, each with its unique purpose. The barn, a large, weathered building, held secrets of its own. A couple of workshops stood close to it, the silent witnesses of countless covert preparations and strategizing. A mobile home, seemingly innocuous, had provided a discreet hideout on more than one occasion.

As they entered, the family began the process of uncovering and rediscovering their former life. Norah, innocent and carefree, danced around the rooms, her laughter filling the space as Sarah suggested they should get her a dog, a thought that brought a smile to both parents.

Removing sheets from the furniture, Noah and Sarah uncovered not just objects but memories. Each item, each mark in the house, spoke of their past missions. A bullet lodged in the wall in the living room was a stark reminder of a close call. A hidden compartment in the barn, once used for secure storage of critical equipment, now lay open, a relic of their previous life.

In the barn, as Norah innocently played with pine cones, placing them in the once-secret compartment, Noah's phone buzzed, breaking the tranquility. He retrieved it from his pocket, his expression shifting as he read the message.

"Already?" Sarah's voice carried a mix of surprise and resignation.

It was a summons from Allison, a call back to duty. The message was clear: Their time of settling in was over. Duty beckoned, and with it, the return to a life of intrigue and danger. Noah and Sarah exchanged a glance, an unspoken understanding passing between them. The tranquility of the farmhouse was but a brief interlude; the real story was about to begin.

***

Minutes later, Noah's '69 Dodge Charger growled to a halt outside the E & E offices, its engine echoing against the buildings of Kirtland. As Noah stepped out, his eyes were caught by the reflection of the morning sun dancing off the car's immaculate finish.

Raising a hand to shield his gaze, he spotted a familiar face that brought a smile to his own. Across the way, leaning casually against the grill of his pickup, was Ralph, the fourth member of their tight-knit group, Camelot.

"Hey, boss." Ralph greeted him with a grin as Noah approached.

Noah returned the smile. "Ralph," he said, and the two men shared a firm, brotherly hug—testament to a bond forged over countless missions.

As they broke apart, Marco and Renée arrived, adding to the reunion. The four of them, each a crucial part of Camelot, stood together, a unit reunited.

"How's the farmhouse treating you?" Ralph asked, looking at Noah with a hint of nostalgia.

"Feels like we never left," Noah replied, a touch of

sentiment in his voice. "Norah's already claiming every corner as her playground."

"And Sarah?" Renée inquired.

"She's good, thinking of getting Norah a dog," Noah answered, a hint of amusement in his tone.

"That'll make it a real home," Marco added, smiling.

The conversation continued as they walked toward the E & E offices, reminiscing and catching up, the ease and familiarity among them as good as ever. As they entered the building, little did the foursome know that their futures already hung in the balance.

A minute later, in the stark, windowless briefing room of E & E HQ, the air was already growing thick with tension. Allison Peterson, the formidable leader known as the Dragon Lady, stood at the head of the table. At fifty, her graying blond hair was a testament to her experience, yet her posture remained as commanding as ever, embodying the strength and grace of a lioness. Her piercing gaze methodically swept over each member of Camelot as they settled in.

Beside her, Molly, her super-smart assistant, stood with an air of solemnity. Her round glasses framed a pair of thoughtful eyes, and her curly brown hair was neatly arranged. Despite her youth, Molly's presence complemented Allison's, a perfect balance of wisdom and innovation.

Allison broke the silence first. "You'll recall, Noah, six years ago, you encountered a rather effective international assassin in England by the name of..."

"Adrian," Noah cut in sharply, his voice tinged with barely suppressed rage. "The bastard killed Moose Conway before I put a bullet through his head."

"Yes, indeed," Allison said. "But I'm afraid American

intelligence has recently received information that is contrary to this."

A frown creased Noah's brow, confusion clouding his features. As for the other members of Team Camelot, they all began looking at each other.

"Molly will explain," Allison said, gesturing toward her.

The lights dimmed, casting shadows across the room as a projector screen flickered to life behind Molly. Images of various men, each bearing a striking resemblance to one another, began to cycle through on the screen: stills from CCTV footage, covert photographs, all pointing to a deeper mystery.

As the images continued to cycle, the similarities between each man became increasingly evident. All were white, with their nondescript appearances almost blending into one. Their hair, though varying slightly in hue, shared a uniformly washed-out palette, ranging from dull browns to muted blonds. These were no ordinary men; they were replicants, sculpted by facial reconstruction surgery to embody anonymity. Through various surgeries, their chins had been deliberately rounded, their cheekbones softened, all in an effort to strip away any distinctive features. It was as if they were molded to be forgotten, their faces a blank canvas, leaving no trace or memory in the minds of those who glimpsed them—perfect for the assassin who wants to get away after a kill. This eerie uniformity cast a chilling air over the room as the team absorbed the implications of what they were seeing.

"British intelligence," Molly began, her voice steady, "had long suspected that Adrian was not just one man, but a network of operatives."

"But someone has to be at the head of it," Noah interjected. "Every organization needs a leader."

"And you're not wrong," Allison said. "We believe there's a single mastermind behind the collective. His name is Henrik Schultz."

The images on the screen stopped at the picture of a man of indeterminate age, his features meticulously average, almost deliberately forgettable. His hair was a nondescript shade of brown, cut in a simple, unremarkable style. His eyes, the only striking feature, carried a depth and sharpness that contrasted with his otherwise plain appearance. He was dressed in a plain dark jacket and a simple shirt. He would blend seamlessly into any crowd. The background of the picture was blurred, offering no clues about his location. His posture was relaxed yet alert, suggesting a man who is comfortable in shadows and adept at melting away into them. The overall impression was of someone who is there and yet not there, a master of blending in, leaving no lasting impression except for those who know exactly what to look for.

"Henrik Schultz," Molly began, "known in covert circles as 'Adrian,' has carved out a notorious legacy as a brilliant assassin. His career, shrouded in shadows, began in the dense forests of Eastern Europe, where he honed his skills hunting elusive targets for local governments. One of his most impressive kills was the dismantling of an underground syndicate in Tbilisi, where he single-handedly eliminated the top echelons of the organization under the cover of a single night. His ability to vanish without a trace after striking made him a legend. Coming west to Paris, he orchestrated a complex assassination of a high-profile arms dealer at a crowded gala, leaving no evidence behind. Schultz's mastery in evading law enforcement and rival factions is legendary. He slipped through Interpol's net during a coordinated international operation in Amsterdam, leaving local authorities embarrassed. With each calculated move, Henrik Schultz and Adrian solidified their status as phantom figures, feared and respected in both espionage and criminal warfare."

The next images were a series of photos that were all too familiar to Noah. The first depicted the outside of St. Paul's Cathedral in the immediate aftermath of Adrian's foiled assassination attempt on Charles III (then the Prince of Wales). The iconic dome loomed large against a gray London sky, police vehicles and ambulances clustered around its entrance.

The next image captured a scene of abrupt disarray inside the grand nave of St. Paul's Cathedral. Scattered chairs and a dropped ceremonial program on the polished stone floor bore silent witness to the sudden panic that had ensued. In the background, the magnificent altar stood unscathed, a stark contrast to the chaos in the foreground.

Another chilling photo revealed the aftermath of the foiled plot: the would-be assassin lying motionless on the cathedral floor, blood pooling from his head and spreading across the three centuries old stone floor. The towering columns and soaring ceiling of the cathedral enveloped the scene, adding a sense of solemnity and gravitas.

"Six years ago," Molly went on, "E & E first encountered Schultz and Adrian. It ended with a member of Camelot dying. This time we need to be careful that we don't lose another."

"So that's why we're here?" Marco said, leaning forward in his chair. "To take another crack at Adrian?"

"That's exactly what you're here for," Allison replied.

"But this time," Noah added, "we need to put the bullet through Schultz's head. Not one of his people."

"That's right," Allison said with a firmness to her voice, her steely eyes fixed to the similarly steely look in Noah's. "This time you're going to cut the head off the beast and bring an end to Adrian. And Molly's about to tell you how you're going to start."

The images on the screen cycled through, pausing on a particular photo. It was a blurry CCTV still—a man making his way along a busy courtyard with a domed building in the background.

"This is the last confirmed photo of a known member of Adrian," Molly declared.

Marco, squinting at the image, recognized the backdrop. "That's Capitol Hill, Washington, D.C."

"That's right," Molly added, confirming his observation.

"When was it taken?" Ralph asked.

"Two days ago," Allison answered.

A sense of urgency gripped Noah. "What's he doing there?"

"That's what we need Team Camelot to find out," Allison said with her usual firmness. "Molly?"

Molly continued with the briefing. "We've received intelligence that he's due to meet with a known arms dealer in Chicago in two days. The dealer is a CIA informant."

She scrolled through the images. The photograph

she stopped on showed a man in his late forties, exuding a blend of sophistication and understated menace. He had a weathered complexion, indicative of a life spent in high-stress environments, and his eyes were alert and calculating, probably missing nothing. His hair was cut short, neat, with hints of gray at the temples suggesting maturity and experience.

"This is James Callahan," Molly told Team Camelot. "Beginning his career as an arms dealer in the underbelly of the Eastern European markets, Callahan quickly made a name for himself with his savvy business acumen and ruthless efficiency. His operations soon caught the eye of the CIA, leading to a complex relationship as both an informant and an operative. He has provided critical intelligence on the flow of weapons and terrorist activities while maintaining his cover."

"And what?" Ralph put to her. "He's meeting up with Schultz?"

"We believe so."

Renée, deep in thought, raised a valid point. "What if it's not Schultz at this meeting? It wasn't him in London."

Allison acknowledged her concern. "Whether it's Schultz or another Adrian operative, it will lead us closer to their operations. I need him followed. Not killed. Well, not for now, at least."

Noah nodded in agreement. "Whoever it is, it's a step toward uncovering their agenda."

Allison concluded, "Our mission in Chicago isn't just about intercepting a meeting. It's about getting closer to Schultz and unraveling his network. He's the key to understanding what they're planning on

American soil. Whatever happens in Chicago is a step closer."

The briefing ended with the team exchanging looks of determination, each member acutely aware of the complexity and danger that lay ahead.

***

The sun was barely halfway across the sky when Noah and his team made their way toward the R&D buildings. The air was crisp, and the morning light cast long shadows across the pavement. As they approached, a figure emerged from the main entrance, his silhouette sharp against the brightening sky.

This was Wally Lawson, the head of Research and Development (R&D) at E & E. Wally was a man whose enthusiasm was as large as his stature. With a thick beard peppered with gray and wearing glasses that perpetually seemed on the verge of slipping down his nose, he exuded a mix of academic brilliance and childlike wonder. His attire was casual—a stark contrast to the high-tech environment he oversaw. Today, he wore a faded T-shirt featuring a Kiss logo and jeans that had seen better days.

As Noah and the team drew closer, Wally's eyes lit up, especially upon seeing Noah. Without hesitation, he bounded forward and enveloped him in a bear hug. "Noah! It's so great to see you back!" he exclaimed, his voice booming with genuine affection.

"You too, Wally," Noah managed to say, his words slightly muffled in the embrace.

Wally released Noah and turned to greet the rest of Team Camelot with equal warmth, though he refrained from any more surprise hugs. "Come on in, I've got some incredible stuff to show you!" he said with barely hidden excitement.

He led the team through the large glass doors of the main R&D building. Inside, the contrast was striking. The high-ceilinged lobby was sleek and modern, with interactive displays lining the walls and a holographic E & E logo hovering in the center. The atmosphere was the blend of a high-tech lab and a place where the impossible seemed routine.

Wally guided them down a hallway lined with doors leading to various development rooms, each one a gateway to another marvel of technological advancement. Noah and his team followed, their steps echoing lightly on the polished floor, each aware that they were stepping into a world where the boundaries of what was possible were constantly being pushed.

As they ventured deeper into the lab, a familiar voice filled the space. "Good morning, Professor Lawson. Noah. Marco. Sarah. Renée," the female announced in her distinctly digital tone.

"Esmeralda," Noah acknowledged.

Wally's face softened with nostalgia. "After the order to decommission Stanley and Esmeralda, I couldn't let go of everything. Using her AI, I've put her in charge of R&D's systems. Esmeralda here, she's now the soul of this place," he said, gesturing around the high-tech lab.

The team gathered around a large table where Wally had laid out three cloth-covered items. With a flourish, he unveiled the first—a sleek, shimmering fabric that had been made into a loose-fitting hoodie.

"This, my friends, is a quantum cloak," Wally began, his voice tinged with pride as he spoke out of a half-smirk. "We've been working on it for years. It makes you completely invisible to digital eyes— cameras, infrared, heat cameras, facial recognition, you name it. Here, Noah, try it on."

Noah draped the cloak over his shoulders.

"Here, look," Wally said to the rest of the team, holding the screen of an iPad up to them. "It's the security footage from this lab," he told them, nodding upward to a camera.

To the team's amazement, Noah was nowhere to be seen on the footage. Only a slight distortion marked where he stood.

"The cloak works by bending digital wavelengths around you," Wally explained. "It's crafted from advanced metamaterials, capable of manipulating electromagnetic waves. The core of this cloak houses a miniaturized quantum computer, which constantly adjusts the fabric's properties in real-time, maintaining invisibility. However, remember, it's still in its beta form. The power supply is limited, lasting only for an hour tops. Also, extreme environmental conditions like heavy rain or sub-zero temperatures can disrupt the metamaterial structure, affecting its performance."

While Noah removed the cloak and placed it back on the table, Wally moved to the second item, a sleek, slim-bodied device resembling a high-tech wand or a miniature version of an avant-garde soundbar. "This is our latest parametric speaker. Watch this." Wally pointed the device toward the team and began whispering into it. Suddenly, his voice was coming from the opposite corner of the room, making the whole team turn around, expecting to see another Wally standing there.

"It sounds like you're right there behind us!" Renée stated with wide-eyed fascination.

"Exactly!" Wally beamed. "This speaker uses ultrasonic transduction to project sound in a highly focused beam. It's like an audio laser, directing sound to a precise location, creating the illusion that it's emanating from somewhere else. The sound waves are modulated in such a way that they only become audible when they converge at the targeted point. This technology is ideal for creating auditory diversions or disorienting targets without alerting others nearby."

Lastly, Wally presented a compact, handheld device with a screen. "This beauty is the TWRI—Through-Wall Radar Imaging. Essentially, it lets you see through walls. Let me show you." Placing the device against the nearest wall of the lab, he activated it. The monitor in its center displayed a live feed of the neighboring labs, with the ghostly figures of technicians and engineers moving around within the walls.

"As you can see," Wally said, "it can scan a large area—around a hundred meters square, utilizing ultra-wideband radio waves to penetrate through different materials. This technology provides detailed images and movement patterns of objects and people behind barriers, offering an invaluable advantage in surveillance and reconnaissance. It means you can map out entire building layouts and monitor activities from a single vantage point without physical intrusion."

Wally demonstrated this, taking them on an X-ray tour of R&D. As they observed, however, an unexpected scene unfolded on the screen. Coming across a storage cupboard somewhere within the facility, they discovered two lab workers engaged in a clandestine embrace. Wally's eyebrows shot up. "Oh my. I never expected to catch that on our demo."

Marco chuckled. "Looks like they're the ones giving the demo, Wally."

The team erupted into laughter. As they left the lab, passing the now-flustered couple emerging from the cupboard, their smiles were a mix of amusement and the focused determination of seasoned operatives gearing up for what lay ahead.

**

In the dimly lit operations room, Team Camelot gathered around a table, their faces illuminated by the glow of a 3D holographic model of downtown Chicago. The air was tense with concentration as Noah began outlining their strategy for the upcoming mission.

"All right, let's break this down," Noah said, his gaze unwavering from the glare of the hologram. "Our target, Adrian, is cautious. The informant, James Callahan, states that he only ever gives the location of the meeting twenty minutes before the drop."

Marco furrowed his brow in concern. "So how are we going to know where to be?"

Noah responded, "Adrian always gives our man a general area of where he'd like to meet. This time, he's picked the Loop in Chicago."

"But the Loop's huge," Ralph cut in, his voice laced with skepticism.

Locking eyes with Ralph, Noah's voice was firm. "Callahan has met Adrian seven times. Three in Chicago. Always the same pattern: a multi-story parking garage. We've got five potential hotspots in the

Loop, each marked here in red."

On cue, the hologram zoomed in, revealing five red-highlighted structures—parking garages. The team leaned forward, their eyes scanning the intricate model.

Noah continued, his finger tracing a laser pointer across the hologram. "As you can see, each garage is roughly the same—three garages with five levels, one with four, another with six. Notice the central ramps, elevator shafts, ticket barriers, and pay stations." With each feature he mentioned, a corresponding part on the model flickered brightly under the laser's touch. "Operated by the same firm, their designs are almost carbon copies. It gives us the tactical edge—knowing the layout of the meeting, we can anticipate and plan our moves, tracking Adrian right from his entry point."

Renée leaned in, her voice tinged with curiosity. "What about listening in?"

Noah shook his head slightly. "Intel states that Adrian won't meet the informant until he's been observed for days by one of their watchers. That rules out getting too close, and it's precisely why we can't risk Callahan wearing a wire."

Ralph's brow furrowed in thought. "So how do we tap into their conversation without being noticed?"

Noah's finger hovered over the hologram, pinpointing a shimmering figure on the third level. "That's where I come in. I'll be in the garage with them, nearby, out of sight. And I'll be using a parabolic microphone that's sensitive enough to pick up their conversation from a distance."

As Renée studied the hologram, a dubious expression took hold of her features. Her hands pressed firmly on the table, she countered, "But according to

Molly's intel report, Adrian's got a hacker team. They've developed malware that hijacks security cameras, giving Adrian full surveillance control. It means he'll be watching every corner."

Noah's eyebrows arched in a mix of challenge and amusement. "Did you forget already about our latest tech demo at R&D?"

A flicker of realization dawned in Renée's eyes. "The quantum cloak, you mean?"

"Exactly," Noah affirmed with a confident nod. "With the quantum cloak, I'll blend seamlessly into the background of the footage. To Adrian's hijacked cameras, I'll be invisible."

Marco, leaning against the wall with his arms crossed, voiced his skepticism. "This feels too easy. Like a setup."

Noah nodded, understanding the concern. "If it's a game he's playing, we'll play along. We're going to use this opportunity to get closer to him, no matter what."

Marco's expression softened into a wry smile. "Just remember, this could backfire."

Noah chuckled. "When does anything in our line of work ever go exactly as planned?"

Their attention returned to the glowing hologram. It now displayed their strategic positions around the five parking garages. Marco and Renée would be stationed inside an inconspicuous SUV, listening into anything that Noah's parabolic microphone picked up, as well as to the stingray device rigged up to the van that would be monitoring local cellphone activity, just in case other Adrian operatives were in the area. Marco and Renée's primary task was surveillance, but they had a secondary, critical role. Whichever garage Adrian selected, they would discreetly position their SUV near the exit, timing their arrival to shadow the target. Then, once he left, the delicate dance of tailing their quarry would begin.

Meanwhile, Ralph's role was watchman. The surrounding high-rises offered perfect vantage points for observation—or a sniper's nest, depending on how the meeting went. Poised on his sleek black Ducati, he would be ready to race to the chosen building as soon as meeting's location was revealed. Once there, he'd ride the elevator to the roof, settling behind his formidable Barrett M82, watching, eyes sharp and patient.

As for the challenge of receiving the meeting location a mere twenty minutes in advance, the team would be hovering at a strategic midpoint of the potential sites—the intersection of Madison and State Streets, the heart of the Loop. From there, they would be able to race to their positions in less than twenty minutes.

Once the general logistics had been worked out, the conversation shifted to the intricacies of the meeting itself. Renée chimed in, "The informant has been coached to draw information out of Adrian."

Noah pointed toward a street-level view on the hologram. "We're using real remote mines for the drop. Adrian's the type to check, and he'll know if they're fakes. We need him to leave the meet confident and unsuspecting. As he exits, that's our cue." He zoomed in on the exit route. "Marco and Renée will initiate the tail from the SUV, and Ralph and I will join the pursuit on our Ducatis. Any concerns?"

The team exchanged glances, a silent consensus forming. Only Marco voiced a lingering doubt. "It still has the stench of a sting operation," he remarked cautiously.

"And, like I said," Noah stated, "it's still another breadcrumb. Look, we can be damn sure that whichever garage the meet is at, Adrian has staked it out thoroughly. If he feels like he's being watched, he'll have an escape route, and he may have others in the vicinity. So we need to be eagle sharp on this one, Camelot."

The others didn't say anything. Instead, they all studied the model, each member mentally rehearsing their roles. The plan was set, the contingencies considered. Team Camelot was ready. As they dispersed from the operations room, there was a sense of quiet resolve. The mission was risky, but they were a team tempered by experience and united by trust.

***

The night had deepened by the time Noah's Charger rolled up the gravel driveway of the farmhouse and parked beside the Durango. He switched off the engine, savoring the moment of silence before stepping out into the crisp night air. The warm glow from the windows beckoned him home.

Inside, he found his wife in the living room, softly lit by a single lamp. She was with Diana, Ralph's girlfriend.

Diana had become like family over the years, especially after she had risked her life to save Norah while the little girl was still only a baby. The two women were sitting on the couch, and it looked like Sarah had been comforting her. Diana's eyes were red-rimmed and puffy, as if she'd been crying.

"Hey, Diana," Noah greeted softly, placing his keys

on the hall table. "Ralph should be home by now. You okay?"

Diana managed a weak smile. "Yeah, I'm fine. Just tired, you know?" But her voice betrayed her, lacking its usual cheer.

Noah gave a comforting nod, watching as Diana gathered her things and Sarah then saw her out. "Take care, okay?"

Once Diana had left, Noah turned to Sarah, a concerned look on her face as she returned to the living room. "What's going on with her?" he asked quietly.

Sarah sighed, leaning against the wall. "Diana and Ralph have been fighting. She didn't go into details, but it's upset her."

Noah frowned slightly, concern etching his features. He hoped Ralph would sort things out soon. It made missions run more smoothly if there were no domestic issues. Shaking off the concern, he made his way upstairs to Norah's room.

Norah was sitting up in bed, having waited up for this moment. Her small face lit up as Noah entered. "Daddy!" she exclaimed, her voice filled with sleepiness and joy.

Noah smiled, sitting on the edge of her bed and gently kissing her forehead. "Hey, sweetie. You waited up for me?"

Norah nodded, her eyes wide and curious. "Mommy says you're going away. For how long?"

He sighed softly, brushing a strand of hair from her face. "Not too long, sweetie. I'll be back before you know it."

With that, he tucked her in, watching her eyelids

flutter shut. He stayed a moment longer, the soft sound of her breathing a comforting rhythm in the quiet room. Watching her, his heart grew heavy with the thought of leaving. With one last glance at his sleeping daughter, he quietly left the room, the weight of the coming mission settling on his shoulders.

CHAPTER THREE

Adrian had called almost twenty minutes ago. Callahan was right—the meet was to take place at one of the garages. The one the assassin chose wasn't far from the starting point, and within seven minutes, Team Camelot was in position.

The Windy City was living up to its reputation. Gusts howled through the concrete skeleton of the garage, adding an eerie undertone to the night. At times, the wind was so strong it interfered with the parabolic microphone, creating a crackling static in their earpieces that sent spikes of tension through the team.

Before the meeting, they'd used the TWRI unit to meticulously map out the location. They identified every car and every potential hiding spot, ensuring they left nothing to chance.

Noah, invisible under the quantum cloak, positioned himself close to the expected meeting spot. His heart beat in a steady rhythm, a contrast to the chaos of the wind. He was a shadow within shadows, watching and waiting.

"How's the cloak working?" he whispered into his comms, his voice barely rising above the howling air flow.

Inside a blacked-out Dodge Durango, Marco was monitoring the grainy CCTV feed of the garage—after all, Adrian wasn't the only one who could hack into live camera feeds. He squinted at the screens, scanning for any sign of Noah. "You're on the third level, right?" he asked, his voice crackling through the static.

"Yes. Beneath camera six," Noah confirmed, his eyes never leaving the meeting spot.

Marco checked the camera feed, focusing on the area beneath camera six. There was nothing but a faint trace of static, a slight distortion that could easily be missed. "Well, if Adrian is watching like we are, he won't see you," he said, a hint of admiration in his voice.

"Good," Noah replied, his voice calm but alert. He settled into his position, ready to observe the meeting. The wind continued its relentless assault, adding an unpredictable element to the night's operation. But inside Noah, a sense of readiness prevailed, honed by years of training and experience. This was what he did best, and he was in his element.

Then Ralph's voice broke through the static. "Looks like we got company."

The first to arrive was the informant, James Callahan, his panel van creeping into the site like a prowling beast. Noah watched from his vantage point, senses heightened.

"That's our guy," Marco confirmed from the Durango.

Just like he'd been told to do, Callahan took the third floor, parking not far from where Noah hid.

For the next few minutes, everyone waited, the tension mounting, until a BMW M8, sleek and predatory, wound its way up to the third floor, pulling up beside the informant's van.

"Looks like this is him," Renée murmured from beside her husband.

Using the TWRI unit, the team tracked every movement within the garage. Noah, from his hidden spot, observed the initial interactions.

The door of Adrian's BMW opened, and a man in sunglasses and a fedora stepped out, his movements confident, almost theatrical.

Inside the Durango, Renée and Marco strained to get a facial ID through the cameras. "I can't get an ID on the face," Renée whispered, frustration evident in her voice.

The man, presumed to be Adrian, met the informant. They exchanged a brief, firm handshake before moving to the back of the van. The doors swung open, revealing a large duffle bag which Callahan dragged to the edge.

Adrian didn't waste any time. He pushed the informant aside and began inspecting the contents. Each item he pulled out was examined with meticulous attention. "And they're magnetic?" he asked, his voice tinged with interest.

"Completely," Callahan responded.

Adrian tested one of the devices, throwing it against the side of the van. The loud clang echoed through the comms, making Ralph, Marco, and Renée wince simultaneously.

"But are they primed?" Adrian's voice was curious yet commanding.

He unscrewed the top of another device, inspecting its interior. "Firing pin's there. And the rest, too," he muttered, almost to himself.

"Be careful with those," Callahan said in a voice edged with nervousness.

Adrian's next question was about the trigger, his hand pulling out a handheld device from the duffle bag. His interest seemed piqued as Callahan explained the dual functionality of the trigger.

"So what do you need this for, anyway?" the informant asked after the explanation, trying to keep the conversation light.

Adrian's response was chilling. "Rats," he hissed, a wide and unnerving grin opening up on his face as he fixed Callahan with his cold eyes. "Great. Big. Rats."

The informant tried to laugh it off. "Funny. Yeah. But really. That's a lot of firepower. Must be something big."

The grin never leaving his face, Adrian said, "It never bothered you before, James. What I do with the things you sell me. Why now?"

Callahan held his hands up. "Okay. Sorry. I'll keep my nose out."

"Yes. Do." Adrian straightened up, placing a hand into his coat. "Now to your payment." But instead of money, he pulled out a gun.

"Hey! What the fuck?!" Callahan spluttered. Then he did something real stupid. He turned to the parking garage, right to where Noah was hidden, and shouted, "Help me!"

Adrian's gaze followed the informant's desperate plea, locking on to the exact location where Noah was hidden. In a fluid, chilling motion, the assassin raised his gun and, without a hint of hesitation, fired a bullet straight into Callahan's forehead. The shot, precise and fatal, sent a paralyzing chill coursing through Noah's veins.

But Adrian wasn't finished. His movements were predatory, calculated. In the same breath, he reached into the duffle bag, his hand emerging with one of the magnetic mines. With a deft flick of his wrist, he hurled it toward Noah's position. The mine spun through the air, a deadly harbinger of the chaos that was seconds from happening.

Noah barely had time to react. He dove behind a nearby SUV as Adrian's thumb pressed down on the detonator. The ensuing explosion was deafening, a violent eruption that shook the very foundations of the parking garage, the SUV taking most of the impact. Smoke and debris filled the air, clouding vision and muffling sounds.

"I've lost eyes on the target," Ralph complained in their ears.

In the midst of the disarray, Adrian displayed a terrifying level of composure. He wasted no time, throwing himself into the M8 and slamming his foot down on the accelerator. The car lurched forward as he made his escape, leaving behind a scene of devastation and a team scrambling to comprehend the full scale of what had just occurred.

"Marco? Renée? He's coming your way," Noah barked into his comms.

Marco and Renée, ready to intercept, maneuvered the Durango to block the exit. But Adrian had an ace up his sleeve. His people had already been here to this parking garage. The place was well prepared for his escape.

Upon reaching the bottom level, he didn't turn toward the exit. Instead of heading for the place Marco and Renée were waiting, he went to the opposite corner, where there was no exit.

Or at least not yet.

Coming up on the outer wall of that corner, Adrian took a second detonator from the dashboard of the BMW and pressed the button on top. A series of hidden incendiary devices exploded, creating a hole in the wall large enough for the M8 to escape through, the car disappearing onto the streets.

"Marco? Renée?" Noah shouted. "You got this?"

"We do. Yes," Marco replied. "We're in pursuit."

"Ralph? Where are you?" Noah's voice was edged with desperation.

"On the move," came Ralph's calm response.

Ralph was already dropping from a fire escape onto the Ducati. The team was now in full pursuit mode, Marco and Renée in the Durango and Ralph on the bike, all charging after the assassin.

Left alone amidst the smoldering wreckage, Noah surveyed the damage. James Callahan lay on his back, a halo of blood spreading out from the back of his head. He was very much now the former James Callahan.

Noah stood gazing down at the dead man when he felt a sudden, sharp prick. His hand flew to his neck, fingers closing around what he instantly knew was a dart. Almost immediately, his vision blurred as he fell weakly to his knees, the world spinning around him.

As he slowly collapsed to the ground, a shadowy figure emerged from the smoky haze, their presence sinister and foreboding as they came to a stop a few feet from him. Noah's consciousness was slipping away, but the figure's words cut through the fog of his mind with chilling clarity.

"You're not the only one who can hide, Noah Wolf."

With darkness gradually enveloping him, Noah realized with a sinking heart that he had just been outplayed at his own game. The last thing he saw was the figure stepping closer, their identity obscured by the encroaching blackness.

***

Outside the garage, the streets of Chicago were quickly transforming into a battleground as the rest of Team Camelot, now aided by the Chicago Police Department, launched into a high-octane pursuit of the notorious assassin Adrian.

Renée beside him, Marco weaved the Durango through traffic with the precision of a surgeon's scalpel, while Ralph, astride the Ducati, sliced through the nighttime congestion with the agility of the best street racers. Above, police helicopters cut through the night sky, their searchlights painting the frozen city in stark, moving beams. The chase was relentless—a high-octane thriller, transforming the city into a canvas of light and sound. Streets blurred into a kaleidoscope of motion and light, civilian cars pulling aside, pedestrians jumping back, their expressions a mix of awe and fear as the cars whipped by like bullets.

The man driving the M8—whether Henrik Schultz or another member of Adrian—was clearly a master of evasion. He pushed his BMW to the limits of its 4.4-liter twin-turbocharged V8 engine. Swerving around corners with the precision of a ballet dancer, his engine roared down narrow alleys, his wheels daringly skimming sidewalks and pedestrian zones. His car's maneuvers were a blend of reckless abandon and calculated risk, the M8 threading through the urban maze, always a step ahead.

In their Dodge Durango, Marco and Renée were a study in focused determination.

"Left on Wacker Drive!" Renée barked into the radio, her eyes locked on the weaving taillights of Adrian's car.

Marco, gripping the steering wheel, replied, "Got it. Ralph, you still on him?"

Through the radio, Ralph's voice crackled. "Right behind him. This guy's slippery, but I'm close."

The Durango groaned under the strain, its engine pushed to the max. Marco and Renée worked in unison, predicting Adrian's next move, trying to corner him at every opportunity.

Meanwhile, Ralph, on the Ducati, was a shadow flitting through the night. He zipped through tight spaces, his bike's agility keeping him tantalizingly close to the fleeing assassin.

Above, the police helicopters hovered like predatory birds, their searchlights slicing through the darkness, directing ground units and trying to corner Adrian from the skies.

At the same time, Marco kept trying to contact Noah. "Noah, come in. Where are you? You with us? We need your eyes up here!" There was a beat of static, then silence. Noah was still unreachable.

Renée's voice was tense but controlled. "Focus, Marco. We can't lose him. Noah must be somewhere."

Adrian's car darted into a narrow alley, the walls barely wide enough for a vehicle. Marco and Renée exchanged a quick, resolute glance, pressing forward, the chase unyielding, the Durango just barely getting through.

At that moment, their pursuit took an almost catastrophic turn. As Adrian's car emerged from the alley, it swerved violently, barely avoiding a pedestrian who had inadvertently stepped into the fray. The near-miss sent a shockwave through Marco and Renée.

"Watch out!" Renée yelled.

Marco's white-knuckled hands tight on the wheel, he navigated the SUV through the same narrow escape Adrian had taken, his heart racing.

Ralph, still close behind, witnessed the chaos unfold. "That was close! Keep your distance," he advised through the radio, his voice a mix of caution and determination.

The chase now wound through the bustling streets, threading between cars and pedestrians, the city a maze of potential hazards. Adrian's desperation was becoming obvious, his maneuvers more erratic and dangerous.

Marco, still trying to reach Noah, felt a surge of frustration. "Noah, if you can hear us, we need you now!" His voice echoed into the void, the response still a maddening silence.

Renée, her focus laser-sharp, announced, "We're heading east, toward Grant Park. If you're out there, Noah, that's where we'll be."

Their Durango barreled down the street, keeping pace with Adrian's increasingly reckless driving as the pursuit wound its way toward the Chicago River, the tension mounting with every second. Adrian, his options dwindling, pushed the BMW M8 to its absolute limits. The engine's growl echoed off the city buildings, a ferocious sound that sent shivers down the spines of the pedestrians who heard it.

Marco, Renée, and Ralph, in their relentless pursuit, sensed the critical moment was upon them. This had to end, and it had to end now—before the chase spiraled into catastrophe.

Ralph, his instincts razor-sharp, saw his chance. He twisted the throttle of the Ducati, surging forward with a burst of speed. He raced alongside Adrian, his bike a blur of motion.

"Ralph, be careful!" Renée's voice crackled over the radio, laced with both concern and urgency.

In a heart-stopping moment, Ralph executed a bold maneuver. He edged his bike closer, clipping the rear of Adrian's car. The contact was slight, but it was enough. The BMW, already at its breaking point, lost control on the icy road. It spun wildly, a whirlwind of metal and momentum, before smashing through the flimsy barrier at the river's edge.

With a sound that seemed to shake the very air, the car plunged into the murky depths of the Chicago River, sending up a massive spray of water. For a moment, time stood still, the only sound the river's disturbed waters settling back into place.

Marco and Renée skidded to a halt, jumping out of the Durango and rushing to the edge of the river. Ralph threw his motorcycle down with a clatter as he followed suit.

Their eyes scanned the gloomy water, searching for any sign of Adrian. Each second stretched out interminably. Suddenly, a figure broke the surface. Adrian, gasping for air, his face a mask of shock and exhaustion, struggled against the river's pull.

The team, along with the arriving police officers, wasted no time. They sprang into action, swiftly apprehending the soaked and almost drowned assassin. As they secured handcuffs around his wrists, ensuring he was firmly in their grasp, a mix of relief and triumph swept through them.

Marco, his focus shifting, reached for his radio. "Noah, do you copy? Adrian's in custody," he announced, expecting a crackling reply.

But the response was only static, an unnerving silence filling the airwaves. He tried again, urgency lacing his voice. "Noah, do you copy? Target apprehended. Please respond."

Still, there was nothing—just the persistent crackle of an empty channel.

CHAPTER FOUR

At the same time that Team Camelot were wondering where their leader had gotten to, halfway across the country, Noah's remote farmhouse on Temple Lake was about to see the serenity of its night abruptly broken into. Six shadowy figures were this minute descending upon it, their movements as silent as a wisp of smoke. Cloaked in tactical gear, they melted into the darkness, advancing with the lethal precision of seasoned predators. Hand signals passed between them, brief and muted, orchestrating their stealthy approach. The leader, a man with ice in his eyes, halted the group with a raised hand. He produced a small device, its screen glowing faintly in the night. Expert fingers danced across it, deploying a program that silently infiltrated and neutralized the farmhouse's security.

Inside, the home was an oasis of peace, undisturbed. Both Sarah and Norah were fast asleep, oblivious to the approaching danger, all the way up until the windows in the living room imploded in a violent cascade of glass.

The sound tore through the quiet like a gunshot, shattering the night's calm. The first intruder slipped through the shattered window, a ghostly figure who began moving fluidly through the house like a snake on the hunt. He was followed by the others, fanning out with practiced efficiency, their footsteps a faint whisper on the wooden floors.

Upstairs, Sarah was jolted out of sleep by the intrusion. Her eyes flew open, the remnants of dreams vanishing in an instant. The distant, muted sounds of the men downstairs sent a surge of adrenaline through her. Her instincts kicked in, honed by years of fieldwork and one other thing—motherhood. She sprang from her bed, her heart thrumming wildly against her ribs.

In the next room, little Norah slept, unaware of the nightmare unfolding. Sarah burst into her daughter's bedroom, her movements swift and decisive. She scooped up Norah, holding her close in a protective embrace. The child, startled awake by her mother's sudden grip, clung to Sarah, her tiny frame shaking with a mix of fear and confusion.

"Mommy, what's happening?" Norah's voice was small, muffled against her mother's shoulder.

Sarah's eyes scanned the house, a fierce determination settling in. "It's going to be okay, sweetheart," she whispered, her voice a blend of comfort and steel. "Stay quiet for Mommy now."

As they moved, Sarah's mind raced, planning their next steps. The safe room was their only sanctuary now. Clutching Norah, she moved swiftly, her familiarity with the farmhouse giving her a fleeting advantage. But as she rounded a corner, her heart dropped. An operative stood before her, a silent sentinel, his face obscured by a mask, his weapon aimed with a dispassionate precision that chilled her to the bone.

With no way out, Sarah's maternal instincts roared to life. She placed Norah behind her, her body a shield between her child and the looming threat. Her voice, though low, was laced with an unwavering resolve. "Stay back, baby."

The operative advanced, a model of cold efficiency. Without hesitation, Sarah launched herself at him. Her movements were those of a mother fighting for her child's life, each strike driven by raw, primal urgency. She aimed for any vulnerable spot—his face, his throat, anywhere she might land a telling blow.

But the operative was not just any intruder. His responses were the result of rigorous training, each parry neutralizing her attacks with mechanical precision. Sarah's desperate strikes, powered by sheer emotion, were no match for his cold, calculated defense. A fist slammed into her stomach, stealing her breath, and a second strike sent her staggering back, pain clouding her vision.

Through a blur of tears and agony, Sarah's eyes found Norah. Her daughter's face was etched with terror, her small body trembling in its nightgown. That image, that moment of pure fear in her child's eyes, ignited a final burst of desperate energy in Sarah. She lunged again, a wild mix of fear and fierce resolve in her movements.

But the gap in skill was too great. Another blow caught her in the side of the head, and she felt her legs give way, the ground rushing up to meet her as she fell.

As Sarah knelt on the floor fighting against the encroaching darkness, the operative she had fought retreated, making way for a more imposing character to step forward. This new assailant, with a menacing determination, advanced toward Norah. Sarah's heart thundered in her chest, her breaths ragged and labored.

She desperately tried to rise, to be the shield her daughter needed, but her body was unresponsive, betraying her maternal instinct.

In the tense silence, Norah's small, uncertain voice pierced the air. "Mommy?" Her wide eyes were fixed on the stranger nearing her, a sense of terror slowly dawning in them.

The man reached out, his grip sure and relentless. Sarah's voice erupted in a raw, anguished scream, "Don't touch her!" But her words were lost in the void of his indifference. With a chilling ease, he scooped Norah up, his movements betraying no hint of compassion. Sarah extended a trembling hand, her fingertips barely brushing Norah's foot in a futile gesture of desperation. But it was in vain; her daughter was being taken away, her small, frightened, despairing cries dissolving into the night as she disappeared out of view.

Another figure then approached Sarah. As he drew closer, the other operatives surrounding her removed their ski masks, revealing their faces. Each face was strikingly nondescript—average white men with features so ordinary they would be impossible to describe in detail. They were the kind of faces that would be described to police as 'just another regular-looking guy.' The type that fade from memory, leaving no trace behind—the very embodiment of anonymity.

This, Sarah began to realize, was Adrian.

The third man, his face as unremarkably average as his cohorts', crouched in front of Sarah, his presence chilling in its calmness. When he spoke, his voice was a whisper, emotionless and cold as liquid nitrogen. "Soon your husband will be waking up into his new reality," he intoned. Sarah's eyes, filled with fear and defiance, met his, but she found no empathy there, only a black void. "In the meantime," he added, "you sleep, momma wolf."

Before Sarah could react, she felt a sharp sting on her neck. A dart, its contents quickly sending a wave of dizziness crashing over her. Her vision blurred, her thoughts scattering like leaves in a storm. She tried to fight the encroaching darkness, to stay awake for Norah, for Noah. But her body betrayed her, succumbing to the forced slumber.

As her eyes fluttered closed, Sarah's last conscious thought was a silent prayer for her daughter and husband. The farmhouse stood eerily silent under the moonlit sky, its peace shattered, its inhabitants torn apart by forces beyond their control.

***

Noah's return to consciousness was gradual, a slow emergence from the dark veil that had been thrown over him. The first sense to claw its way back was his hearing, initially just a low hum, like distant waves, gradually sharpening into the distinct, mechanical sounds of an unfamiliar environment. The buzzing of fluorescent lighting mingled with the faint hum of electronics.

Next came his sense of touch. He felt the hard, unyielding surface beneath him, the chill of the cold metal chair against his skin. He was sitting, his back pressed against something rigid and uncomfortable. His arms and legs were heavy, not just with the grogginess of his drugged state, but also because they were being held in place. As he moved, the metal restraints around his wrists and ankles clinked softly.

His eyes flickered open, struggling against the

harsh, artificial light that filled the small room. The walls were a stark, unadorned gray concrete, the kind that seemed to absorb rather than reflect light, adding to the oppressive atmosphere. The room was bare, save for the chair he was strapped to and a telescreen mounted on the wall directly in front of him.

The air in the room felt heavy, thick with a sense of foreboding that settled on Noah's chest like a physical weight. There was a staleness to it, as if the room had been sealed off from the outside world for far too long. It was a space designed to isolate, to intimidate, to make one acutely aware of their vulnerability.

Noah's instincts came alive. He began to struggle against the restraints, muscles straining as he tested the strength of the clasps that held him. They were mechanical, clearly designed to hold someone of his strength and training. His efforts were met with the unrelenting resistance of the chair, a harsh reminder of his helplessness.

As he paused, panting slightly from the exertion, the telescreen flickered to life. The sudden burst of static made him tense, his eyes fixed on the screen as it stabilized to reveal a face. The image was grainy, the colors washed out, but the plain-looking face on the screen was unmistakable. The man's eyes locked with Noah's, a cold, calculated stare that seemed to pierce through the screen and into his very soul.

Noah stilled, his struggle ceasing as he faced the reality of his situation. The person on the screen was about to speak, and Noah knew that whatever was coming next, it would be pivotal. The atmosphere in the room seemed to tighten, the air growing even heavier with anticipation. This was a moment of reckoning, and Noah braced himself for what was to come.

"Do you recognize me?" the man said, his voice smooth and taunting.

Noah's eyes narrowed. "Adrian," he managed to say, his voice a low growl. "Or should that be Henrik Schultz?"

"That's right. You can call me either."

"I thought I'd killed you."

"No. You only killed a part of me. Not the head. Just a limb," Schultz replied with a chilling calmness. "Now listen up, Noah Wolf, because this next part is pretty important, so I'm going to go slowly."

The footage on the screen panned out, revealing the room behind Schultz. Another man stood in the background, an eerie mirror image of the one speaking. Nevertheless, it wasn't Schultz or any other member of Adrian that drew Noah's immediate attention. It was the small figure next to the man in the background. The little girl, her mouth covered, her eyes wide with terror, was unmistakably his daughter, Norah.

The revelation hit Noah like a physical blow. For a fleeting second, his hardened exterior faltered, revealing a glimpse of the father beneath the assassin. His heart pounded in his chest, a mixture of fear for his daughter's safety and a deep, burning rage toward the man who dared to use her against him.

As he processed the sight of Norah, his muscles tensed, and he once again strained against the bindings, every fiber of his being radiating a desperate need to protect his child. His teeth gritted together, the strain etched into every line of his face.

"Wow," Adrian observed with a tone of detached curiosity. "And I was always under the impression that you were devoid of emotions, Noah Wolf."

The comment was a taunt, designed to provoke, but Noah's focus was laser-sharp on his daughter. The realization that she was in danger, that she was a pawn in this twisted game, fueled a primal, protective fury within him. Henrik Schultz, Adrian, had just escalated the situation to an intensely personal level. Noah's resolve hardened; this was no longer a mission—it was a fight for his family.

The camera refocused on Schultz. Noah's breath came in short, ragged gasps as he continued to struggle against his restraints, his glaring eyes never leaving the screen.

"What do you want?" he snarled.

"I want you on my side," Adrian replied. "Or at least the side of your daughter."

"Where's Sarah?" Noah's voice was a mix of fear and demand.

"Asleep, but alive and well," Adrian responded with cold indifference. "She's waiting for you at home."

As Adrian continued, his words became measured and precise. "Now the reason I'm in America, the reason you and your team were trying to trap me, is because I have been awarded a rather lucrative contract. A kill list that will take all my powers to complete."

"And now," Noah interjected, his mind racing to keep up with the unfolding situation, "I take it you want me to complete it for you, right?"

The smile that crept onto Schultz's face was chilling. "Yes, Noah Wolf. That's exactly it. I want you to complete it for me. I will pass you one name at a time…"

"How many?" Noah cut in, desperate for any

semblance of control.

Schultz shook his head, a gesture that conveyed both authority and a hint of mockery. "No. Only when I am giving you the last name will you know it is finished."

"Then this could go on indefinitely."

"I can tell you that it is less than ten. That will have to do you for now."

"So you want me to kill people for you; otherwise you'll..." Noah's voice trailed off, the realization dawning.

"Kill your daughter," Schultz finished for him, his tone chillingly matter-of-fact. "Yes. That's exactly how this works. And just so you know—as a kind of inspiration, should we say—I am going to show you something."

The screen shifted abruptly, and Noah's heart clenched in his chest as he took in the new scene. It was a pit, sunk deep into a concrete yard, its walls scarred and weathered. Inside prowled several pit bull terriers—beasts with rippling muscles and jaws capable of breaking bones. Their eyes glinted with a savage intelligence, and their snarls reverberated through the room, a chorus of primal rage and hunger.

The camera shifted, focusing on a hand that emerged into the frame. In it, Noah immediately recognized Norah's favorite stuffed animal—a small, well-worn bunny with one eye missing and a patchwork ear. The hand shook the toy, making it dance mockingly in front of the camera. The dogs below grew more agitated, their growls intensifying, a cacophony of impending violence.

With a heartless flick, the hand tossed the toy into

the pit. The dogs exploded into action, leaping at the stuffed bunny with a ferocity that was both terrifying and mesmerizing. In mere seconds, the toy was ripped to shreds, its cotton innards strewn across the pit like snowflakes in a tempest. Then, in a frenzy, the dogs turned on each other, their snarls and yelps filling the air, a chilling soundtrack to the chaos below. It was a brutal, visceral display of raw power and aggression, a vivid reminder of the danger that Norah was in. The toy's destruction was a clear message from Adrian: This could very well be Norah's fate should Noah fail to comply.

He felt a cold sweat break out all over his body as the weight of the moment crashed down on him. This was no longer just a fight for his daughter's life; it was a battle against an enemy who was willing to use the most depraved means to achieve his ends. The stakes had never been higher, and Noah knew that he had to do whatever it took to ensure his daughter's safety.

"You understand the gravity of your situation, Noah Wolf?" Schultz said, his voice as steady as ever.

Noah exhaled slowly through his nose. "Yes. I understand," he said, trying to keep his voice as steady as his interlocutor despite the storm raging within him.

"There's no room for refusal or error," Schultz continued, his tone leaving no doubt about the seriousness of his threat.

"None," Noah affirmed, his jaw setting in a hard line.

"Are you ready for your first target?" Schultz asked, his eyes locked on to Noah's through the screen.

"Yes," Noah replied, his voice barely more than a whisper.

"The first name on the list is Allison Peterson," Henrik Schultz announced, watching closely for Noah's reaction.

A pause hung in the air as the name sank in. Noah's mind raced to process the implications. "Are you that dumb?" he finally asked, his tone laced with disbelief. "You kill Allison Peterson and you're not just starting a war, you're signing a death warrant for everyone involved. Including myself."

"Then consider it motivation to avoid getting caught," Schultz retorted. "You do this properly, and no one needs to know that you murdered your boss."

"Not just my boss," Noah corrected him, his voice tight with emotion. "The woman who saved me from death row. The woman who is godmother to my only child."

"And that's where you need to think, Noah. Your only child. She's mine now, and if you want her back, you need to get this done. Think about Norah. Whilst you're on my side, I will do everything in my power to make her stay with me as comfortable as possible. So get this done. You have three days," Adrian stated, his words laced with a stone-cold finality. "Plenty of time to plan it accordingly."

Noah's jaw clenched tighter, his mind a whirlwind of strategies and countermeasures. "And if I do this... you'll release my daughter?" he asked.

"Complete the list and she's yours. Fail, and the last thing you'll remember is her screams as the dogs—"

"She's just a child!" Noah implored, his voice thick with emotion. "This is between you and me."

"Now, Noah Wolf, you of all people should know... in our line of work, there are no children, no innocents, no lines that can't be crossed," Schultz replied, the irrevocable certainty in his voice reverberating through the small, concrete room as he laid out his ultimatum.

"You'll get what you want," Noah spat back angrily.

"Remember, stay in the shadows," Schultz instructed with a clinical, calculating tone. "Explain your absence to your team any way you can, but you must get me the head of Allison Peterson within three days. Am I clear?"

"That won't work."

"Why?"

"I'll need others onboard. People that can help me complete the list. I usually don't work alone."

"I foresaw this. Okay. You can allow others into it, people you trust with your daughter's life, but if knowledge of what is happening goes beyond the few you need for the completion of the list, then, again, Norah pays."

"I understand," Noah replied, the two words heavy with the burden of the choice he was being forced to make.

"After you have completed the first assassination, I will feed you the next name. Goodbye, Noah Wolf. I wish you luck in your endeavor," Schultz said, a hint of mockery in his tone.

The screen went blank, plunging the room into near darkness. The sudden, oppressive silence echoed in Noah's head. He sat motionless, the reality of his situation weighing heavily on him.

Suddenly, the mechanical clasps over his wrists and shins clicked open, releasing him from the chair's grip. The sound resonated through the room, followed by the door clicking as it slowly swung open, the dim light from outside casting a long shadow across the floor.

Noah stood up slowly, every muscle in his body tense. At the door, he looked out. The building he was in was under renovation, construction materials scattered everywhere. It appeared he was the only one here.

It also appeared he was free to leave, but the freedom was an illusion, overshadowed by the daunting task that Schultz had set him. As he walked out of the room into the hallway of the derelict building, Noah's mind swirled with plans and possibilities, each more desperate than the last.

***

In the sterile confines of the Chicago Police Headquarters, tension hung in the air like a fog. Marco and Renée paced the hallways, their minds racing with the unfolding events. The sudden disappearance of Noah added a layer of urgency to their mission.

Marco's phone buzzed, snapping him back to reality. He hoped that it was Noah, but it wasn't. It was Ralph, calling from the bombed-out parking garage. "There's no sign of him. No blood or evidence he got hit by the explosion. Where the hell could he be?"

"I don't know," Marco replied, trying to mask his own worry. "Keep looking. Renée and I need to speak with our friend here. I'll keep you posted."

As the phone call ended, a short, middle-aged man approached them. His features were rounded with a face weathered by time and marked by a gnarled complexion. His expression conveyed a mix of annoyance and impatience.

"Captain Morelos," he announced, extending a plump hand lined with stubby fingers.

Marco reached out, his grip firm despite the dampness of Morelos' hand. "I'm Marco," he introduced himself, then gestured to his wife, "and this is Renée."

Renée, maintaining a professional demeanor, offered a brief, efficient handshake to the captain.

Morelos, retracting his hand, eyed them with a scrutinizing gaze. "So you two are the ones who have the governor calling me out of bed," he remarked, his tone carrying a hint of reluctance. "I suppose that means you should come with me." With a curt nod, he gestured for them to follow. His demeanor suggested a mix of resignation and wariness, setting the tone for what was to come.

In the interrogation room, Detectives Miller and Johnson sat across from Adrian, their expressions a mixture of frustration and determination. The air crackled with an edginess, the recent violence casting a heavy shadow over the proceedings.

Detective Miller leaned forward, her eyes locked on Adrian. "Let's talk about the parking garage. Why did you shoot that man you were meeting? What was your motive?"

Adrian, his hands cuffed on the table, regarded her with a cryptic smile, his demeanor unnervingly calm. "Shootings happen every day, Detective. Why is this one so special?"

Detective Johnson, who had been observing quietly, interjected with a hardened tone. "This isn't a game. A man is dead because of you. And those explosions could have hurt dozens more. So I need you to start talking."

Adrian's smile widened slightly, but his eyes

remained cold. "Explosions make a statement, don't they? They're much louder than bullets."

Miller slammed her hand on the table, her patience waning. "You're facing serious charges. Help us understand why you did this."

But Adrian simply leaned back, the smile never leaving his blank face. "Understanding is a luxury, Detective. And I'm not feeling very generous today."

The interrogation was interrupted as Captain Morelos entered, followed by Marco and Renée. The detectives, already on edge, turned with a mix of surprise and annoyance. "Captain Morelos?" Miller queried, her tone hinting at the foreboding news to come.

"I gotta ask you two to leave," the captain said in a weary, disgruntled tone.

Both detectives furrowed their brows.

Johnson was the first to speak. "I don't get it."

"Eh, well, guys, I just got a call from the governor," Captain Morelos announced.

"The governor of Illinois?" Johnson asked, his brow furrowing in confusion.

The captain's frown deepened. "What other governor could it be? The governor of Kentucky?" he retorted, his sarcasm cutting through the tension in the room.

"What'd he say?" Miller inquired.

"Says these guys have got jurisdiction," Morelos answered, gesturing toward Marco and Renée.

With visible reluctance, the detectives vacated the interrogation room, leaving Marco and Renée alone with Adrian. The room was small, the air thick with the smell of blood and old sweat. Adrian sat handcuffed to a table that was bolted to the floor, his expression unreadable.

"So you're not Schultz," Marco stated immediately, cutting to the heart of the matter, his gaze fixed on Adrian, searching for any sign of deceit. "Your leader wouldn't sacrifice himself for something like this."

Adrian's upper lip quivered slightly, the only hint of emotion on his otherwise impassive face.

"So who are you?" Renée asked, her voice steady but her eyes sharp, locked on to Adrian's.

Blinking twice, Adrian met her stare. "It is simple who I am," he declared, his voice devoid of emotion as he leaned forward as far as his chained hands would let him, adding, "I am Adrian."

This left more questions than answers in the minds of Marco and Renée.

**

Noah's footsteps echoed through the icy early morning streets of Chicago. Storm clouds churned overhead, obscuring the moon and casting the world in a shadowy gloom. As he emerged onto a wider street, a figure materialized from the darkness as if he'd been waiting —a disheveled tramp, his clothes worn and tattered. He held out a trembling hand.

Noah's first instinct was to dismiss him as another soul lost to the unforgiving city streets, but something halted him. The tramp's eyes, clouded by years of hardship, flickered with an unusual sharpness as he clutched a nondescript metal case about the size of a cellphone.

"Take it," the tramp rasped, his voice as rough as the wind that swept through the streets. "And don't ask any questions. I don't know nothin' 'cept what he told me when he picked me up 'bout ten minutes ago. I'm to give the man in the strange hoodie—I'm pretty sure that's you—this and then the guy will text me the location of more money when it's done."

Noah, his senses heightened by his recent ordeal, cautiously took the case.

"He said you had to put the thing inside in your ear," the tramp told him, the stench of unwashed clothes and life on the streets wafting toward Noah with the gusting wind.

The scene was surreal, a strange interlude in the midst of chaos, and Noah couldn't shake the feeling that every step was leading him deeper into a web from which there was no escape. The night air felt heavier as he clutched the case, aware that its contents would only further entangle him in Adrian's deadly game.

"Open it and put it in," the tramp urged. "He said you had to. Said you knew what that would mean."

Noah opened the case, flipping the lid. Inside was what looked like a very small communications earpiece. It looked to be designed to contour perfectly to the user's ear canal. The outer surface of the earpiece, only a few millimeters in diameter, had been finished with a skin-matching tone that would blend seamlessly with Noah's complexion.

"You gotta put it in."

The smell and the tone of the tramp was starting to annoy Noah. He lifted the minuscule earpiece from the case and inserted it, feeling its cold touch against his skin. The night seemed to press in around him, the distant sounds of the city muffled as if underwater. The earpiece nestled comfortably and securely, becoming an almost indistinguishable part of Noah.

"Good." Schultz's voice was a hiss of satisfaction. "I can speak to you now at all times. Right there with you."

The sense of invasion was immediate and profound; Schultz's voice was not just in his ear, but in his head, as if the man had crawled inside his mind.

The tramp, his part played, turned abruptly and disappeared into the night, leaving Noah alone with the case and the haunting words of Adrian echoing in his skull.

"So you know," Schultz said next, "this earpiece you've just put in utilizes state-of-the-art quantum encryption algorithms, rendering its transmissions impenetrable to any known method of eavesdropping. This level of encryption ensures absolute privacy between us as the quantum keys used are theoretically impossible to replicate or intercept. Additionally, the earpiece operates on a dynamic frequency-hopping spectrum, further muddying its signal and making it virtually undetectable to conventional tracking devices."

"Why are you telling me this?" Noah replied dryly. "You want my admiration?"

"No. All I want is for you to understand. Your friend Wally at Research and Development won't be able to find me using the earpiece. So don't waste your time and your daughter's time on trying. As well as that, it contains a tracker and can read both your temperature and heart rate just by being inside your ear."

"What use to you is that?"

"Easy. I want to know when you take it out. Because

the first rule of this is that you can't. Ever. Understood?"

Noah said nothing. He merely waited for Schultz to continue.

"I'm going to be listening in to your every move, Noah Wolf. And not just that. I'll be watching you, too. I am everywhere. Now. Less chat. It's time to follow my directions. You need to be somewhere."

"Where?" Noah asked, though he knew the answer would be as elusive as the man himself.

"You'll find out when you reach it."

With those inevitable words, Noah felt the invisible leash tighten. He was no longer just a hunter or a soldier; he was a puppet, dancing to the tune of a master who held not only his strings but also those of his loved ones. The night seemed darker, the wind even harsher. As he moved forward, each step took Noah further into the unknown at the behest of a voice in his ear.

The city lights flickered in the distance, casting long shadows as Noah navigated the deserted streets. Above, CCTV cameras under Schultz's control shifted with a mechanical precision, tracking his every movement. The low hum of their motors was a constant reminder of Adrian's watchful stare.

When the first drops of rain began to fall, Noah knew that time was of the essence; the clouds would soon unleash their fury. He had to act fast, make his move before the heavens opened and took away the only advantage he had left: the quantum cloak. Schultz's people must've thought it was just some ordinary piece of fashion.

Rounding a corner, Noah seized the moment of transition as Schultz switched between cameras. In one fluid motion, he pulled the hood of the quantum cloak over his head, vanishing from the digital eye that had been tracking him.

Somewhere far away, confusion registered on Henrik Schultz's face as he flicked back to the previous camera, only to find Noah gone from that one too.

"Wolf? Wolf? Where are you?" His voice crackled with frustration over the earpiece.

Noah ignored him, focusing instead on the task at hand. The rain was intensifying, slowly turning into a downpour that blurred the neon reflections of Chicago on the wet pavement. He quickened his pace, the quantum cloak crackling as droplets hit it, momentarily revealing his silhouette in the footage before cloaking him again in its protective invisibility. It wouldn't be long before he was no longer invisible.

It had to happen now.

"Wolf, where are you?"

Up ahead, he spotted it: a relic of a bygone era, a payphone. Noah approached it swiftly. He needed to make a call, a call that could change everything.

Under the shelter of the phone booth, Noah removed the earpiece, closing it up inside his fist. He fished in his pocket for a quarter, the cold metal a stark contrast to the warmth of his palm. He dialed the number with practiced precision, each digit echoing in the confined space of the booth.

It rang, the shrill tone cutting through the sound of the rain pounding on the booth. Noah held his breath, waiting for the other end to pick up. This call was a risk, a desperate gamble, but it was the only move left to him.

The line clicked, the call going to voicemail. Noah waited for the beep. Then, holding the earpiece tight, he whispered two words: "Protocol 9."

Putting the phone down, he quickly left the booth and entered the rain, the cloak faltering under the assault. When Noah was far enough away from the booth, he put the earpiece back in and switched the cloak off.

"Wolf?" Schultz's voice held a note of uncertainty.

"What?" Noah responded, his voice a blend of feigned ignorance and subtle defiance.

"I lost you for a moment."

"Must be the rain," Noah replied, his gaze fixed on the dark horizon.

"Yeah. Must be. Now listen. You turn left onto Maple Avenue in about a hundred yards."

"Got it," Noah replied mechanically.

As the rain intensified, Noah moved forward, each step taking him deeper into the heart of the storm.

CHAPTER FIVE

Rain hammered against the stone façade of the Chicago Police Headquarters. The storm outside mirrored the storm within—of worry, of frustration, and a whirlwind of unanswered questions that swirled around Noah Wolf.

Noah stood for a moment outside the precinct, the rain plastering his hair to his forehead. The voice in his ear whispered final instructions. "Now I leave you," Schultz said. "Go see your friends. And remember. No one is to know unless absolutely necessary." The line went dead, leaving Noah with the heavy burden of a mission that felt like a noose around his neck.

He pushed open the door to the precinct, his appearance causing a few heads to turn. Water dripped from his cloak, pooling on the floor as he walked across the scarred linoleum. He felt the weight of every gaze, the room pretty full with people for such an odd hour.

At the desk, he flashed his ID to the cop on duty. Words were exchanged, brief and functional, before he was led through the maze of the precinct. The sterile light of the hallway cast long shadows, adding to the sense of unease that had been his constant companion since he woke up in that gray concrete room.

Finally, Noah was ushered into the interrogation

suite. The door opened to reveal Marco, Renée, and Ralph clustered around a table littered with takeout containers and coffee cups. Their expressions shifted from relief to confusion and then to a guarded kind of concern as they took in their leader's disheveled state.

As the rain lashed against the windows, Noah's entrance felt like the final piece in tonight's puzzle, but it was a piece that didn't quite fit.

Marco's voice cut through the tension like a knife as he spotted Noah. "Boss?" he said, his relief evident. "I thought something had happened."

Noah strode forward, feeling the weight of their stares. "Sorry I went dark," he began, his voice steady despite the weight of the situation. "Right after Adrian took off, I saw someone. Looked like another one of them. I had to follow."

Marco's brow furrowed in disbelief. "Follow? Without telling us? What happened to your comms? Or your phone?"

Noah could feel the lie sit heavy on his tongue. "It was a split-second decision," he said. "The guy started climbing down the outside of the parking garage. I had to go after him. In the middle of the climb, I slipped, almost fell. In the scramble, the earpiece fell out, and my phone dropped out of my pocket. Gone."

"Did you catch him?" Renée pressed, her gaze sharp.

Shaking his head, Noah's expression was filled with frustration. "Lost him in the alleys. I doubled back as soon as I could."

Marco's concern was clear. "It was risky, going alone like that. You could've been captured."

How prescient, Noah thought.

Ralph added, "At least you're back unharmed." He paused, a hint of something else in his voice. "But you missed quite a bit."

Curiosity piqued, Noah leaned in slightly. "What happened?"

"We got him," Marco said, a note of triumph in his voice.

"Who?"

"The guy from the garage."

Noah's eyes lit up. "You caught him? That's... that's very good news."

The door to the interrogation room had a small window. As Noah turned toward it, he caught sight of the man whose leader had Norah. Adrian sat inside at the table, his pink hands cuffed to it, his gaze fixated out the window, looking directly at Noah.

Noah's heart pounded in his chest, a storm of emotions swirling within him. Without a word, he sprang toward the door, flinging it open with a determination that bordered on fury. He quickly shut it behind him, locking it and pulling down the blind, obscuring the view from outside. The action was swift and decisive, leaving no room for hesitation.

"Noah?! Noah?!" The calls from Marco, Renée, and Ralph were muffled but urgent, their hands trying the handle in vain. Confused cops in the corridor also converged on the door, their voices blending into a cacophony of concern and confusion. "Is there a key for this?" Ralph asked, but Noah was beyond hearing them.

Inside the room, the air was getting thicker by the second. Adrian, still chained to the table, looked up at Noah with a smirk playing on his lips. His face was like a blank rubber mask, altered by so many surgeries that the boy his mother had once known had been completely erased, his eyes holding nothing but a calculating coldness.

Noah moved around the table with a predator's grace. He withdrew a knife from his belt, its blade glinting under the harsh interrogation room lights. Adrian's smirk wavered slightly, a flicker of uncertainty crossing his features. "You gonna cut me?" he asked, trying to maintain composure.

But Noah had other plans. He swiftly cut through Adrian's shirt, revealing the man's torso. He sheathed the knife, then gripped Adrian's left shoulder with a hand that seemed almost inhuman in its strength. Adrian was immobilized, his body fixed to the chair by Noah's unyielding grip.

Noah's eyes busily scanned Adrian's back, his gaze sharp and calculating. He leaned in closer, his focus narrowing on the area where the neck meets the right shoulder. It wasn't the skin or the muscle that interested him, but what lay beneath—the brachial plexus, a network of nerves that was key to his purpose.

The tension in the room was suffocating as Noah prepared to extract the information he needed in the only way he knew how.

He leaned in close, the air between the two men charged with a dangerous intensity. Outside, the rain continued to pound against the windows, but inside, all that existed was the confrontation unfolding in the dimly lit room.

"You know when I first joined E & E," Noah began, his voice low and steady, "Allison had me take courses in pressure point and nerve torture." His eyes never left

Adrian's, searching, probing.

"I'm aware of its practice," Adrian replied, his voice betraying a hint of unease.

"I'm sure you are. But have you ever been on the receiving end of it?" Noah's question hung in the air, laden with threat.

Suddenly, without warning, his hand shot out, delivering a sharp, focused strike to the brachial plexus. The effect was immediate and devastating. Adrian's face contorted in agony as a wave of intense pain shot through him, akin to being struck by lightning. His right arm went limp, paralyzed by the shock to his nervous system.

Adrian swayed, nearly toppling out of the chair, saved only by his handcuffed arms. The precision of the strike had disrupted the nerve signals, throwing his body into turmoil. Noah kept him upright, his grip unforgiving.

Outside, the sounds of the team's concern grew more urgent. "Boss? Boss?" Ralph's voice was clear through the muffled din. "The local PD won't take kindly to us using our methods in their precinct."

But Noah wasn't listening. He held Adrian by the hair, the man's breaths coming in ragged gasps as he tried to control the pain. "Where is he keeping my daughter?" Noah demanded, his voice a snarl.

Adrian's response was a smile, one that ignited a fire of rage within Noah. He was poised to smash Adrian's face into the table when the door burst open. Captain Morelos, having obtained the key, stood in the doorway, an angry expression on his face.

"Stop right there," he commanded. "You wanna do it that way. Fine. You got jurisdiction. He's all yours."

His gaze shifted to Adrian, still reeling in pain. "But I'm telling you this. If that's the way it's gonna be"— he nodded at Adrian—"you take him elsewhere. Not my precinct."

Noah held the captain's gaze for a charged moment before relenting. Turning to Ralph, who stood by the door, he said, "Ralph, organize us a pickup. This bastard is coming with us on a little trip to international waters."

"Sure thing, boss," Ralph replied, nodding in understanding.

As Noah released his grip on Adrian, the room seemed to exhale, the tension dissipating as quickly as it had developed.

***

The relentless downpour seemed almost deliberate, each raindrop a harbinger of the chaos to come. Less than an hour after Captain Morelos had essentially kicked them out of his precinct, an E & E employee pulled up to the back of the building in an armored van. Parking it in one of the bays by the gate, he got out, ducking under the deluge, and met Team Camelot at the back door.

The keys glistened with rainwater as they were handed to Marco. "Orders are I'm to make my own way from here on in," the guy said.

"That'd be right," Marco replied.

The guy merely nodded and left through the rain.

"Okay," Noah said when he was gone. "Let's do this."

They escorted the handcuffed Adrian across the precinct's courtyard, Marco holding his right elbow,

Ralph holding the other. Noah led, Renée at their rear. The storm assaulted them with its full might, the wind whipping around them, their ears filled with a cacophony of howling gusts and pelting rain, as if nature itself was protesting the unfolding drama.

Adrian, in the midst of this tempest, paused for a moment and closed his eyes, his face upturned to the heavens.

"Hey," Marco complained. "Keep moving."

But Adrian wasn't listening. It was as if he was savoring the sensation of the rain on his skin, a man resigned to his fate, finding a moment of peace before the inevitable end. He inhaled deeply, the rain tracing paths down his pale face.

"Come on!" Ralph snarled, shoving him forward.

As they continued their short journey toward the van, its back doors gaping open like the maw of some beast, a shot pierced the racket of the crashing storm—a sharp, unmistakable crack, distinctly different from the rumble of thunder.

Adrian collapsed in an instant, the bullet's impact unmistakable.

Noah's eyes darted to the fire escape stairwell of a surrounding building, catching a glimpse of the sniper descending it with practiced ease, scaling down the steps to a waiting motorcycle. By the time Noah and the team burst out of the courtyard, the sniper was a ghost, disappearing into the storm-lashed streets.

Gasping for breath in the relentless downpour, Marco looked at Noah, his face a mask of confusion and concern. "You think it could be the same guy you chased out of the garage?" he asked, his voice barely audible over the din of the storm.

Noah didn't answer. His mind was racing, piecing together the fragments of this rapidly unraveling puzzle. He turned back toward the courtyard, his decision made.

"Come on," he called over his shoulder to Marco, who still stood rooted to the spot. "We need to get back to Kirtland. Speak to the Dragon Lady. Try to see what happens next."

They were words spoken not just as a command, but as a grim acceptance of the twisted path that lay ahead. Each step forward would be an unknown into the storm of betrayal and conspiracy that surrounded them.

CHAPTER SIX

The team's return to Kirtland was marked by a subdued air, their movements sluggish, reflecting the weight of their recent failure. Their cars lined the front of the airport building with a sense of defeated resignation.

Before getting in them, Marco, Renée, Ralph, and Noah gathered briefly, their expressions a blend of frustration and fatigue. The typical post-mission debrief was absent, replaced by a palpable sense of disappointment.

Marco broke the silence, his voice tinged with disbelief. "Can you believe it? All that planning for nothing."

Renée nodded, her eyes downcast. "It's like we were always one step behind."

Ralph, ever the pragmatic, chimed in with a sigh. "At least we're all back in one piece. That's something."

The group fell into a brief, uneasy silence, each lost in their own thoughts. Ralph was the first to break away, his car engine purring to life as he drove off, leaving a trail of unsettled dust behind.

Marco took this moment to pull Noah aside, away from Renée, who waited patiently by their SUV. His voice was low, filled with a mix of concern and suspicion.

"What the hell do you think this all was, boss?" he asked, his eyes searching Noah's.

Noah met his gaze. "How do you mean?"

Marco's frustration was evident. "First, the easy intel leading us straight to him. Then killing the informant like that before taking out one of his own guys. It feels like he was just bringing us out there to tease us."

Noah listened, his expression betraying nothing, yet inside, the wheels turned, analyzing each of Marco's points. He placed a reassuring hand on Marco's shoulder, his tone firm yet calming.

"We're dealing with a cunning adversary, Marco. He's playing a complex game. But remember, we've overcome worse. We'll regroup, reassess, and hit back harder."

Marco nodded, slightly appeased by Noah's words, yet the shadow of doubt lingered. He turned to join Renée at their SUV.

As they parted ways, Noah's gaze lingered on the departing figures of his team, the weight of leadership and the burden of the unknown pressing heavily on his shoulders.

***

Noah's drive back to the farmhouse was a blur of anxious thoughts and grim determination. The rain had followed them from Chicago, a steady drumming against the windshield of the Charger, each drop echoing his mounting dread.

Upon arriving home, he found the farmhouse eerily quiet. He pushed the front door open, his eyes immediately falling on Sarah, unconscious on the hallway floor. His heart clenched at the sight. Swiftly, he crossed the floor, gently lifting her into his arms and carrying her upstairs to their bed with a care that belied his urgency.

As he laid her down, Sarah stirred, her eyes fluttering open, confusion and dizziness clouding her gaze. Noah fetched her a glass of water, his movements mechanical.

While he fed her sips of water, Sarah's senses began to sharpen. Once the dizziness subsided a little, she started recounting the night's events, her voice shaky but gaining strength. Not even halfway through, though, she paused, her eyes narrowing as she studied Noah's face. "You already know, don't you?" she asked, a note of realization in her voice.

Noah met her gaze, his own filled with a turbulent mix of sorrow and anger. He nodded slowly. "I know about them taking Norah," he admitted quietly. "It was Adrian. The same people we were after in Chicago."

"What do they want?"

Sarah waited, her breath held in anticipation.

Noah's voice was low as he revealed the darker truths. "There's a kill list," he told her, his words hanging heavy in the air.

Sarah's face drained of color, her hands gripping the bedsheets. "A kill list?" she whispered, disbelief and fear mingling in her voice. "And what? He wants *you* to complete it?"

Noah nodded.

"Who's on it?" Sarah asked.

"I only have one name so far."

"Who?"

"Allison. The first target is Allison Peterson." His eyes never left Sarah's, conveying the gravity of the situation.

Sarah's reaction was a mix of shock and despair. Tears brimmed in her eyes as the reality of their situation set in. "Allison..." she murmured, her voice barely audible. "What are we going to do, Noah?"

Noah's jaw set, his determination resolute despite the turmoil inside him. "We'll protect Norah, Sarah. Whatever it takes."

His words were a promise, a vow made in the face of an unseen enemy. The moment was intimate and fragile, a brief sanctuary as Noah and Sarah clung to each other, seeking solace in the warmth of their embrace. But it was rudely shattered by the unwelcome intrusion of Schultz's voice, resonating through the secret comms unit nestled in Noah's ear. "What a poignant scene, Mr. Wolf."

Noah tensed, his body stiffening at the sound. The intimate moment evaporated, replaced by a cold sense of dread. Sarah, sensing the change, looked up at him, her eyes filled with concern. "What is it?" she asked, her voice laced with worry.

"He's speaking to me now," Noah replied, his voice a strained whisper. He moved away, distancing himself from Sarah as if to shield her from the venom in Schultz's words. "What do you want?" he demanded, trying to keep his voice steady.

Schultz's response was chilling in its casual cruelty. "The device in your ear has Bluetooth. Does your house have speakers?"

Noah's heart sank. "Yes," he answered, wariness

creeping into his tone.

"And do they connect to Bluetooth?" Adrian pressed on, his voice betraying a hint of perverse satisfaction.

Again, Noah answered, "Yes. Why?" His mind scrambled into action, trying to anticipate the assassin's next move.

"Because your wife may want to hear this next part." Schultz's words were like blades of ice, sending a shiver down Noah's spine.

His eyes met Sarah's, and in that brief exchange, a world of unspoken fears and questions passed between them. The atmosphere in the room shifted, charged with a new tension, a palpable sense of foreboding that hung heavy in the air. The storm outside seemed to echo their inner turmoil, its relentless battering against the windows a grim soundtrack to the unfolding nightmare.

Then something happened. Noah's heart clenched as the tender, innocent voice of his daughter Norah filtered through the earpiece. She was conversing with someone in the background, her tone light and carefree, blissfully unaware of the gravity of the situation. Schultz called out to her, his voice uncharacteristically gentle, a stark contrast to the harshness he seemed to reserve for Noah.

"How do I get this thing connected to Bluetooth?" Noah asked, urgency lacing his voice. Sarah watched him, her eyes wide with fear and anticipation.

"It's on seek now," Schultz instructed, his tone business-like. "Connect to it through the speaker."

Noah's fingers moved swiftly over the home stereo system, driven by a desperate need to hear his daughter.

He followed Schultz's instructions mechanically, his mind in a storm. As he completed the setup, Norah's voice suddenly filled the room, broadcast through the home speakers. Her innocent chatter, so normal and yet so heartbreakingly distant, echoed through the house.

The effect on Sarah was immediate and profound. The sound of her daughter's voice, so close yet so far away, was too much for her to bear. Tears burst forth, streaming down her face in a torrent of raw emotion. She sobbed, each cry a testament to her pain and longing, her maternal love palpable in every tear.

Noah stood, torn between comforting his wife and the harsh reality of their situation. His jaw was set, a hard line of determination and barely contained fury. The sound of Norah's voice was a bittersweet agony, a reminder of what they had lost and what he was fighting to regain.

The room filled with a tense, desperate energy as the couple listened. Noah's voice trembled slightly as he spoke, trying to mask his fear with reassurance. "Hey, sweetie, it's Daddy. Are you okay? Are they treating you well?"

Norah's reply was innocent, tinged with a hint of confusion. "Yes, Daddy. They have lots of toys here. But, Daddy?"

"Yes, sweetie?"

"Daddy, Mr. Henrik says that it was a game."

"What was a game?"

"Last night when he put tape over my mouth. He said we were all playing a game. He said Mommy was playing too, that she isn't really hurt."

"No no. She isn't…"

Sarah, her voice a fragile whisper amidst her tears, quickly interjected to maintain the façade for Norah's sake. "That's right, honey. Mommy is okay, it was all a game. We're all playing it together, and soon we'll be back together. We love you so much, sweetheart."

Norah, appeased by her parents' assurances, shifted the conversation with the blissful ignorance of a child. "Okay, Mommy. But when are you and Daddy coming to get me?"

Sarah, tears streaming down her face, managed to choke out words of comfort. "Soon, honey, we'll be there soon. We love you so much."

Schultz's voice suddenly cut in, his tone a chilling hiss compared to the tender exchange. "Let that be a motivation to you, Mr. Wolf. So far, I have kept my part of the bargain. You have two days left."

The line went dead, leaving a heavy silence in its wake. Sarah, overcome with emotion, threw herself into Noah's arms, her body wracked with sobs. Noah held her tightly, his own emotions a tumultuous mix of fear, anger, and a fierce determination. His eyes were hard, his mind already pulsating with plans and contingencies.

It was as the room seemed to close in around them, the storm outside mirroring the turmoil within, that Noah's new phone chimed.

"Who is it?" Sarah asked when he checked the screen.

"It's Allison," he replied. "She wants to debrief."

"Oh Noah," Sarah practically sobbed, throwing herself once more into his arms.

In that moment, they were united not just in their

love for each other and for Norah, but in their resolve to do whatever it took to bring their daughter home.

***

Less than ten minutes later, Team Camelot sat in a semi-circle in the dimly lit briefing room, fatigue all over their faces but eyes alert. The air crackled with anticipation. Allison Peterson, stern and composed, stood at the head of the table, Molly beside her, flipping through a dossier.

"All right, team," Allison began, her voice firm. "So the mission wasn't exactly a success."

"It was a disaster," Marco added.

"Well, Molly has a little information on the man you apprehended."

All eyes turned to Molly. "We've identified him. Thanks to running his DNA profile through the databases of several companies that test people's DNA, a match with three US citizens was found. A little detective work and we found a male relative that looks like our guy."

"Who was he?" Ralph asked.

"Michael Torres," Molly said, bringing his picture up on the screen behind her.

It depicted the head and shoulders of a man in his mid-thirties. His hair was dark, cropped short in a military style, with hints of premature graying at the temples. He had a strong, angular jawline and deep-set blue eyes. Noah recognized those eyes: they belonged to the man from Chicago.

"He's an ex-Green Beret," Molly went on. "After his discharge, things got murky. Financial troubles, a few run-ins with the law, and then…"

"And then he crossed paths with Adrian?" Renée suggested.

"Exactly," Molly explained. "Adrian recruited him, offering a way out of his debts. Trained him up, and soon Torres was one of their most efficient operatives."

Noah leaned forward, interjecting, "So a skilled soldier turned assassin. It just shows how deep Schultz's network goes."

Molly added, "Exactly. Perhaps if we take more of a look at Torres' recent activities, we might be able to find a way to get at them."

Allison added, "We need to dismantle this network before they strike again. Noah, what are your thoughts?"

Noah exchanged a glance with his team. "I have a feeling that we won't have to wait long before Adrian makes his next move. I think our only option is to wait. It's risky, but…"

"But necessary," Allison finished his sentence. "I agree. The only thing left is to wait. I don't think we'll find much with Torres. I'll leave him to the FBI. No. Noah is right. We have to be patient. Let Adrian make his move and be there when it happens."

The rest of the debriefing continued with some tactical discussions, strategic planning, and assignments of new roles. The atmosphere was one of determination mixed with the reality of the danger they faced.

The whole time Noah did his best not to think about the things he would have to do. Every now and then, he would catch himself casting a look across the dim light of the briefing room at Allison. In those moments he couldn't believe that soon, he would have to kill her.

***

Noah's '69 Dodge Charger cut a solitary figure on the rain-slicked roads of Kirtland as he drove away from the meeting. His journey was shadowed by overcast skies that seemed to mimic his internal conflict.

As he turned onto Temple Road, the earpiece crackled to life, Schultz's voice sliding into his ear with unsettling familiarity. "Home is the other way, Mr. Wolf," he pointed out, his tone casual yet laced with suspicion. "Where are you going?"

"Nowhere," Noah replied, keeping his voice neutral, his hands steady on the wheel.

"The Temple Road's not nowhere," Schultz retorted, his words revealing a disturbing level of surveillance. "It's where Research and Development is."

Noah's mind clicked into action, calculating his response. "You told me I could incorporate anyone into the conspiracy to help me with the kill list, as long as they kept it secret." His gaze flickered to the rearview mirror, half-expecting to see Schultz's eyes staring back at him.

"I did," Adrian conceded, a hint of curiosity in his tone.

"So I'm going to see the man I trust more than anyone else. He can help me." Noah's voice carried a faint note of defiance.

"But I can't access R&D's security system. I won't be able to see you," Schultz countered, his voice betraying a hint of frustration.

Noah smirked, a small victory in this high-stakes game of cat and mouse. This was something he had wanted to test—whether Adrian could penetrate the fortress that was R&D. Its security system, still in its experimental phase, was a standalone marvel, separate from the rest of Kirtland. The AI behind it was powerful, a little too powerful for some, and it provided a haven beyond Adrian's prying eyes.

"I need the help of Wally Lawson," Noah explained, laying his card, "and his tech if I'm going to get this done without being identified."

There was a pause, filled with the buzz of static— Schultz weighing his options. After a tense few seconds, he gave in, his voice grudgingly accepting Noah's plan. "Fine. But remember, I'm watching everything else."

As Noah pulled into the parking lot of R&D, the large building loomed ahead. He stepped out of the Charger, the rain peppering his jacket, and headed toward the entrance.

As he strode through the corridors, the soft hum of machinery and the distant clatter of keyboards created a symphony of progress and potential. Pushing open the doors to the main lab, Noah stepped into a world that felt both futuristic and slightly otherworldly. The air was filled with the faint buzz of activity, the scent of solder and circuitry mingling with the sterile cleanliness of the room. Tables laden with gadgets, screens displaying streams of data, and the constant flicker of LED lights painted a picture of relentless innovation.

At the center of this technological maelstrom was Wally Lawson, the eccentric genius completely engrossed in his latest creation. Surrounding him was a swarm of tiny drones, each designed to mimic the appearance and movement of a bee. Their amplified buzzing filled the room, creating a surreal ambiance. The swarm of drones danced around Wally in eerie coordination, their mechanical wings catching the light as they moved.

Noah watched for a moment, marveling at the sight. Wally, oblivious to his presence, continued his work, his hands deftly manipulating a control tablet, his eyes alight with the fervor of a man in his element.

Taking a deep breath, Noah stepped forward, his boots echoing slightly on the polished floor. "Wally," he called out, his voice cutting through the hum of the drones.

Wally looked up, startled, his concentration broken. His eyes, wide with surprise, locked on to Noah's. For a moment, time seemed to stand still, the only sound the continuous buzz of the mechanical bees.

The swarm of drones parted slightly, creating a tunnel of space between the two men. Through this corridor of buzzing wings, their gazes met.

"Wally, I need your help," Noah said, his voice steady but laced with an urgency that resonated in the space between them.

"In what?"

Taking a deep breath, Noah told him. "In assassinating the Dragon Lady."

The words hung in the air, a poignant echo amidst the whirring of the drones. Wally's expression shifted, a mixture of curiosity and outright concern, as he processed the weight of Noah's request.

CHAPTER SEVEN

Early next morning, Noah stood motionless at the bay window of the farmhouse, his gaze fixed on the framed picture in his hands. Beyond the glass, Lake Temple shimmered under an uncertain sky, its surface reflecting the tumultuous clouds above. The small boat they kept bobbed gently on the lapping waves, tugging at its mooring line at the base of the dock.

Noah saw nothing of the scene outside. His entire world was in the picture he held—Norah. It had been taken a few months ago at the beach. Her delicate little smile, revealing a row of milky baby teeth, was a bittersweet reminder of her innocence and purity. Noah's heart clenched in his chest, an ache so profound it transcended physical pain. In this moment, he was acutely aware that only two people in the whole wide world had the power to evoke such deep emotions within him: Norah and Sarah.

A shadow of a memory flickered in his mind— a much younger version of himself, witnessing the unthinkable. His own father, in a moment of madness, had taken the life of his mother before ending his own, cruelly leaving Noah orphaned and all alone. Those young eyes, once filled with innocence, had been stained by horror, the trauma leading to something doctors called 'blunted affect disorder.' His emotions, too painful and overwhelming, had been stifled by his own brain, seeking to shield him from further torment. They had become dormant, hidden deep within the recesses of his psyche.

Sarah and Norah had changed that. They had unearthed those buried emotions, rekindling his ability to feel, to connect, to love. They made him feel human again. They were his anchor in a life that had often felt adrift in numbness.

Now as he held the picture of Norah, Noah grappled with the gravity of the choice before him. To save his daughter, he had to betray Allison Peterson—the woman who had once saved him from death row, the woman who was Norah's godmother. The irony was cruel and unrelenting.

He felt the weight of his decision, the immense pressure of what he was about to do fixed heavily upon his back. It was a choice that pitted his past against his future, his gratitude against his love. The internal struggle was almost unbearable, each breath laden with doubt and resolve all at the same time.

As he gazed at Norah's innocent smile, a resolve hardened within him. He knew what he had to do, no matter how excruciating the cost. For Norah, for Sarah, he would walk through fire, battle his own demons, face the darkest parts of himself. Allison Peterson had once given him life. But now, to save his daughter, he was prepared to take hers.

Noah felt the warmth of another presence. Sarah's arms encircled around him from behind. She rested her chin on his shoulder, her voice soft but tinged with the weariness of countless sleepless nights. "Couldn't sleep either, huh?" she whispered into his ear.

Noah remained still, his eyes locked on Norah's picture. "I will get her back, Sarah. I promise," he said, his voice firm yet heavy with unspoken burdens.

Her embrace tightened slightly. "Does that mean what I think it does?" Sarah's voice was a fragile blend of hope and fear. "That you're going to do it? Do what he wants?"

Taking a deep breath, Noah gently placed the picture down. He turned to face Sarah, his eyes searching hers for understanding, for forgiveness for what he was about to do. "I have to go. Prepare things," he said, the words laden with a gravity that stretched beyond their simple meaning.

Sarah nodded, her eyes glistening with unshed tears. She understood the enormity of his decision, the sacrifices that loomed ahead. "Just... be careful, Noah. Please," she implored, her voice barely above a whisper.

He cupped her face in his hands, the touch a silent promise, a vow that transcended words. For a moment, they stood there, locked in an embrace that spoke of shared pain, unyielding love, and the daunting journey that lay ahead.

Noah finally released her, stepping back with a resolve that seemed to steel his entire being. He knew the path he had chosen was fraught with peril, a tightrope walk between morality and necessity. But for Sarah, for Norah, he would traverse any darkness, confront any demon.

As he walked away, each step felt like a march toward an inevitable confrontation with destiny. He left the farmhouse under the shroud of the early morning, the world around him still asleep, oblivious to the storm that was brewing in one man's heart. The choice he had made was irrevocable, a line crossed from which there was no return. Noah was no longer just a man fighting for his family; he was a soldier marching into battle, where the stakes were life itself.

***

Less than an hour later, Noah sat tensely in a surgical chair in one of the labs at R&D, his left forearm exposed and laid out on the arm rest, the limb feeling oddly detached under the influence of local anesthetic. Wally, hunched over the arm with a concentration that bordered on reverence, worked meticulously on the implant.

"Is the anesthetic still working?" he asked without looking up, his hands steady as he made delicate adjustments to the device nestled just under Noah's skin.

"Yes. It's still numb," Noah replied, trying not to focus too much on the bizarre sensation of disconnectedness where the implant was being installed.

"Good. This shouldn't take much longer. It's nearly complete." Wally's voice was calm, especially when compared to the storm of thoughts that raged in Noah's mind.

As Wally continued his work, he began to explain the features of the implant he was inserting into Noah's arm in a tone that was both clinical and tinged with a hint of pride.

"This device is powered by your body's own bioelectric energy. It harnesses the kinetic and thermal energy you naturally produce. So as long as you're moving and, well, warm, it'll keep working."

Noah nodded, intrigued despite the surreal situation.

"It's also equipped with state-of-the-art encryption. The messages you send and receive will be secure, undecipherable to anyone but you and your intended recipient. And for added security, we've included biometric authentication. Only your specific biometric markers can activate and access the device."

Wally paused, selecting a tool and continuing the surgery. "Now for the stealth aspect. We've constructed it from advanced non-metallic composites. It won't set off metal detectors, and it's designed to be virtually invisible to X-ray and other imaging technologies."

Noah's brow furrowed. "What if it's detected electronically?"

"We've thought of that too," Wally continued. "It's shielded against electromagnetic detection. The material not only blocks signals from escaping but also prevents external signals from interfering with its operation."

He glanced up at Noah, a slight smile playing on his lips. "Best of all, though, it'll allow you to communicate without Adrian being aware—as well as haptic feedback for silent alerts."

Wally refocused his attention on Noah's arm. "We're almost done here," he said. "To activate it, press gently under your left ribcage where there's a pressure sensor. It's designed to feel like a natural extension of your body. And... voilà! There you have it!"

He rolled back in his chair, giving Noah a clear view. Bringing his left forearm in line with his face, Noah gazed at the message glowing beneath his skin.

"Esmeralda?" Wally called.

"Yes, Wally?" replied the AI's voice, echoing through the lab.

"Would you be so kind as to dim the lights, please?" Wally requested. To Noah, he explained, "It's more effective in low light."

Indeed it was. As the room darkened, the message on Noah's forearm became more pronounced against the shadows. 'Hello, Noah,' it read.

"Now try sending a message back," Wally encouraged.

Beneath the fingertips of Noah's right hand, pads had been positioned to interact with the implant. He started tapping on his left forearm, treating it like a keyboard. Before long, 'Hi, Wally' appeared, and he sent it.

Wally's phone vibrated. He held the screen out to see—the message had been successfully sent.

Noah mulled over the implications of such a device —the secrecy, the power, the potential risks. Gazing down at his forearm, he felt the weight of the responsibility that now literally rested within him.

As Wally sat admiring his handiwork on Noah's arm, the lab door opened. One of Wally's assistants, a young woman with an intense gaze, approached them, holding Adrian's minuscule earpiece between her fingers.

"We've finished the analysis," she announced, handing the earpiece to Wally. "Esmeralda has scanned it completely."

Wally got up from his chair, took the earpiece, and walked toward a central computer console. "Esmeralda, report," he commanded.

The room was soon filled with the clear, artificial voice of Esmeralda. "The earpiece's encryption is sophisticated, approaching the standards of our own security protocols at R&D. Tracing back to its origin or intercepting its communications remotely will be impossible with current technology. However, if we had access to at least two additional devices similar to this one, we might stand a chance at locating Adrian by intersecting the multiple signals. With only one, however, such a task remains unfeasible."

Noah's expression tightened. This meant they couldn't use the earpiece to track Adrian or eavesdrop on his communications.

Just then, Noah felt a strange sensation on his arm—a gentle vibration that tickled his skin. Startled, he remembered the implant Wally had just installed. Pressing the discreet activation button under his ribcage, he saw the skin of his forearm light up, revealing a scrolling message that moved like a digital whisper under his skin:

'This is 9,' it read. 'We are ready and everything is in place.'

Noah's eyes narrowed as he read the message. He was still adjusting to the bizarre feeling of receiving communications through his own body.

Wally, noticing Noah's focused gaze on his arm, asked, "Everything all right?"

Noah looked up. "It's 9," he said, trying to mask the urgency he felt. "They're ready."

Wally nodded. "Good. You will need to stay in contact with them. Remember, Noah, that device is more than just a tool. It's a lifeline, a link to those you trust. Use it wisely."

As Noah processed this, he realized the gravity of the situation. The message from 9—a key player in his plans to thwart Adrian—meant that the game was changing, and he had to be ready to adapt.

With a determined nod to Wally, Noah stood up. "Thank you, Wally. This... this changes everything."

As he left the lab, the weight of his mission felt heavier than ever. But armed with Wally's tech, Noah knew he had a fighting chance. The next steps were crucial, and time was of the essence.

***

Since he'd started wearing the earpiece, Noah had mastered the subtle cues of Schultz's presence and absence on the other end. Each time Schultz was near, the earpiece emitted a faint, barely perceptible hiss, a signal Noah had become attuned to. It was his way of discerning when his adversary was directly listening in, though he harbored no illusions: someone, or something—perhaps an AI algorithm sifting through keywords—was likely always eavesdropping.

As Noah stepped out of the R&D building clutching a heavy-looking duffle bag, the earpiece stirred to life, emitting that telltale whisper of a hiss. It was promptly followed by Schultz's inquisitive voice echoing in Noah's head. "What were you doing at R&D?" he demanded.

Noah walked toward his Dodge Charger, a faint smirk on his face. "What do you think? If I'm going to do this job for you, I need Wally's tech. You see the jacket I'm now wearing?" he replied, subtly enjoying the back-and-forth with Schultz.

"Yes" came the wary response, Adrian watching

him from a nearby security camera.

"It's a quantum cloak," Noah said, adding an undertone of mock secrecy to his voice.

"And what does a quantum cloak do?" Schultz inquired, his curiosity evident.

Noah couldn't resist a bit of showmanship. He slipped the hood over his head. "Now you see me," he announced and then activated the cloak. "Now you don't."

There was a significant pause from Schultz's end, undoubtedly as he scrutinized every camera feed he had hacked into.

"Clever," he finally conceded.

Noah removed the hood and deactivated the cloak, a small smile playing on his lips. "I thought you'd appreciate the trick," he quipped as he reached the Dodge and placed the duffle bag in the trunk. "With Kirtland crawling with cameras," he went on in a more serious tone as he slammed the lid down, "I'm gonna need this if I have any hope of getting away with murdering Allison."

There followed a short pause, nothing but the sound of breathing and the hiss in Noah's ear. Then, with a hint of suspicion in his voice, Schultz pointed out, "You were wearing that jacket the night we picked you up."

"I was," Noah confirmed, climbing into the car.

"When you disappeared in the alley," Schultz added.

"Getting paranoid, Henrik?" Noah teased lightly, starting the Charger's engine with a roar.

"No. But it is the same jacket," Schultz countered,

trying to maintain a tone of authority.

As Noah reversed out of his space and began to turn around, he responded, "It's not the exact same. Wally has made this one to look like my normal jacket —the one I was wearing in Chicago—so that no one will suspect. That's what he's been working on for me today. We were fitting it out."

Schultz appeared to buy this explanation. "And Wally Lawson?" he inquired. "What is his view of you killing Allison Peterson? I thought you people at E & E were all practically family."

"He's onboard for the same reason I am: Norah," Noah said, his voice more solemn as he drove off. "She's an innocent. Wally's a logical thinker, like me. He understands. Allison has lived her life. Norah hasn't."

"The cold logic of killers," Schultz acknowledged.

"Wally's no killer."

"But he invents things for you to use in the process of killing."

"I suppose."

"You don't think Oppenheimer wasn't just as guilty as everyone else for all those dead Japanese?"

Noah said nothing. The conversation was touching on an almost personal level, and he didn't want to get pally with the guy holding his daughter hostage.

"And what's in that duffle bag?" came Schultz's next question, sharp with curiosity.

"Tools for the job," Noah replied casually, navigating through the busy streets of Kirtland. He could sense Schultz's unsatisfied curiosity, like a shadow looming over their conversation.

Schultz pressed, "And these tools are?"

Noah exhaled slowly, his grip tightening on the steering wheel. "I haven't got all day to list every piece of tech, Henrik. It's just what I need to get the job done. Okay?"

There was a brief silence, the hiss of the earpiece filling the void. Then Schultz relented, "Just so long as you get this done, I don't care what you use."

Noah nodded to himself, feeling a momentary sense of triumph. As he merged onto the highway, his thoughts lingered on the task ahead, the weight of it pressing down on him. The conversation with Schultz had been another step in their intricate dance, a dance that was edging ever closer to its next, decisive moves.

CHAPTER EIGHT

A short while later, Noah stood in the shadows of an alleyway, his eyes fixed on the entrance of the E & E offices across the street. He was a ghost in this world of passersby and bustling traffic—a silent observer meticulously charting every movement of his unwitting target, Allison Peterson.

As Allison emerged from the office for lunch, accompanied by Molly, Noah checked his watch, noting the time with robotic precision. Remaining out of sight, he followed the women at a safe distance as they made their way to a nearby diner.

From a vantage point across the street, Noah watched the women enter, then, through the diner's window, he watched them take their seats. There sat Allison, lively and animated, laughing at something Molly had said. The normalcy of the scene gnawed at him. It was such a stark contrast to the grim reality he was orchestrating.

As he observed them order, his mind drifted to Norah's innocent smile. He could practically hear her sweet little chuckle in his ears. Only the day before yesterday she had filled their home with so much joy. The memory was a sharp blade, cutting through his moral quandaries. He reminded himself that this was for Norah, for Sarah. Yet the justifications did little to ease the turmoil within him.

It was then that Noah's blood froze in his veins as a familiar voice broke his attention.

"Hey, boss," Marco greeted, his approach casual and unsuspecting.

Noah turned to him. "Marco, hey," he replied, masking the intensity of his surveillance with a practiced ease.

"What you up to?" Marco inquired, his eyes scanning the street.

"Just about to go pick up some lunch for Sarah and Norah," Noah responded, smoothly diverting the conversation.

"Oh, ay. That's what I was about to do." Marco's gaze followed Noah's, landing on Allison and Molly in the diner. A smirk played on his lips as he added, "Looks like the Dragon Lady and Molly beat us to it."

"Yeah. Looks like it."

Marco gestured toward the diner with an easy grin. "You know, I've heard their pastrami sandwich is something of a legend around here."

Noah nodded, playing along with the casual banter. "Yeah, but have you tried their club sandwich? It's a game changer."

Marco chuckled, his eyes twinkling with amusement. "A game changer, huh? Big words for a sandwich."

"It's not just a sandwich, it's an experience," Noah quipped, keeping his tone light despite the undercurrent of tension he felt.

"The way you talk about it, sounds like it should

have its own fan club," Marco replied, his laughter genuine.

Noah smiled, the ease of their conversation a temporary respite from the gravity of his mission. "If it doesn't, it should. I might just start one."

"Yeah, right," Marco replied. "Anyway, you were gonna get those sandwiches."

Caught in an unexpected turn of events, Noah found himself walking into the diner alongside Marco, entering the very scene he had been observing from a distance. The air inside was filled with the aroma of coffee and freshly baked bread, a stark contrast to the tension Noah felt.

As they approached Allison and Molly's table, the diner murmured with the easygoing chatter of a casual lunch outing. Smiles lit up the faces of the two women as Noah and Marco drew near, a picture of warmth and familiarity.

"Hey, Noah, Marco." Allison greeted them with a bright smile, her voice infused with genuine pleasure. "Fancy seeing you here."

Molly chimed in, her tone equally welcoming, "Yeah, join us! The more the merrier."

Marco responded with his characteristic Cajun charm, "We wouldn't miss it for the world, mademoiselle."

Noah and Marco took seats in the booth next to them.

"You two often come here to Ray's?" Noah asked the ladies as they got comfortable.

"All the time," Allison replied. "Especially when we're working late in the office, like tonight, so a good lunch is exactly what we need."

Noah's mind clicked. The cover of night. Less people in the offices. Easy to find. Could it really be so easy?

Marco's voice pulled him from his reverie.

"I've heard too many good things about the sandwiches here. Looks like I'm about to discover what all the fuss is about."

Noah slid into the conversation seamlessly, his smile never faltering. "That's right. Best sandwiches in town."

"I'll second that," Allison agreed.

"That's praise indeed," Marco jokingly remarked. "'Specially if the big bad boss lady gives it her stamp of approval."

The table erupted in light laughter, the kind that comes from shared jokes and comfortable friendships. For the next minutes, the easygoing conversation flowed effortlessly, topics meandering from the food to casual office banter.

Yet beneath the easy façade, Noah's mind was a tumultuous sea. Every laugh, every light-hearted comment was overshadowed by the grim reality of what lay ahead. His smile remained unbroken, his responses sharp and witty, but behind his calm exterior, he wrestled with an internal storm of emotion. The dichotomy of his actions and his true intentions created a surreal contrast, casting a shadow on the otherwise sunny atmosphere. No one at the table, not Allison, not Molly, nor the unsuspecting Marco, could have guessed the turmoil raging within Noah. They were oblivious to the fact that in less than twenty-four hours, their lives, as they knew them, would be irrevocably altered. Noah, the man they knew as a colleague and a friend, was harboring a secret that, if revealed, would shatter the very foundation of their reality.

As laughter and light conversation filled the diner, Noah was acutely aware of the ticking clock, each second bringing him closer to a decision that would define the rest of his life. The weight of what lay ahead hung heavily on his shoulders, a burden disguised by a veneer of normalcy in an ordinary diner on an otherwise unremarkable day.

**

Later, in the quiet confines of the farmhouse basement, Noah sat hunched over a laptop, the screen glowing in the dim light. Scattered around him were plans of Kirtland with particular emphasis on the E & E building. As he methodically made notes on a notepad beside him, each stroke of the pen was a step closer to formulating a plan.

A half-eaten chicken and bacon club sandwich lay forgotten beside the keyboard. The room was a hub of strategic planning, filled with maps and diagrams, each a piece of the puzzle he was desperately trying to solve.

The sound of soft footsteps announced Sarah's presence. Having been asleep in Norah's room when Noah had returned, she looked somewhat rested yet still carried a weight of concern in her sunken eyes. She moved gracefully across the room and took a seat beside him, her presence a comforting warmth. Resting her head on his shoulder, she gazed at the screen and the myriad of notes.

"This how you're going to do it?" she asked softly, her voice tinged with a mixture of fear and resolve.

"Yeah," Noah replied, his voice low but steady.

Sarah's eyes scanned his notes, absorbing the details of his plan. After a moment, she looked up at him, determination etched on her face. "Let me help you," she said, her words not just an offer but a plea to be a part of this battle they were fighting together.

Noah leaned back slightly, turning to face Sarah, his eyes reflecting a mixture of appreciation and concern. "It's not going to be easy," he began, his voice low and serious. "The E & E building is like a fortress. Armed security guards, patrols, cameras with facial recognition... It's designed to keep people out—or in, depending on how you look at it."

Sarah nodded, her blue eyes fixed on the laptop screen. "What about the personnel?"

Noah tapped a few keys, bringing up detailed employment files. "They work in shifts. Changeover is my best bet. Earlier on, I bumped into Allison and Molly at Ray's Deli."

"That must've been odd," Sarah remarked.

"It was. Nevertheless, I learned that Allison is working late tonight. The final shift change of the day is at nine. It means there'll be a brief window where things are in flux," Noah explained. He scribbled something on the notepad, underlining it twice.

Sarah's gaze followed his pen. "Escape routes?"

He sighed, running a hand through his hair. "That's the tricky part. There's the main entrance, of course, but that will be watched—especially if the body is discovered before I leave or if I'm seen. There are service exits, but they're likely to be locked down quickly." He paused, his finger tracing a line on the map. "I'm thinking the old service tunnels that run underneath R&D."

She frowned. "And if things go wrong?"

Noah met her gaze, his eyes resolute. "That's where the contingencies come in. I've got multiple scenarios planned out." He hesitated, then added, "You understand, though, Sarah, that getting away with it will only be the first part. After that, the real work will begin. We'll have to lie to the faces of our friends. They'll want to know who killed her, and they'll expect me to find out."

Sarah reached out, placing her hand over his, and looked deep into her husband's eyes. "I understand. But do we really have no choice in all of this, Noah?"

Noah shook his head. "I've wracked my brains, baby." He took a deep breath. "There's no other way... At least not in the short term. Not if we want Norah back."

She squeezed his hand reassuringly. "You're the best father, Noah. Don't let anyone say different. You're doing this for our little girl, and that's all there is to it."

He gave her a small, grateful smile. "Thank you, baby." The determination in his voice was unmistakable. They were in this together, facing an uncertain future with a shared resolve.

Noah went to add something to this when his cell phone suddenly chimed. He glanced at it, a message from Adrian, his expression stoic as he inserted the earpiece that lay on the table beside him. The room fell silent for a moment, the tension palpable, before Schultz's voice filtered through the small device.

"You should keep that thing in at all times," came his stern rebuke.

Noah responded calmly, maintaining his composure. "I didn't think it was necessary to wear it every waking moment."

There was a brief pause on the other end, and Noah could almost picture Schultz weighing his words. "This operation doesn't afford you the luxury of being off-grid, even for a moment," he finally replied, his tone more controlled but still firm.

"I understand," Noah said, his voice betraying no emotion. "It won't happen again."

"Make sure it doesn't," Schultz warned, his words tinged with a sense of smug superiority. "I've been two steps ahead of you since the beginning, Noah," he boasted, his tone dripping with condescension. "I knew about you coming back to Kirtland before you did. Knew Allison Peterson would make that journey to the Sunshine State to beg you to come back. Knew you'd bring your family back to the lake."

The casual mention of specific details sent a chill down Noah's spine. Schultz continued, oblivious to the storm he was stirring within Noah. "I even watched that little escapade at the diner in Florida. The robbery. You taking out those two thugs who snatched the old man's wallet. Impressive, but it just showed how predictable you are."

Noah's mind went into a spin. That incident hadn't been widely known. It was a private moment, a fleeting incident in their past. The realization that Adrian had been watching them for so long was a jolt.

But it wasn't just that. It also pointed to an unsettling truth: There was a mole in Kirtland, possibly within E & E. Because only a select few knew about them being in the Florida Keys, and they were all part of Noah's inner circle.

Noah kept his voice steady, giving nothing away. "Thank you for that, Henrik," he said, his tone polite but laced with an undercurrent of cold calculation.

As the line went dead, Noah's mind went into overdrive, analyzing every interaction, every conversation with his team. Who among them could betray him? The thought was a bitter pill stuck to his tongue.

Turning to the notepad, his face a mask of grim determination, he began scribbling something down: *There's a mole inside Kirtland, and we need to find them.*

Sarah's eyes widened, a mix of shock and understanding in them.

CHAPTER NINE

It was a black night, and nine o'clock was fast approaching. Consumed by the weight of what lay ahead, Noah's mind was sharpened to a point. The late-night stillness of the farmhouse felt more oppressive than peaceful, each silent moment heavy with the anticipation of what was to come.

In the dimly lit hallway, Sarah and Noah stood close, their eyes locked in a moment that spoke volumes without a word being spoken. There was an intensity in the air, a palpable mix of fear, love, and determination. They both understood the gravity of the situation, the unspoken possibility that this could be their last moment together.

"Be careful," Sarah whispered, her voice barely above a breath. The words were simple, yet they carried the weight of all their unspoken fears and hopes.

Noah nodded, his eyes never leaving hers. "I will," he replied, his voice steady yet thick with emotion. His hand reached out, gently touching her cheek, a tender gesture that belied the harsh reality of what lay ahead.

They lingered in their embrace, a silent farewell charged with the hope of a safe return. As Noah finally pulled away, there was a finality in his step, a resolve that spoke of his commitment to do whatever it took to protect his family.

Leaving the farmhouse quietly, Noah moved through the shadows to the lake where a small motorboat waited. Equipped with a soundless electric outboard motor, it was a ghostly vessel that glided silently across the still waters of Temple Lake.

As the boat cut through the water, the vast lake unfolded in the dim light of the moon, its surface shimmering with its glowing refection. The kidney-shaped lake curved around the small mountain range that cradled one side of Kirtland, a natural barrier that Noah would be using to his advantage.

Mooring the boat, Noah carefully donned the hood of the quantum cloak. As he pulled it over his head, he became a digital ghost—knowing that even the mountain range was covered in surveillance cameras hidden in the rocks and trees.

His hike up the mountains was a solitary journey, each step a deliberate move toward his objective. The terrain was rugged, but Noah moved with the ease of someone accustomed to such challenges. The only sounds were the soft rustle of his movements and the distant call of nocturnal birds of prey.

As he reached the entrance to Kirtland on the other side of the range, the world seemed to hold its breath. The atmosphere was one of eerie calm, the quiet before the storm. Noah's approach had been methodical, each movement calculated, his senses heightened to every nuance of his surroundings.

Across the road, the gatehouse loomed like a sentry. The stillness of the night hung heavy in the air, punctuated only by the occasional whisper of the fallen leaves being blown about in the breeze. From his vantage point, Noah could see the outlines of the two guards moving inside the gatehouse as the men started their shift, their silhouettes casting shadows against the dimly lit interior. He took a deep breath, steadying himself for the task ahead, then made his way across the road into destiny...

***

Minutes later, the air in Allison Peterson's office hung heavy with the finality of what had just occurred. The Dragon Lady lay dead behind her desk, a bullet hole in her forehead.

Molly's eyes, wide behind her glasses, met Noah's with a mix of shock and disbelief.

"Noah?" she whispered.

"I'm so sorry, Molly."

For a fleeting second, time seemed to freeze, the world reduced to the space between them. But then reality snapped back with the harsh whisper of the silenced gunshot.

Molly, a woman Noah had known practically his entire life, crumpled to the floor, her disbelief etched forever in her lifeless eyes.

Noah, his heart pounding in his ears, turned on his heel and fled, Schultz's voice in his earpiece, cold and detached. "Good work, Mr. Wolf. Now it's time to get out of there so you can terminate the remaining names on the list."

Noah activated the TWRI and placed it to the door of the office, Molly's body lying about a meter from his right foot. The device buzzed softly in his hands, its screen painting a ghostly blueprint of the building layout and the positions of the people inside. He used it to plot his escape through the hallways, avoiding the paths that showed signs of movement, and left the room, closing the door behind.

His every step was a blend of trained precision and raw instinct. The quantum cloak's fabric fluttered silently around him, keeping him invisible to the cameras that were everywhere.

Approaching a junction of corridors, he paused. Ahead, two guards conversed, blocking his only route forward. They hadn't been there a minute ago when he'd checked with the TWRI.

It was a hassle. But he did have other tricks.

Noah's hand moved deftly to the parametric speaker clipped to his belt. He adjusted the settings, aiming the wand down the corridor. A moment later, he activated it, releasing a faint, directional sound—a distant whisper of someone calling for help, just audible enough to pique curiosity.

The guards, their conversation interrupted, tilted their heads, listening. Confusion etched their features as they tried to discern the source of the phantom sound. "Did you hear that?" one guard murmured to the other, his voice laced with uncertainty.

"Yeah, sounded like it came from down there," the other replied, nodding in the direction Noah had intended.

As they moved off to investigate, Noah seized the moment. He slipped past the spot they had vacated, his presence nothing more than a fleeting shadow. Behind him, the guards' murmurs faded into the distance, their footsteps resonating off the walls as they moved farther away.

However, only seconds later, all hell broke loose. Someone had discovered the bodies. The building instantly became a hive of activity. Alarms began to blare, a shrill sound that pierced the air and set Noah's nerves on edge. The once quiet corridors were now thrumming with the sound of running feet and urgent voices, his planned escape route disappearing.

Schultz's voice filled Noah's ear. "Keep moving. You need to get out now," he urged, his tone laced with an edge of anxiety. "The whole place is on alert. They'll be locking down exits."

Noah's steps quickened, his mind a whirlwind of calculations and strategies. Every second mattered now, every movement had to be precise.

"Into the storage cupboard on your right," Schultz commanded. "Quick!"

Noah dived into the cupboard just as two armed men ran around the corner.

"Stay there," Schultz whispered. "They're passing you now."

Noah checked the power of the cloak. There was only one bar of battery left. It would be useless in a matter of minutes. The safety of invisibility was slipping away with each passing moment.

"Go!" Schultz snapped.

Noah left the cupboard, head down, bolting along the corridor. "There's an open window in the third room on the left." *One, two, three,* Noah counted off, then dived through the door.

The room was empty, and the window was straight ahead. Checking outside, he saw the beams of flashlights bobbing about in the dark as additional security headed to the building. More importantly, however, there was no one close enough to see him climb out the window and shimmy down a drainpipe to the ground.

The cold night air pinched his skin, his breath stretching before him as he hid behind an air-conditioning unit at the edge of the building. With the power of the quantum cloak waning, every moment he remained was a gamble.

"Stay low and move toward the parking lot." Schultz's voice crackled in his ear; Noah's enemy was now his protector. "I'm watching the cameras. I'll guide you."

Noah moved cautiously, keeping to the shadows, his senses hyper-alert. The parking lot was a minefield of potential exposure, dotted with cars and intermittent pools of light from the overhead streetlamps.

"Stop," Schultz commanded suddenly. Noah ducked behind a nearby minivan, his heart pounding in his chest. "There's a guard to your left. Wait for him to pass."

Peering from his cover, Noah watched the silhouette of a guard stroll past, oblivious to the ghost in his midst. Once the coast was clear, Schultz's voice ushered him forward. "Go now, quickly but quietly."

Noah advanced, his steps silent on the asphalt. The cloak made him invisible to the cameras, but a careless move could still betray his presence to the naked eye.

"Stop. Someone's coming out of the building to your left," Schultz warned. Noah's reflexes were instantaneous, ducking behind an SUV just as a pair of guards emerged from a small office block, talking animatedly. They passed by without a second glance, lost in conversation.

"Okay, move. Head to the northeast corner. There's less activity there."

Noah navigated the maze of cars, his progress a careful dance between light and shadow. The tension was a physical thing, a tight wire stretched to its limit. Each command from Schultz was a step further toward safety—or a plunge deeper into danger.

"You're close to the tunnel. Just another fifty meters."

Noah's legs carried him swiftly across the last stretch. The utility station loomed ahead, his way into the service tunnels lying on the other side of a padlocked door. His sanctuary was a windowless building with a flat roof, and as he made his way quickly toward it, Noah only had eyes for the utility station.

Maybe that was why he didn't see him.

Noah had the lock open and his hand on the door when a voice pierced the quiet. "Noah?" It was a call, tentative yet clear.

Noah froze, the name echoing in his ears, the door open an inch. Who could have recognized him?

Slowly, he turned to face the speaker.

Ralph stood there, his pistol drawn and aimed right for Noah. His face was a mask of shock, betrayal, and most of all confusion. The familiar lines of camaraderie and trust were now etched with a deep, unsettling conflict. "I recognized your jacket," he said, his voice cutting through the silence.

Noah's mind spun, searching for words that could explain the unexplainable. "It's not what it seems,

Ralph," he managed to say. "There's more to it all than you know—and much more that I can't explain to you right now. Can you just trust me, Ralph?"

"They say a guy matching your description was just seen leaving the offices. You know the Dragon Lady and Molly just got shot, right?"

All Noah could do was look at him, hoping that five years of knowing each other meant something, his fingers still wrapped around the handle of the door.

"Damn it, Noah! She was more than just our boss, she was our friend! Our family! How could you?" Ralph's anguish was obvious, his voice wavering, his finger twitching on the trigger.

"I had no choice, Ralph. It's… it's complicated," Noah tried to explain, but the words sounded hollow even to his own ears.

"There's always a choice!" Ralph's voice rose in a crescendo. "We trusted you! *I* trusted you!"

Noah could see the turmoil in Ralph's eyes, the struggle between duty and friendship. He knew he had to act fast. "I'm sorry, Ralph. I truly am." With those words, Noah turned and ripped the door open, throwing himself into the utility station and jamming the door behind him.

Ralph ran for the door, but by the time he got there, Noah had secured it, and there was no immediate way through.

As Noah ran into the service tunnel, the sound of Ralph's anguished pounding at the door faded into the distance, replaced by the pounding of his own heart and the rush of blood in his ears. The betrayal he knew Ralph now felt weighed heavily on him, but there was no turning back. Ahead lay the path he had chosen, a road paved with shadows and secrets, leading him further into the darkness.

CHAPTER TEN

After what felt like hours, but in reality was only a fraction of that, Noah reached the end. He paused in the dimly lit service tunnel, a few steps from the exit.

If it hadn't been for Ralph spotting him like that, he would have gone left instead of right at the fork about five hundred meters back. That would have taken him just underneath the barn in his yard. There, he would have climbed out of a hatch and been back home with Sarah already, ready to receive the call that Allison and Molly were dead. But that's not what happened.

Because Ralph had seen him, he had to go left. To the place he was now, a place he hoped he'd never need: his escape route from Kirtland.

Here, underneath some ordinary street in the next town over and tucked away in a concealed compartment, lay the items he had meticulously prepared for a scenario just like this one. The air was musty, filled with the earthy scent of damp soil and concrete. Several loose bricks shuffled easily out of the gap they sat in. From the cavity, Noah retrieved a simple yet effective disguise kit, a set of nondescript clothing, and most importantly, the documentation of a new identity. With practiced speed, he changed his appearance, discarding his recognizable attire for something far more inconspicuous. He then skillfully inserted a dental prosthetic inside his mouth, subtly altering the shape of his mouth and cheeks, adding a distinct but unrecognizable fullness to his face. A fake beard and glasses completed the transformation, significantly altering his recognizable features. He also added a little tradecraft, stooping his back a little and widening his gait.

The final touch was a set of forged identification papers. Noah inspected them briefly, ensuring they matched his new appearance. These documents would be his shield in the outside world, a necessary façade to evade the intense scrutiny he was sure to be under.

Climbing out of the tunnel via a manhole, he found himself on a quiet, residential street, the world fast asleep under the starry sky. Houses lined the road, their inhabitants likely still nestled in bed or in front of the TV. His footsteps were silent as he moved toward a black Chevy Silverado parked a short distance away. It was an average pickup, chosen because it was one of the most popular vehicles in this area.

Noah slid into the driver's seat, the interior of the pickup as plain as its exterior. He started the engine, the sound barely audible in the tranquil night air. As he drove away, he kept his movements calm and measured, just another night worker going off to start his shift.

The journey was long, a relentless drive that took almost an entire day. He avoided major roads and populated areas, sticking to back roads and lesser-known routes. His vigilance never wavered, eyes constantly scanning for any signs of pursuit. The landscape gradually changed, the mountains and rolling plains flattening out into picturesque deserts before transforming into lush, fertile valleys.

As he neared his destination, a sense of surreal familiarity washed over him. The streets and houses of his childhood neighborhood came into view, a mosaic of memories, some dark and some light. He approached his childhood home, a place heavy with history, now a refuge in his hour of need. The house, a silent witness to the tragedies of his past, stood as the last place anyone would think to look for him. A place both haunted and safe, it was his sanctuary amidst the chaos that his life had become.

He arrived at a modest two-story house that looked like any other in this area of northern California. To any passerby, it was unremarkable, but to Noah, it was a place heavy with memories. It was his childhood home, the scene of a tragedy that had shaped his entire life.

A few years ago, when he had seen the 'For Sale' sign in front of the house, something had compelled him to buy it. It was a decision driven by a mix of sentiment and strategy. For him, the house was a reminder of a past he could never escape, but it was also the perfect hideout—the last place anyone would think to look for him.

He entered the house. It was just as he had left it: sparsely furnished, the walls bare, the air stale with disuse. It was a stark contrast to the warmth and life of the farmhouse he shared with Sarah and Norah.

Noah moved from room to room with a sense of detachment. Each one held a memory, a ghost from the past. This was where he had grown up, where he had witnessed the unspeakable horror of his father's actions. The walls seemed to whisper with the echoes of that day, the day when everything had changed.

In the kitchen, the memories were worst. Still, in his numbed emotional state, Noah was able to keep them at arm's length as he pressed a button hidden at the back of the fridge. With a mechanical hum, the floor retracted several feet from the far wall, revealing a square hatch underneath. He quickly tapped in a code on the keypad beside it, and the hatch opened outward with a click. Dropping into the safe room below, he found himself surrounded by all he needed: communications gear, supplies, weapons, and a computer connected to a secure network.

As he sat down at the computer, the hatch door closed above him, and the kitchen floor extended back over it. Noah was now a fugitive, hunted by those he had once called allies. But he was not without resources or resolve. He was already planning his next move, his mind already racing through the possibilities.

Outside, the world went about its business, unaware of the man hidden in the depths of an old, forgotten house. A man who was now a ghost in his own life. Noah was well aware of the chaos he had left behind. He knew his first priority should be to check in on Sarah.

Now he was safely cocooned away, he picked up the fully encrypted phone and dialed her number. As it rang, each tone echoed in the silence of the room. When Sarah answered, her voice was laced with a mixture of fear and sadness.

"Hello?" she said softly.

"Hey, babe," he said back.

"Noah," she cried, her voice cracking with emotion as she breathed heavily into the phone. "Noah, why? Why did you do it, baby? Tell me."

Noah knew they were listening in. This was her way of letting him know—pretending she knew nothing about what he had planned. What *they* had planned. Nevertheless, despite that, despite him knowing her sadness was an act, his throat still tightened, hearing the pain in her voice.

"Sarah, I... I don't know what to say," he started, making his voice sound strained. "Just know that I love you. I love you and Norah more than anything."

His words were a blend of truth and deception, a necessary façade to protect her. To make those listening trust her. After all, she'd need to find the mole on her own now, so Noah needed her to be above suspicion.

"Where are you?" she asked.

They'd told her to say that.

"Somewhere safe," he replied, dodging the question.

"Come home, Noah," Sarah managed to say between sobs. "Whatever has happened, we can work through it. Together. I love you."

"I love you, too, babe." Noah ended the call, his heart aching with the lies she would have to tell on his behalf. Why did Ralph have to spot him like that? *Why? Why? Why?*

He sat in the silence of the room, the gravity of his actions and their consequences settling around him like a suffocating cloak. He knew he had to stay focused, to plan his next moves carefully. But in that moment, all he could think about was the pain in Sarah's voice and the uncertain future that lay ahead.

The aftermath of the phone call had left Noah in a state of emotional turmoil, but he was quickly jolted back to reality by Schultz's voice.

"Cheer up," Adrian said. "So you got spotted and everyone knows you murdered the Dragon Lady. You can still complete the kill list. Just remember your daughter."

Noah's jaw clenched at the mention of Norah. "I want to speak to her," he demanded, his voice a mix of anger and desperation.

"You're in luck," Schultz sneered. "That's exactly what I'm calling for. A little treat for you now you've completed the first name. Oh, and shooting your old pal Molly—beautiful. That was when I really knew I had you in the palm of my hand, Mr...."

"Get my daughter!" Noah shouted.

Half a minute later, he was hearing the sweet tones of Norah.

"Hello?"

"Hi, sweetheart, it's Daddy. How are you doing today?"

Norah's little voice, tinged with longing, filled the line. "Hi, Daddy! I'm okay. When are you and Mommy coming to get me? I miss you."

The words hit Noah like a punch to the gut, his voice trembling slightly as he replied. "Oh, my little star, we miss you so much too. You're on a special vacation, remember? We'll be there as soon as we can. Are they treating you well?"

Norah's innocence tore at his heart. "Yes, but I don't like this vacation, Daddy. I want to come home."

Noah fought back emotions that threatened to tear him in half, his voice barely a whisper. "I know, honey, I know. You're being so brave. Daddy is working very hard to bring you home. Do you have teddies with you?"

A moment of childish simplicity shone through as Norah responded. "Yes. But they took Peter Rabbit and say they can't find him."

Noah couldn't help picturing the dogs ripping the bunny apart.

"I wish I could hug you and Mommy," Norah added.

"And we wish we could hug you too, sweetheart. Very soon, okay? I promise. Daddy loves you so much," Noah managed to say.

The call with Norah ended there, Schultz replacing her, his tone business-like. "Let that be an incentive," he said.

"You better not…"

"Hurt her or you'll kill me," Schultz impatiently finished for him. "Yes, I know. You've made yourself clear on that. Look, get this done and you and Mrs. Wolf can take your little wolf cub and go live happily ever after."

"Yes. But you're forgetting one thing."

"What?"

"They know I did it," Noah pointed out. "Ralph saw me."

"It doesn't matter that you're a fugitive. I trust your skills enough to know you'll be able to evade capture while working on the list. Which reminds me. You're ready for the next name. Same as before. Three days from now."

"But I can't work it on my own," Noah protested, wary of the implications of being a lone wolf in this deadly game.

"Then get help," Schultz replied dismissively. "Same

as before. So long as they don't ruin this, then I don't ruin your precious little daughter."

The words stung Noah hard, and his fists clenched. But he didn't let it slip, didn't let Schultz know that he was getting to him.

"Who's the next name?" he seethed, doing his best to keep his tone flat and even.

"The next name is Harmeet Singh. She's an Indian citizen but lives in Berkeley, California. That should be enough to get you started. Three days, remember. Get it done."

The line went dead. In a moment of frustration, Noah yanked out the earpiece and hurled it against the wall. He needed a moment to gather his thoughts, to plan his next move.

That's when his forearm tingled, a subtle vibration signaling an incoming message. He pressed the activation button on his ribcage. Feeling the familiar sensation as his skin lit up faintly, the text scrolled across his arm just beneath the surface.

The message from 9 was brief but filled with urgency: "Are you safe?"

He texted back: "Yes. How did it go your end?"

He waited, his eyes fixated on the glowing script beneath his skin. The reply wasn't long in coming. "Perfectly. What about you?" scrolled 9's message. Noah's own reply was terse, reflecting his dire circumstances: "No. I got spotted by Ralph as I left."

A pause hung in the digital conversation, the weight of this revelation hanging heavy. Then 9's response appeared, a flicker of concern in the otherwise impersonal exchange: "What did Adrian say about it?"

Noah's fingers moved swiftly over the sensitive pad under his skin, typing out: "Strangely, he said it was okay."

Even as he sent it, his mind was a storm of strategy and foresight. Schultz's casual dismissal of such a critical slip-up didn't sit right with him. It was a dangerous game they were playing, and Noah knew he was the one on the edge.

The conversation continued, 9 asking about the next target.

"Harmeet Singh, Berkley, California," came his swift answer.

"Okay," 9 replied. "We'll see what we can do our end. Let you know. 9 out."

As he deactivated the device, the glow fading from his skin, Noah's mind was a tumult of thoughts. The success of 9's end of the mission was a small victory, but his own exposure had escalated the stakes to a new height. He was now a fugitive, a ghost on the wind with the real possibility of capture looming over him. It was something he hadn't really planned for. The escape route, this house, it was all just some contingency plan ready to be used on the spot. This wasn't how it was supposed to play out.

The quiet of the safe house enveloped him, a stark contrast to the storm raging within. Every decision from here on out had to be calculated with the utmost precision. There was no room for error, no chance for second guesses. The game had indeed changed, and Noah was at its epicenter, a rogue wolf navigating a landscape fraught with danger and deceit.

***

Back at Kirtland, the mood at the farmhouse was bubbling with tension and disbelief. Team Camelot, once a tightly knit unit under Noah's leadership, now found themselves adrift in a sea of confusion and betrayal.

Despite the swirling chaos of emotions, Sarah's performance had thus far been impeccable; not a single crack showed in her façade of shocked innocence. Renée, her maternal instincts in overdrive, had taken it upon herself to comfort her.

The two women sat in the living room, the waters of Lake Temple shimmering under a watchful gray sky on the other side of the bay windows. Just outside the room, in the hallway, Marco and Ralph stood eyeing them with curious looks.

Renée eventually left Sarah's side to join them. They were deep in conversation, their voices low and laden with a mixture of anger and disbelief. Renée, pulling Marco aside, whispered with a hint of hope, "I really don't think she knew what he was going to do."

Marco's response was tinged with frustration and sadness. "What about *why* he did it?"

Renée shook her head. "She doesn't know that either. She said he showed no sign that he was going to do it. Said he's been acting just fine."

"That's the bossman," Ralph interjected from the side. "Never one to show his emotions or his cards."

"Well," Marco said, "we need to find out what his cards are and what he intends to do next. Because right now, he's an enemy of E & E." His words were heavy with the reality of their situation.

Renée's gentle scolding did little to alleviate the

tension. "You don't have to be so dramatic, Marco," she said softly, trying to inject some calm into the situation.

But Marco was resolute. "Not dramatic? You know what the Dragon Lady did for us—for Noah, right? I was looking at the rest of my life in jail, and Noah was looking at the lethal injection. Allison Peterson came along and saved us, Renée. Me, you, *this*. None of it would have happened had it not been for her—so more than anything, I want to know why he did it."

It was then that Ralph chimed in, his voice cutting through the thick air. "Where's Norah, anyway?" His question was like a stone dropped into a still pond, the ripples spreading out and unsettling the fragile balance of the room.

"That's a good point," Marco acknowledged, his brows furrowed in concern.

They returned to Sarah, their expressions a mix of concern and suspicion. When they posed the question about Norah, Sarah's answer came too quickly, too rehearsed. "She's at my aunt's," she said, but the discomfort in her voice was discernible. Renée noticed it, the mother in her sensing something amiss, but she chose to remain silent.

"An aunt?" Marco put to her.

"Yes. She went there for the weekend and was supposed to be back today. But since this all happened, I can't have her back just yet. Not while her dad is a fugitive." Sarah's voice wavered as she continued, "I don't want Norah caught up in all this. She's safer there, away from the chaos."

Marco nodded slowly, but his eyes betrayed his skepticism. "Probably for the best. Especially if Noah is mixed up in something serious that puts a threat on one of you. Because that's the only explanation I've got for any of this so far."

Ralph, usually the more easygoing of the two, agreed. "He was probably doing it to protect you, Sarah. We should get someone to stay here with you. I'll get Diana to come."

Sarah smiled. "That'd be nice," she said.

It was then that Marco touched his ear as something came over his comms. "It's Doc Parker," he said to the others a few seconds later. "He wants us back at base."

The three members of Team Camelot left, Ralph promising Sarah that Diana would be there soon. Once they had left, Sarah sat and shivered. It had been a long time since she'd felt so lonely.

Meanwhile, the gray sky outside seemed to mirror her turmoil, as if nature itself was in sync with the storm brewing within the walls of the farmhouse. As the day drew to a close, Sarah knew one thing for certain: Her world had irrevocably changed, and there was no turning back from the path that lay ahead.

CHAPTER ELEVEN

Noah sat in the safe room under the kitchen, his gaze fixed on the laptop screen. The dim light cast shadows that seemed to dance across the concrete walls, reflecting his troubled thoughts. He scrolled through the details of Harmeet Singh, his next target, his mind struggling to connect any dots that might link her to Allison Peterson or E & E.

Harmeet Singh's profile was impressive, even by his seasoned standards. At the age of thirty-five, she had already carved a formidable reputation in the technology sector. Renowned as a maverick, she had a flair for disrupting traditional industries with groundbreaking innovations. Singh's expertise wasn't confined to one field even; she had made significant contributions across various technological domains, from AI and machine learning to renewable energy solutions.

In the world of technology, where change is the only constant, Harmeet Singh had not only adapted but thrived, continuously pushing the boundaries of what was possible. Her profile was not just impressive; it was a narrative of resilience, innovation, and unwavering determination.

But none of it linked her to E & E or Allison

Peterson. This lack of connection troubled Noah. Harmeet's profile depicted a visionary, a leader in her field, far removed from the dark world of espionage and assassinations in which he and E & E operated.

Going over her X account, however, he did find it mentioned that Harmeet was scheduled to attend a major technology charity gala in Silicon Valley in two days. Noah noted the dates and location, a plan beginning to form in his mind.

He leaned back in his chair, his eyes not leaving the screen. The pieces were there, but the puzzle remained unsolved. Noah knew he had to tread carefully. Every step forward would be shrouded in uncertainty.

He was about to log off when his forearm vibrated, a message scrolling across the implanted device. It was from 9, his only real ally in this tangled web he found himself trapped in.

"Everything in place," the message read.

Noah replied, his fingers tapping against his arm: "Same here. Any idea why her?"

The response came quickly. "Not yet. Still looking for link. What now?"

Noah stared at the words glowing through his forearm for a moment longer, his mind working through the possibilities, the risks. He typed his response, a plan forming in his mind. "Now I go see some old friends."

***

Sarah sat alone in the living room of the farmhouse, the weight of her thoughts pressing heavily upon her. The presence of Diana in the house, though meant as a comfort, felt more like a silent watch, a reminder that the eyes of E & E were upon her. She couldn't shake the feeling of being observed, scrutinized for any sign of complicity in Noah's actions.

While Diana made coffee in the kitchen, Sarah's mind whirred, sifting through the list of people who knew about their time in Florida, trying to pinpoint the mole. The list was short but complicated, each name carrying a history, a connection to her and Noah.

First were Allison and Molly, but they were out of the question for the most tragic of obvious reasons. Sarah's heart ached as she thought of them, casualties in a game they hadn't even known thcy were playing.

Then there was Doc Parker, who had seamlessly stepped into Allison's shoes. Could his sudden ascent be more than mere coincidence? Was he part of a grander scheme? The thought sent a shiver down her spine.

Wally Lawson came to mind next, but Sarah quickly dismissed him. Wally's loyalty to Noah was unshakeable, his dedication to their cause proven time and again. No, it couldn't be Wally.

Her thoughts turned to the team. Marco, a longtime friend and comrade to Noah, shared a bond with him that was forged in the fires of countless battles. It was unimaginable that Marco would betray that brotherhood.

Renée, however, was a more complex story. Her past undercover mission with Spear and the subsequent revelation of her being drugged and hypnotized had exposed a vulnerability. Could Adrian have exploited that, manipulating her as he had done with Sarah and Noah?

Ralph Morgan's history was also tainted with

personal tragedy and tough decisions. Ralph's father, Jimmy Morgan, had been a notorious crime lord, controlling a vast network across Arkansas and its neighboring regions. Under Morgan Sr.'s reign, the area had become a wild den of drug trafficking and violence with local politicians and law enforcement under his influence. Noah had gone in undercover and dismantled this criminal empire, culminating in the death of Ralph's father at his own hands. He was supposed to have killed Ralph, too. However, Noah saw untapped potential in Ralph. He offered him a stark choice: join the secretive organization E & E for a chance at redemption or face certain death. Ralph chose the former, swearing allegiance to the organization that had upended his world.

Sarah wondered if old grudges and hidden agendas might have resurfaced, that beneath Ralph's loyalty, the embers of old resentments and concealed motives were smoldering, waiting to ignite.

Lastly, there was Diana, Ralph's beau and Sarah's current guardian angel. Out of everyone, Diana seemed the least likely. Three years prior, in a harrowing ordeal, Norah's life had hung in the balance. She was just an infant when Meredith Bascom, the unhinged ex-director of the CIA, infiltrated their home with a sinister intent. It was Diana, in a moment of sheer courage and resolve, who intervened at the critical juncture, thwarting Bascom's grim plans and saving Norah's life. This act of bravery had not only rescued their child but had also left an indelible mark on the family's history. After all that, why would Diana now help someone place Norah in harm's way?

Despite turning each possibility over in her mind,

Sarah found herself at a dead end. The idea that any of them could betray her and Noah, endangering Norah, seemed unfathomable unless they were under immense pressure.

If only they knew the true motive behind the assassination list, perhaps then they could unravel the identity of the mole within E & E. But for now, Sarah was left with only theories, suspicions, and the chilling reality that the enemy might be closer than she'd ever imagined.

The silence in the farmhouse was broken by the sounds of Diana's footsteps. She approached Sarah carefully from the kitchen, holding two mugs of steaming coffee. Her eyes, filled with empathy, carried a hint of unspoken worry that seemed to weigh heavily on her. As she sat down next to Sarah on the couch, she placed the mugs on the coffee table with a soft clink, breaking the tension in the air.

Diana then took a moment, gathering her thoughts. She knew the question she needed to ask might upset Sarah, but it was essential for their predicament. With a deep breath, she turned to Sarah, her expression a mix of determination and hesitance. "Sarah," she began cautiously, "there's something we need to discuss. It's important, but I understand it might be difficult for you to hear." Her voice, though steady, betrayed the gravity of what she was about to say. "I know this is tough, Sarah, but I need to ask you this. Have you had any thoughts in the last twenty-four hours as to why Noah would do this?" The question hung in the air, delicate yet heavy.

Sarah looked up, her eyes momentarily meeting Diana's before drifting away. She felt a knot in her stomach, a mix of fear, confusion, and the burden of unspeakable secrets. "I... I can't believe he did it, Diana," she said softly, continuing with the act. "Noah loved Allison; she saved us, both of us. And Molly... she was innocent in all this." Her voice trembled slightly, betraying the turmoil within.

Diana nodded, her expression somber. "I know. It doesn't make sense. Noah isn't a traitor. There must be something more, something we're missing." She hesitated before adding softly, "Have you spoken to him?"

Sarah shook her head. "No. I... I don't even know where he is. And Norah..." Her voice broke as she mentioned her daughter, the fear for her safety overwhelming.

Diana's eyes narrowed slightly, like she'd spotted something.

"Well," Sarah continued, averting her eyes, "Norah's lucky to be at my aunt's and out of it."

"Norah is strong, just like her parents," Diana reassured her, placing a comforting hand on Sarah's shoulder. "When's she coming back?"

"Not until this is all over," Sarah said, her trembling voice betraying her.

A moment of silence fell between the two women. It was then that Diana, seemingly lost in thought, mentioned something offhand. "You know, it's strange," she began, her brow furrowing slightly. "But I saw Renée yesterday, talking on the phone in hushed tones. She seemed... anxious, almost secretive."

Sarah's attention snapped to Diana, a flicker of curiosity igniting in her eyes. "Secretive? In what way?" she asked, trying to keep her tone casual but her mind already racing with possibilities.

Diana shrugged, her demeanor expertly crafted to appear unconcerned. "I don't know. She was in her front yard, facing away, talking in whispers. When I waved, she pretended not to see me and rushed back in the house. It could be anything, personal stuff, you know? At the time, I wondered if it wasn't something between her and Marco. But with everything going on, it just struck me as odd."

The seeds of suspicion planted in Sarah's mind began to grow shoots. Renée, always composed and in control, behaving secretively? In the turmoil of their current situation, any abnormality felt like a potential clue. As Diana continued to speak, Sarah's thoughts spiraled, considering the possibilities. Could Renée be involved in some way? Or was it merely stress taking its toll?

As she sat there, Sarah felt all alone with her thoughts, the weight of suspicion and fear pressing down on her. Gazing across at Diana, a sense of resolve began to crystallize within her. She realized she needed an ally, someone to confide in, and Diana seemed the only logical choice. Despite the whirlwind of doubts and possibilities circling her, Sarah knew she had to take a leap of faith.

Taking a deep breath, she broke the silence that hung between them. "Diana, there's something I haven't told anyone," she began, her voice quivering. "Norah... she was kidnapped by Adrian. He's using her as leverage against Noah and me."

Diana's eyes widened in shock. "Oh my God, Sarah, that's... that's horrifying. How have you been coping with all this?"

Sarah's gaze dropped to her hands, knotted together in her lap. "We've been... we've been living in fear, constantly looking over our shoulders. That asshole in charge of them, Schultz, made us swear not to tell anyone, or he'd... he'd hurt her."

There was a pause as the gravity of the revelation hung heavily in the air. Diana leaned in closer, her voice soft but firm. "You need to tell Doc Parker about this. He can help."

Sarah shook her head vehemently. "I can't risk it, Diana. Not after what we've already done..." Her voice trailed off, a reference to the dark deeds that haunted both her and Noah.

Diana nodded slowly, understanding the depth of Sarah's dilemma. "Then how can I help?" she asked.

After a moment of contemplation, Sarah hesitantly revisited the earlier conversation. "You mentioned something about Renée earlier... about her being on the phone?"

"It was probably nothing, maybe a call about a missed package from Amazon or something." Diana paused, then continued, "But given the circumstances, nothing can be taken lightly. I suppose we could keep an eye on Renée, see if there's anything unusual."

Sarah nodded, a plan forming in her mind. "We should follow her discreetly. If she's the mole, she might lead us to something."

Diana agreed, the gravity of the situation reflected in her determined gaze. "Let's do it. We need to find out what's really going on and if Renée is a part of this."

The decision made, the two women stood up, a new sense of purpose driving their actions. They were going to uncover the truth and save Norah, no matter what secrets lay hidden in the shadows of their close-knit community.

CHAPTER TWELVE

In the light of morning, Noah Wolf blended seamlessly with Silicon Valley's early risers. He moved with purpose, his attire that of a nondescript blue collar worker, eyes hidden behind dark sunglasses. The fifteen-story glass building of Neil Blessing's social media company The Hive loomed ahead, its sleek, black façade reflecting the awakening Californian sky.

As he made his way toward the building, a van caught his eye. It was parked on the edge of the next street, the front of it poking out from the end of a wall. Inside, Marco and Ralph sat, their focus on the building's entrance. A smirk tugged at Noah's lips. He had trained them better than this; their obvious stakeout position was amateurish. But he couldn't afford to linger on their mistake; his mission was critical.

Using a maintenance worker's guise, Noah didn't use the main entry point. Instead, he slipped around the back to the service entrance, getting through the security turnstile there using a manufactured ID badge that granted him unchallenged access. Just to make sure he wasn't rumbled, he carried a toolbox with him, completing the look. As he made his way to a service elevator, every step he took was measured, every glance calculated to avoid drawing attention.

Reaching the appropriate floor, Noah navigated his way through the maze of cubicles and glass-walled meeting rooms, each step taking him closer to his goal.

Finally, he reached Neil's office. The door was ajar, a sliver of light spilling into the darkened hallway. Noah paused, listening intently. Inside, the soft sound of typing resonated, the rhythm steady and focused.

With a deep breath, he pushed the door open and stepped inside. Neil, immersed in his work, didn't immediately notice his entrance. It was only when Noah closed the door with a soft click, sealing them in the room, that he did.

Neil looked up, surprise flashing in his eyes before recognition set in. A mixture of relief, apprehension, then anger crossed his face as he met Noah's gaze.

Neil stood up, rigid. "What the hell are you doing here, Noah?" His voice was sharp, tinged with betrayal. "Molly? Allison? They're saying you killed them—"

Noah's face was a mask of desperation and resolve. "Neil, it's not that simple."

Neil's frustration boiled over. "Make it simple for me, then. Because from where I'm standing, it looks like you've crossed a line and murdered them."

Noah took a deep breath, his voice weighed down by an unbearable burden. "I know how it looks. But you have to trust me, there's more to this. He's got Norah."

Neil paused, his anger momentarily replaced by shock.

"Who's got Norah?"

"Adrian. Schultz. Whoever he's working for." Noah's voice cracked slightly. "And he won't stop until I've done what he wants."

"You mean killing two of your closest friends? Who next, Noah—me?" Neil's voice was laced with disappointment and disbelief.

"Please, Neil. I need your help."

Neil turned away. "I don't know. I thought I knew you. After all those years we fought together, side by side, I thought I did. But now, I'm not so sure."

"The man you fought alongside is trying to save his daughter."

Neil turned back to him. Noah's eyes were fierce, his stance unyielding.

"You think I wanted any of this?" Noah asked him. "You think I don't know how it looks? Know what I have done?"

Neil's logical mind sought for a way out. "Then let me help you go to the authorities—"

"And get Norah killed? No, the authorities can't go anywhere near this. It's just us, Neil. Like it always was. The original Team Camelot." Noah's plea was earnest, a call to the bond they'd once shared.

Neil's expression turned incredulous. "This is insane. You're asking me to believe in you. Asking me to trust you after what you did."

Noah's voice was low, a mix of plea and command. "I'm asking you to remember who I am. And who we are to each other. I need your help, Neil. Not your judgment."

Neil's internal struggle was evident, his conscience at war with his loyalty. After a long, heavy pause, he sighed deeply.

"Damn it, Noah. This goes against every protocol,

every ounce of my conscience."

Noah's expression softened, a glimmer of hope in his eyes. "I know. I wouldn't ask if there was any other way. You know me. You know I'd never put you in this position if there wasn't—"

"—If there wasn't a world at stake," Neil finished for him. "Yeah, I know the speech. But this... If I do this, if I step into this with you, it's on your head, Noah. Your plan, your play." Neil's voice was resigned, a reluctant ally in a battle he hadn't chosen.

Noah nodded, a heavy burden accepted. "On my head, then. I just hope when all this is over, you'll see I had no choice."

Neil's resolve finally broke, his decision made not out of conviction but out of a deep, unshakable bond. "For Norah, then. Not for you, not for the damned agency. For that little girl who shouldn't be in the middle of any of this."

Noah's reply was simple, yet filled with a world of meaning. "For Norah."

Neil's hand hovered over his phone, a grim determination settling on his face.

"What are you doing?" Noah asked him as Neil picked it up.

"If I'm involved," he replied, "then Jenny will have to be in, too." He dialed quickly, his voice steady as he summoned his wife to his office.

Moments later, the door swung open and Jenny stormed in, her athletic frame radiating an intensity that filled the room. Her eyes, fierce and immovable, locked on to Noah, and the air seemed to crackle with her barely contained fury.

"You killed them!" Her scream sliced through the tense silence, echoing off the walls with a raw, palpable anger.

"Hey, Jenny," Noah said softly, his expression a complex tapestry of guilt, resolve, and regret. Neil stood at his desk, a quiet observer as his wife stormed up to Noah with evil intent burning in her eyes.

**

Marco and Ralph sat in the nondescript black van, discreetly stationed opposite the sleek glass façade of the high-rise building. Marco's gaze was intently fixed through the lenses of his Steiner Military-Marine 10X50mm tactical binoculars, surveying the scene with the sharp focus of a hawk. The office floors bustled with activity, but his attention was zeroed in on one specific area: Neil's office.

Suddenly, a figure was pressed backwards against the glass from the other side. Marco's heart skipped a beat. "You see this?" he said, passing the binoculars to Ralph without taking his eyes off the scene.

Ralph took the binoculars and peered through them. His eyes widened as he saw the back of someone, pinned against the window by Jenny Blessing, her face a mask of anger. "Looks like we got action," Ralph muttered, the urgency in his voice unmistakable.

Marco didn't reply. He was already opening the van door, his movements swift and decisive. Stepping out onto the street, he checked his pistol, a fluid motion born of years of experience.

Ralph threw down the binoculars and jumped out of the van, following Marco's lead. The staccato beat of their racing boot heels echoed on the pavement as they moved with purpose toward the building.

As they reached the entrance, the figure was still visible through the glass. Marco and Ralph, two seasoned warriors in their own right, were about to step into the heart of a storm.

***

Inside Neil's office, the tension crackled in the air like electricity. Jenny's hand reached for her hip, and she whipped a hunting knife from her belt with deadly intention, her eyes blazing with fury as she faced Noah.

"I'm gonna gut him here and now," she declared in a voice laced with venom.

Neil, with a calmness that belied the chaos, stepped between them.

"Baby, baby," he implored, his hands gently reaching for hers. "Listen. They have his daughter. They have Norah."

Jenny's rage faltered, replaced by confusion. She turned to Neil, her expression a mix of anger and confusion. "Then why didn't he go straight to Allison? That's what he always taught us, right? Never compromise the team."

Noah, his back still against the glass, spoke up. "Jenny, I had no choice. I was being watched. Coming here was a risk, but I didn't know where else to go."

Neil nodded in agreement. "He's right. If they're watching him, they could be watching all of us. We have to be careful."

Jenny's grip on the knife loosened slightly, her posture softening. "But why kill them, Noah? Why after all this time would you do that?"

Noah's voice was earnest, his eyes meeting hers. "Because it's Norah, Jenny. I needed to protect her, no matter what. You understand that, don't you?"

There was a brief silence, a moment of contemplation. Jenny's features softened, the motherly instinct in her recognizing the desperation of a parent.

Downstairs, Marco and Ralph reached the elevator, their expressions grim. They pushed past startled office workers, ignoring the protests and shouts. "You can't just go up there!" someone yelled, but they were undeterred, their focus singular.

Back in the office, Jenny finally lowered the knife, her posture relaxing. "Okay," she said, the word heavy with reluctance. "Okay, we'll help. But no more secrets, Noah. We do this together."

Noah nodded, a wave of relief washing over him. Neil glanced at his wife, pride and love evident in his eyes. "Together," he echoed.

Just as the atmosphere began to settle, Noah glanced out the window. The van was empty. "I probably need to leave now," he said abruptly. He turned to Neil with a crucial question. "Is there a window in your bathroom?"

***

Marco and Ralph, their movements swift and precise, burst into Neil's office. The scene before them was disarmingly mundane. Neil sat behind his desk, the epitome of calm, while Jenny was perched casually on the corner, her demeanor effortlessly cool.

"Marco, Ralph," Jenny greeted with a hint of amusement. "Decided to drop in, have you? How nice."

Marco, his gaze darting around the room, cut straight to the chase. "Where is he?" he demanded.

"Who?" Jenny replied, feigning ignorance.

The tension in the air was palpable as Marco's attention was suddenly drawn to the open door of the ensuite bathroom. A fresh breeze wafted through, suggesting recent activity. "Who'd you just have up against the window?" he asked, his voice edged with suspicion.

Neil, maintaining his composure, leaned back in his chair. "That was me," he said, a faint smirk playing on his lips. "You should always think first before telling your wife her new shoes make her feet look fat."

Marco and Ralph exchanged a quick, puzzled glance. Despite their skepticism, the apparent normalcy of Neil and Jenny's behavior cast doubt on their suspicions.

Jenny's expression remained unreadable, while Neil exuded a casual confidence that only served to deepen the mystery.

CHAPTER THIRTEEN

It was an hour after Noah had climbed out the bathroom window of Neil's office that Marco and Ralph finally left. Noah was sitting at a small outdoor seating area, surrounded by an eclectic mix of tech workers. In front of him, lining the sidewalk, was a bustling taco truck, one among several food vendors that adorned the forecourt of The Hive's office building.

Around him, the air was filled with the lively chatter of the lunchtime crowd, their conversations a blend of tech jargon and Silicon Valley slang that was almost alien to Noah.

Not long after watching Marco and Ralph's van disappear from view, his burner phone vibrated to life. Neil's voice crackled through the speaker, a mix of relief and excitement in his tone.

"We got away with it," he announced without preamble.

"Good. How come it took an hour?" Noah asked, his eyes scanning the line of food trucks, lingering momentarily on Sal's Hoagies.

"It was Marco and Ralph. We haven't seen them in almost six months. They stayed for lunch," Neil explained.

"What did you get?" Noah queried, a hint of curiosity in his voice.

"We got one of the guys from the office to pick us up hoagies from the food truck outside," Neil replied.

Noah's gaze shifted back to the taco in his hand. He had considered the hoagies before settling on Mexican. "I went for tacos," he said. "How were the hoagies?"

"The best," Neil responded enthusiastically. "How's your taco?"

"Good." Noah's tone then shifted, the lightness fading as he returned to the matter at hand. "And you're sure they don't suspect you?"

"Of course they do. They're E & E through and through. After they left, Jenny did a sweep of the office. Not only did they leave two listening devices —one under the sofa, the other in a flowerpot—but they also placed a tracking sticker on my phone. It was underneath the protector, so I'm gathering it was Marco using the pickpocket skills he learned from his adolescence on the streets."

Noah's expression hardened, his mind already calculating the implications. The thoroughness of Marco and Ralph's approach indicated their deep-seated suspicion and professionalism. He took another bite of his taco, the flavors now a distant sensation as his thoughts raced. The game of cat and mouse was escalating, and every move had to be meticulously planned. Trust was a luxury he could no longer afford, and every conversation, every interaction, was a potential chess move in a much larger game. Noah knew the stakes were high, and the margin for error was razor-thin.

"You sure your office is clear?" he pressed Neil, ensuring no stone was left unturned.

"Very. And before you ask, this line is clean. Now what's the plan, boss?" Neil responded, his tone more businesslike.

Noah paused, taking a moment to express his gratitude before delving into the details. "My next target is Harmeet Singh…"

"Wait, hold up. What the hell?!" Neil interjected, his voice rising with incredulity. "I know her. She's invested in my company. She's a shareholder. We had dinner at her house only three weeks ago."

"Yes. That's why I had to come to you specifically. You're integral to my plan."

"Oh, and there was me thinking it was our long friendship."

"That as well," Noah said, before adding, "But also this. Tomorrow night, you and Jenny are both attending a gala tech thing. You, Neil, are going to get me into the venue and up close with Harmeet Singh…" Noah explained, his voice steady.

"So that you can kill her?" Neil's question was loaded with apprehension.

"Please, Neil. He's got my daughter," Noah implored.

There was a heavy silence on the line as Neil processed the gravity of the situation. The fact that Harmeet Singh, a prominent figure in Neil's professional circle, was now a target obviously brought the reality of the situation crashing down on Noah's friend.

In the end, Neil sighed, the sound heavy with the

weight of the decision he was about to make. "All right, Noah. I'll help you get in. But this… this is far beyond anything we've done before. You realize that, right?"

"I do," Noah affirmed, his voice resolute. "But I don't have a choice. *We* don't have a choice. It's the only way to get Norah back."

The line was quiet again, the tension palpable even through the phone. Finally, Neil spoke up. "Okay. I'll set it up. But after this, we're going to need to have a serious talk about where we're heading with all this. Adrian has to have an end game."

"Agreed," Noah replied. "For now, let's focus on tomorrow night."

"Okay. I'll get you close to her. But I don't feel good about this, Noah. Harmeet Singh is a friend," Neil conceded, his voice tinged with unease. "She's also a good person."

"I know. I know. Look, do you think you can come meet me without being followed?" Noah asked, shifting gears to logistics.

"Piece of cake," Neil responded with a hint of his old confidence.

"And this line is definitely secure?" Noah pressed.

"Yes," Neil confirmed.

"Then I'll send you my location. Bring Jenny and come meet me when you can. I have the plan all laid out," Noah instructed, his voice firm.

The call ended, and almost immediately came the hiss. Schultz's voice chimed in Noah's ear. "Good idea getting Mr. Blessing involved."

"You mean dragging more people into the swamp with me," Noah retorted, a hint of bitterness in his tone.

"I admire your sacrifice, you know," Schultz said, his voice unnervingly calm. "You truly love your daughter, Noah. I wish I had been blessed with parents like you."

"Me too," Noah quipped, unable to resist a jab. "Then maybe you wouldn't have turned out to be such a psycho."

Adrian chuckled lightly. "You know, Noah, your sense of humor in dire situations is something I've always found... intriguing."

"Is that so? Maybe you should try it sometime. Humor. Lightens the mood," Noah shot back, keeping the tone light.

"Oh, I have my moments. But unlike you, I don't find myself often in situations requiring such... levity," Schultz replied, his voice dripping with sarcasm.

"Must be lonely at the top, huh? All that brooding and scheming, no one to share a good joke with," Noah said, a smirk in his voice.

Schultz sighed theatrically. "You have no idea. My colleagues at Adrian are simply pupils and soldiers. They need only discipline, not friendship."

"Sounds tough. Maybe you should take a vacation. I hear the Bahamas are nice this time of year," Noah suggested mockingly.

"Ah, but who would watch over our little game then, Mr. Wolf? You need me more than you care to admit," Schultz countered, the amusement evident in his tone. "It's men like me who keep the great Noah Wolf motivated."

Noah chuckled. "Keep telling yourself that, Henrik."

The playful banter between Noah and Schultz suddenly shifted back to the grim reality of their situation when the assassin asked, his tone once more serious, "How do you intend to do it?"

"That's where you come in," Noah replied, his voice taking on a steely edge.

"Me?" Schultz sounded surprised.

"Yes. Since I've burned all my bridges, I need a new source for weapons," Noah explained.

"What type of weapon?" Schultz inquired, his curiosity piqued.

"Poison."

"Ooh, interesting."

"Do you know what Cardiotox-A5 is?" Noah asked.

There was a brief pause before Adrian responded, a smirk audible in his voice. "Yes, I do, Mr. Wolf. I'll arrange for someone close to you to meet up for the exchange. Is there anything else you'll need?"

"Just two things."

"What?"

"My daughter back," Noah replied before going silent.

"That's just one thing. What's the other?"

"Your head on a spike."

CHAPTER FOURTEEN

Sarah and Diana crouched behind a row of shrubs, their eyes fixed on Renée, who was walking briskly along Kirtland's bustling streets. The sun was starting to set, the shadows growing longer. All of which added a layer of intrigue to their clandestine observation—one which they had been at since late last night.

"Doesn't she seem a bit too cautious?" Diana whispered, her sore, sleepless eyes narrowing as she watched Renée glance over her shoulder as she entered a park on the other side of the wide boulevard.

Sarah followed Renée's movements, noting the slight hesitation in her steps. "Maybe she's just being careful. This place isn't exactly low-profile."

Renée stopped near a secluded bench that sat within the shade of an Ohio buckeye tree, pulling out her phone. Making a call, it wasn't long before she seemed absorbed in conversation, occasionally looking around, her expression a mix of urgency and wariness.

"Who do you think she's talking to?" Sarah murmured, trying to keep her voice steady despite the growing suspicion in her mind. "She looks like she's scared someone will see her on the phone."

"It could be anyone," Diana replied, her tone suggesting more than she was saying. "But in our line of work, 'anyone' rarely means something innocent."

Sarah watched as Renée ended her call and sat on the bench, her posture tense. "Could she really be the mole?" she thought aloud, the idea knotting her stomach.

"Look at her, Sarah. She's nervous, secretive. It's not definitive, but it's definitely suspicious," Diana said, offering a perspective that nudged Sarah further into doubt.

As Renée stood up from the bench, Sarah and Diana exchanged a quick, determined glance. They cautiously shifted their position, ensuring that they remained unseen as they followed her from a safe distance. Renée's brisk pace took them toward a parking lot, where she quickly unlocked her car and got in.

Diana nudged Sarah. "That's our cue. Let's see where she's heading." They hurried back to their own vehicle, Sarah's Dodge Durango parked a few streets away. Slipping into the car, Diana started the engine, her eyes fixed on Renée's car as it began to pull out of the parking space.

The following journey was tense, with Sarah and Diana maintaining a careful distance to avoid detection. Renée drove with purpose, her route taking them toward the main highway leading out of Kirtland. The setting sun cast a golden hue over the mountainous landscape, contrasting sharply with the seriousness of their mission.

"Where's she going?" Sarah pondered aloud, her eyes fixed on the car ahead.

"Could be anywhere. But it's clear she's in a hurry

to get there," Diana reflected, her hands steady on the wheel.

The highway stretched out before them, the traffic thinning as they moved farther away from Kirtland. With each passing mile, Sarah's apprehension grew. The possibility that Renée, one of their own, could be involved in Norah's kidnapping was a thought she couldn't bear. Yet the unfolding events seemed to point in that direction.

As Renée's car took an exit off the highway, Diana followed suit. The destination was still unknown, but the unfolding mystery only deepened their resolve to uncover the truth.

***

Halfway across the country, Neil, Jenny, and Noah huddled around a makeshift table in the dimly lit safe room under the kitchen.

"So this is really where it all happened, huh?" Neil asked, looking about the room, a hint of unease in his voice. "Where your dad…?"

"Yeah, it is," Noah replied, his voice steady despite the memories the house evoked. "Right above our heads, in the kitchen," he added chillingly.

Jenny shuddered slightly, her eyes scanning the concrete walls. "Nice," she remarked dryly, her attempt at humor doing little to lighten the mood.

They turned their attention to the plan. A short while ago, Neil had hacked into the IT system of the company providing the catering for the gala, ensuring Noah's addition to the serving staff under a carefully constructed alias. Disguised as a waiter, his mission was clear: administer the Cardiotox-A5 into Harmeet

Singh's wineglass.

"The layout of the Villa Montalvo where the gala is taking place is complex," Neil explained, pointing to a blueprint of the venue, "but there are multiple exits. You'll need to be quick and discreet."

"The biggest problem will be getting close enough to Harmeet without raising suspicion," Noah noted, his eyes tracing potential routes on the map. "Having gone over footage of her at previous functions, I've noticed that her security is pretty tight."

"Then thank God you'll be using Cardiotox-A5," Jenny added, her tone clinical. "Once you've administered it, you've got a few minutes before it starts to work. After that, it'll look like a heart attack. There'll be chaos, but that should cover your escape."

As they discussed the intricacies of the plan, Neil and Jenny couldn't help but reflect on their personal interactions with Harmeet.

"She really is nice, you know," Neil said, a hint of regret in his voice. Turning to his wife, he added, "That dinner party at her place last month was something else, wasn't it, babe?"

"What about the weekend at her Aspen cabin?" Jenny reminisced, her usual hard demeanor softening for a moment. "That was amazing."

"Gosh, yes, Aspen," Neil said. "I almost forgot."

"How could you forget Aspen?"

The room fell silent as the reality of their task settled in. It was Jenny who then broke the quiet when she said, "Shame we've now got to murder her."

Noah's response was firm, yet heavy with the burden of his choices. "Just remember that a four-year-old little girl's life is on the line."

"I guess," Jenny conceded, her gaze drifting to the floor. "It's not like I'll feel guilty for it. I never do. But that was one hell of a weekend in Aspen."

A sudden knock at the front door exploded the basement's tense silence like a razor to a balloon. Jenny and Noah reacted instantly, their pistols appearing in their hands as if by magic. They shared a glance, a wordless communication honed by years of working together under pressure.

"Who else knows you're here?" Neil's voice was a mix of concern and accusation.

"No one," Noah replied in a tone as hard as the steel in his grip.

With careful, silent steps, Noah and Jenny ascended the ladder into the kitchen, the rhythmic knocking growing louder with each step. The front door stood like a barrier to an unknown threat, unassuming yet fraught with potential danger.

As they reached the hallway, the knocking ceased abruptly, leaving behind a haunting echo. Noah exchanged a nod with Jenny, and with a swift, coordinated movement, they flung the door open.

An empty street greeted them. Nothing but the lazy swirl of fallen leaves and the distant hum of city life. But the stillness was deceptive; the air was charged with a sense of the uncanny.

Then the knock came again, impossibly close, as though someone were still knocking on the door. Noah's instincts kicked in, and he spun around, pistol at the ready.

There, standing nonchalantly in the hallway behind them, was Wally Lawson, a half-smile playing on his lips as he lifted his hands in a gesture of peace, the parametric speaker, the source of the phantom knocks, held within his fingers.

"Wally, what in the hell are you doing here?" Noah's voice was a mix of surprise and irritation.

"I thought you could use my help," Wally replied, his tone casual but his eyes scanning the room with a professional's alertness.

Jenny lowered her pistol, but her posture remained tense. Noah was the same. He holstered his weapon but didn't relax.

"We're in deep, Wally," he said. "This isn't just another mission."

"I know," Wally said, his smile fading into a serious expression. "That's exactly why I'm here. You're playing a dangerous game, Noah Wolf. And I want in."

CHAPTER FIFTEEN

As the others lowered themselves into the safe room, Neil looked up from the blueprint of the gala venue, his brows furrowed in confusion. "Wally, how did you find us? This place is supposed to be off grid."

Wally, leaning against the cool concrete wall of the underground safe room, gave a half-smile. "It's all about patterns and anomalies, Mr. Blessing. Esmeralda and I, we looked at Noah's history, his tendencies. Then we checked property records, shell companies, digital footprints. His former family home here popped up as a recent purchase by an unknown entity. The timing was too coincidental."

Jenny, her arms crossed, nodded slightly, impressed despite herself. "Smart. But how did you know for sure we were here?"

"I've been listening," Wally said, a twinkle in his eye. "With a little help from my friend."

"Your friend?" Jenny echoed, a hint of skepticism in her voice.

"Yes," Wally replied, extending his finger. The room watched in amazement as what looked like a bee, previously unnoticed on the wall, set its wings to flight and buzzed toward him, landing gently on his fingertip. Except it wasn't a bee. It was a meticulously crafted drone.

Bringing it up to his eyes, Wally added, "He's been watching and listening to everything you've been saying and doing for the past twenty minutes."

Neil whistled softly. "That's some tech, Wally."

Wally's eyes gleamed with pride. "Thank you, Neil. And having listened to your plans, I think I can refine one particular part."

"Which part?" Noah asked, his curiosity piqued.

"The delivery of the toxin," Wally said, his gaze fixed on the drone bee. "Instead of risking exposure by tampering with the wineglass, why not let my little friend here do the job? It's less conspicuous, and we can ensure a precise dose. I've even made a minor adjustment to this one for just that purpose. Watch."

He held the bee up to them as they gathered around.

"Bee 1-9-8," Wally said, "would you arm yourself, please."

As its legs gripped the finger, the mechanical bee lifted its abdomen, and to the amazement of everyone watching, a stinger suddenly shot out of it.

"This is a hypodermic needle," Wally said. "So just like a normal bee, it will deliver a toxin by stinging the target and then flying away. Anyone witnessing it will think the target was merely the victim of an insect."

Jenny's eyes narrowed as she considered the idea. "A bee delivering the Cardiotox-A5 at a high-profile gala. That's... actually brilliant."

Neil leaned back, rubbing his chin thoughtfully. "It's risky. But if we can pull it off..."

Noah watched the drone bee intently. "It's

unexpected, untraceable, and exactly what we need." He turned to Wally, a newfound respect in his eyes. "Wally, you're a genius."

Wally nodded, a hint of satisfaction in his smile. "It has been said." He then placed the bee on the desk and turned to Noah. "Now before we get into the finer details, could you help me with something? I've got a few things in the car that need to be brought in."

Neil and Jenny went to move, but Wally held a hand up. "Just Noah will do," he said.

Noah raised an eyebrow, curious but willing. "Sure thing."

As Noah followed Wally out of the safe room, he glanced back at Neil and Jenny. "Keep an eye on our little friend here," he said, nodding toward the drone bee. "I'll be back in a few minutes."

Neil and Jenny watched as Noah and Wally disappeared up the ladder. Left alone with the bee, they exchanged a glance that mixed wonder and apprehension. Jenny reached out, hesitantly extending her finger toward it. The drone then crawled onto her fingertip, its mechanical wings gently buzzing. "Incredible," she whispered.

Neil, still leaning back, watched with interest. "Technology like this changes the game," he mused. "Makes you wonder what else Wally's got up his sleeve."

Upstairs, Wally led Noah out of the kitchen into the hallway, his expression transforming into one of deep seriousness. He paused and reached into his pocket, pulling out a small, pen-shaped device. With a subtle click, he activated it, and a faint hum filled the air—a signal blocker designed to jam Adrian's earpiece.

Wally glanced at Noah, his eyes conveying the

gravity of the moment. "Just a precaution," he murmured, ensuring that their conversation remained private. Satisfied that the device had effectively blocked the listening device in Noah's ear, he leaned in close, speaking in a low, conspiratorial tone. "I hope they believed me about how I found you." His words carried a weight that suggested there was much more behind his story than he had let on to the others.

Noah glanced over his shoulder toward the kitchen, then whispered back, "I'm sure they did."

Wally's eyes narrowed slightly. "Do you suspect them?"

Noah shook his head, but his own eyes didn't quite match his certainty. "I don't think so. They seemed genuinely upset that I'd killed Allison and Molly. And so far, they've offered their complete support. But they're still on my list of suspects just because they knew we were in Florida. At least until I know for sure who the mole is, I can't take any risks."

Wally nodded, then added, "What about 9?"

"9's ready their end. And now that you're here, everything's in place."

Wally gave a solemn nod, understanding the gravity of the situation. As they turned to leave, the gravity of their mission, the delicate dance between trust and suspicion, hung heavily in the air. The path ahead was fraught with uncertainty, but one thing was clear: The truth was closer than ever, and every step they took could either lead them to salvation or further into the abyss.

***

Sarah and Diana sat in the Durango, the hum of the

engine a subtle soundtrack to their silent vigil. The sun had long since set, casting the world in a palette of shadow and streetlight. The drive from Kirtland had been long, marked by stretches of silence and the occasional murmur of a radio host drifting into the late hours.

The city of Denver appeared ahead of them, its skyline a distant silhouette, the buildings like slumbering giants against the night sky. They had followed Renée's truck with methodical caution for the past four hours, always mindful of the distance, always wary of being too close.

It was nearing seven o'clock when Renée's truck finally slowed, pulling into the parking lot of an all-night diner. Its neon sign flickered intermittently, casting a warm, inviting glow over the otherwise drab exterior. The diner, a relic of a bygone era, seemed almost out of place amidst the city's modern sprawl.

As Diana placed the Durango within a line of parked cars, Sarah watched Renée step out of her truck. She seemed oblivious to the possibility of being followed, her focus solely on the diner's entrance. Entering, she disappeared into the warm embrace of the diner's interior, hidden behind the steamed windows.

Diana shifted in her seat, her eyes never leaving the entrance. "She's in," she whispered, her voice barely audible.

In the passenger seat, Sarah's fingers deftly opened a small container that resembled a ring box. Inside rested a mechanical bee—a gift from Wally before he left. Its metallic wings gleamed faintly in the dim light of the car's interior.

"What's that?" Diana asked, her curiosity piqued by

the tiny device.

"It's one of Wally's drones," Sarah replied, her voice low. She pulled out her encrypted burner phone and began tapping on the screen, connecting to the drone through the appropriate application. The mechanical bee buzzed to life, its wings fluttering in a silent acknowledgment of activation.

The phone's screen came alive with the images from the bee's camera, offering them a unique vantage point. Sarah then rolled down the window. The bee rose up, flew out of the inch gap and made its way toward the diner, zigzagging across the street as Sarah struggled to control it via the phone.

An air vent stood out above the closed doors. As the drone entered the diner through it, Sarah and Diana's view shifted to the interior of the throwback eatery. The diner was a capsule of time, adorned with nostalgic décor—checkerboard tiles, red vinyl booths, and a jukebox in the corner playing soft tunes from a bygone era. It felt like stepping into a scene from a classic movie. You expected to see Jimmy Dean and Natalie Wood drinking a root beer float in the corner or Elvis tossing quarters into the jukebox. It was certainly a stark contrast to the high-tech espionage playing out in their hands.

The drone buzzed quietly over the heads of the diners, its presence unnoticed as it navigated to Renée's booth. She sat in an end one, her back against the wall, engaged in conversation with a man whose face was obscured from the drone's current angle. Sarah maneuvered it subtly, positioning it on the big green leaf of a potted plant that stood close to their booth.

From this new vantage point, the camera feed on

Sarah's phone showed a clear view. The man's features were rugged, his expression serious as he conversed with Renée.

Sarah and Diana watched intently, their attention fixed on the phone's screen. This was a crucial moment, one that might shed light on the shadowy events that had been unfolding around them. In the quiet of the Durango, with the drone's feed acting as their window into the diner, they waited, ready to piece together whatever secrets the night was yet to reveal.

"You recognize him?" Diana asked as she leaned across the SUV.

"No. You?"

"Nuh-uh."

For all the good quality of the images, however, the sound wasn't very good. Sarah strained to hear the conversation through the AirPod nestled in her ear. The sound quality was frustratingly poor, marred by the clanking and hissing of an ancient dishwasher laboring in the background. As well as this, the diner's other ambient noises, a cacophony of late-night chatter and the scraping of cutlery, added to the challenge. Nevertheless, something the man said soon made her hair go on end.

"Does Sarah suspect anything?" His voice cut through the din.

"No," Renée replied. "Or at least I don't think so."

"Does Noah?"

"Only Marco does. Now..."

Diana couldn't contain her curiosity. "What are they saying?" she asked, leaning closer.

"I'm not sure," Sarah whispered back, her focus

on the conversation. "He asked if Noah or I suspect anything."

"Who is he?" Diana inquired further.

"I told you, I don't know. Look, keep quiet, and I might be able to hear them."

Sarah concentrated, trying to filter out the background noise. Amid fragments of conversation, she caught something significant. "Parker suspects something," Renée's voice said clearly.

Suspects what? Sarah wondered.

"It doesn't matter," the man replied dismissively. "It won't be long. But for now, you need to take this." There was a rustle of paper as he handed across a manila envelope. "You'll know what to do with it when the time is right."

Having said this, the man stood up.

"You're leaving?" Renée asked.

"Yes. Stay safe and stay hidden, Renée."

And with that, he left without saying another word.

Sarah sat back, stunned by the revelation. Her thoughts were a whirlwind of questions and fears. What won't be long? And what was in the envelope?

"What do we do now?" Diana asked as the man left the diner.

"We follow him," Sarah said decisively, her eyes tracking the man's retreating figure as he quickly walked off. "He could lead us to Norah."

With a nod, Diana started the Durango, and they eased into the steady flow of city traffic, keeping a cautious distance. The man's pace was brisk, his familiarity with the city's rhythm evident as he weaved through the dwindling crowds of downtown Denver.

The chase led them to the heart of a bustling nighttime market, an impromptu carnival of sights and smells that seemed to spring from the city's very soul. Here, amidst the throng of night owls and treasure hunters, the man became a ghost, his outline blurring with the masses.

They parked and hurried on foot, Sarah's eyes scanning the sea of faces while Diana checked each alley and stall. But it was too late; the man had vanished, swallowed by the chaos of the market.

Breathless and frustrated, they returned to the Durango, the disappointment heavy in the air. "We lost him," Diana admitted, her voice tinged with defeat.

CHAPTER SIXTEEN

Noah stood in the dimly lit safe room, his gaze fixed on his forearm. The message from 9 shimmered through his skin, a glowing beacon in the shadowy room: *Everything is set.*

Dressed in the classic attire of a high-end waiter, Noah looked the part of a seasoned professional ready to blend seamlessly into the upscale gala. His uniform was meticulously tailored—a crisp, white shirt complemented by a neatly knotted red bowtie, a sharp, white coat with tails that added an air of sophistication. The entire ensemble was polished off with sleek, black trousers and shiny shoes that reflected the faint light.

In the background, Neil, Jenny, and Wally were immersed in last-minute preparations, their voices a low murmur as they discussed the finer details of the plan. Maps and blueprints were spread out on a table alongside various gadgets and tools. The atmosphere was charged with a mix of anticipation and apprehension.

Noah glanced over at his companions, taking a deep breath. He knew the stakes couldn't be higher. Every element of their plan needed to work flawlessly for them to administer the Cardiotox-A5 without detection. The weight of the responsibility pressed heavily on him, but his resolve was unwavering.

With a final check of his appearance and equipment, Noah nodded to himself. It was time to put their plan into action. The next few hours would determine the fate of his daughter, and he was ready to do whatever it took to ensure her safety.

That was when his phone rumbled. Picking it up, he saw *LOML* (love of my life) flashing across its screen. It was Sarah.

He didn't answer right away. Instead, he did something first.

Before leaving Kirtland, Wally had developed a unique device to counter Schultz's constant surveillance through the earpiece. The device, which he called the "Sound Blocker," was based on principles of sound manipulation and redirection. It resembled a sleek, metallic ear cuff that sat snugly on the upper part of Noah's ear. Its design was not just for aesthetics but served a functional purpose. Embedded within the device were miniature transducers, capable of emitting sound waves at frequencies that interfered with the specific frequency range of Adrian's earpiece.

These transducers utilized a method akin to active noise cancellation but with a twist. Instead of simply canceling out sound waves, the sound blocker was programmed to create a localized sound vortex. This vortex would funnel sound waves around the earpiece, creating a sort of sound 'blind spot' directly where the earpiece sat. As a result, Adrian's earpiece would be enveloped in a bubble of silence for anything that Noah said or heard through his phone while still picking up ambient sounds from farther afield in the environment. This ensured that Schultz would remain unaware of being cut off, as the background noises of the room would continue to reach him uninterrupted.

With a discreet press of a tiny button on the sound blocker, Noah activated the device. Instantly, the earpiece went silent to his conversation, though the rest of the room's sounds continued as normal. Satisfied with the effectiveness of Wally's invention, Noah then answered his wife's call, confident that this conversation would remain private from Schultz's prying ears.

As soon as Noah answered the call, Sarah's voice, tense and laden with urgency, filled his ear. "It's Renée," she blurted out, "And I think Marco's in on it too."

Noah's voice was a calm anchor in the storm of revelations. "Now calm down, baby. Tell me what you know."

Sarah poured out the evening's events in a rapid stream—the diner, the mysterious man, the exchange of the manila envelope. As she spoke, she sent Noah the footage captured by Wally's drone. It was a patchy visual and auditory account, but the implications were clear enough to chill Noah's blood.

After absorbing the footage, he sighed. "There's not much I can do about it right now. Marco's with Ralph, hot on my trail, and I've got less than four hours to terminate the next target."

A pause hung in the air as Sarah digested his words. The weight of their predicament seemed to solidify between them, a tangible presence in the room. Sarah's next words were barely audible, choked with emotion. "When…" she began, struggling to continue. "When are we going to get our daughter back, Noah?"

A sharp blade of pain lanced through Noah's heart.

The desperation and fear in Sarah's voice was a harsh reminder of the stakes they were playing for.

"Soon, baby. I promise," Noah replied, his voice a mixture of determination and despair. "I'm doing everything I can. We'll have her back with us. I won't stop until she's safe."

As Noah's conversation with Sarah reached its emotional peak, her voice cracked under the strain of unimaginable fear. "I can't stop thinking about what she's doing... What he's doing to her..." The words dissolved into sobs, the sound tearing through Noah's heart.

He struggled to maintain his composure, his voice steady yet heavy with his own concealed anguish. "Don't think like that, baby. I know how hard it is, but we have to understand that he won't hurt her so long as I do exactly what he says."

For almost a minute, he just listened to her sob into the phone, his fists tightening the whole time, every cell in his body compelled by the fury he felt for Henrik Schultz, Adrian, and whoever was behind them —whoever had looked at his sweet little girl and seen nothing but a pawn to use against him.

"Look," Noah said, his voice a mix of resolve and sorrow, "baby, I gotta go. I'll call you when it's done. I love you."

"I love you too," came Sarah's reply, a whisper of hope against the tide of darkness.

The call ended, leaving Noah in the grip of his turbulent emotions. He turned to face Wally, Neil, and Jenny, who were all looking up from the plans, their faces expressing a combination of concern and determination.

"We all ready?" he asked, his voice now firm with the resolve of a man on a mission.

They nodded in unison, a silent pact of commitment and solidarity.

"Then let's do this," Noah declared, the words a clarion call to action. The team rose, each member steeling themselves for the daunting task ahead. They were a unit, bound by a shared goal, ready to face whatever lay in wait.

CHAPTER
SEVENTEEN

This year the Code for Care Global HealthTech Summit was taking place at the opulent Villa Montalvo in Saratoga. The evening air was alive with anticipation as the sprawling gardens of the villa welcomed the tech industry's elite. Floodlights carved swaths of gold against the twilight, and the gentle splashing of fountains played a harmonious backdrop to all the chatter.

Guests meandered along the cobbled pathways, their silhouettes draped in lavish clothing that whispered wealth and sophistication with every movement. Men in tailor-fitted tuxedos and women adorned in gowns that flowed like liquid silver and gold mingled with ease, their laughter and conversation as light and sparkling as the champagne flutes they carried at the ends of their slender fingers.

Amidst the opulence, Noah Wolf navigated the sea of glittering guests, his form camouflaged by the crisp white uniform of the serving staff. He moved with a practiced anonymity, the waiter's silver platter balanced on his hands holding an array of meticulously arranged hors d'oeuvres. The delicate canapés, each a small masterpiece in itself, were rapidly depleting as he weaved through the clusters of guests, who were more engrossed in their conversations about mergers and innovations than the server offering them bites of gourmet flavors.

As Noah made his way across the patio, a sharp voice cut through the hum of technology-laden chatter. "Christian?!"

Christian. That was the name he was using.

Noah turned to find Brad, his supervisor for the evening, standing there with a hawkish gaze and a demeanor that brooked no inefficiency.

"Your tray is almost empty," Brad snapped. "This isn't a garden stroll, you know. And stop dawdling—we have guests to serve!"

Noah met Brad's gaze with a careful blankness. "Apologies, I'll restock immediately," he replied, his voice as nondescript as his uniform.

Brad's eyes narrowed slightly, the sheen of his own black suit seeming to absorb the ambient light, casting him in a more ominous silhouette. "Make sure it's quick. We can't have you drifting around like a fart in the wind. Be sharp, be invisible, and for goodness' sake, be quick about it!"

Noah nodded, his expression betraying none of the irritation that prickled beneath his calm veneer. As Brad turned on his heel and marched away, he exhaled silently before slipping back into the crowd to refill his tray.

While Noah was busy with the demands of the service industry, Neil and Jenny Blessing stood among the throng of innovators and influencers. Jenny was resplendent in a sleek, form-fitting dress that seemed to catch and play with every beam of light that fell upon it. The dress, a deep burgundy that complemented her athletic frame, managed to look both elegant and fiercely modern. It was the kind of outfit that drew appreciative glances from the other attendees, the cut and drape of the fabric accentuating her poise and the subtle strength that lay beneath.

Neil, on the other hand, looked as if he had been teleported straight from his natural tech habitat, forced into a suit and bowtie that felt like a costume rather than an extension of his persona. The suit was impeccably tailored, no doubt, but the slight stiffness in his shoulders and the way his fingers occasionally fiddled with the bowtie betrayed a man more accustomed to smart casual than black-tie.

Together, the couple navigated the event with an air of practiced ease. Champagne flutes in hand, they mingled, Neil's arm occasionally finding a natural rest around Jenny's waist. They laughed on cue at the tepid jokes that punctuated the conversations, their expressions carefully curated blends of amusement and interest. But their laughter, though convincingly merry to the casual observer, failed to reach their eyes, which remained ever watchful and assessing.

Noah weaved his way through the clusters of guests toward Neil and Jenny. Approaching them with the subtlety of a shadow, he presented the tray of hors d'oeuvres, his eyes briefly meeting theirs in silent communication.

When their company ebbed away, leaving them in a momentary pocket of privacy, Noah leaned in, his voice a low murmur meant for their ears alone. "You see her?"

Neil and Jenny gave a slight nod, their gazes

shifting across the room to where Harmeet Singh stood. She was a vision of success and influence, her career as a leading tech visionary almost as striking as her appearance. Clad in a sleek, metallic gown the color of platinum, she exuded an aura of confident sophistication. Her jet-black hair was styled in a chic updo with a few artfully arranged strands framing her sharp, intelligent eyes. The soft light of the villa's ballroom highlighted her features, which were composed with the grace of someone accustomed to the public eye.

Beside her loomed a colossal figure, her bodyguard Curtis, a man-mountain whose very stance was a deterrent to anyone with ill intentions. His suit, though expertly tailored, did nothing to conceal the sheer physicality of his build. His eyes, dark and menacing, scanned the crowd with eagle-eyed vigilance, resting on each person with a silent threat lurking beneath his stoic façade. His scrutinizing gaze seemed to challenge them. "Go ahead. Try it," it said. "I'll break every bone in your body before you so much as touch her."

With each new waiter that approached, the bodyguard's eyes would narrow, not a single movement escaping his notice. When a flute of champagne was offered, he was quick to intervene, producing a small, discreet wipe from his pocket. Noah, Neil, and Jenny watched as he swabbed the rim of the glass, his gaze never leaving the server's face. The wipe was obviously designed to detect the slightest trace of toxins.

Jenny's gaze shifted back to Noah as the bodyguard passed the champagne flute to his boss. "Looks like your original plan of delivering it via her glass wouldn't have worked," she mentioned, a note of satisfaction edging her voice.

Noah's lips twitched in agreement, the hint of a strategist's smile. "No," he mused aloud before pressing a discrete earpiece deeper into his ear canal. "Hey, Wally? You all set?" he whispered into the comms, voice low.

The response crackled through. "I'm almost there."

Above their heads, unnoticed by the revelers, a solitary bee, ingeniously mechanical, buzzed through the air, its flight path directed with precision. It came to rest on a flower arrangement on the table closest to Harmeet Singh.

"In position now," Wally's voice confirmed through the comms.

Unfortunately, that was when Brad the supervisor caught sight of Noah lingering next to Neil and Jenny. With a smile plastered on his face that was all servitude and subservience, he approached the group, nodding obsequiously at Neil and Jenny. "Enjoying the evening, I trust?" he oozed in an oily tone before gripping Noah's arm firmly, steering him a few steps away from the power couple.

As soon as they were a safe distance from the guests, Brad's smile dropped, his features twisting into a visage of contempt. "You shouldn't be hanging around the guests like that, hovering like a fly around a turd. What's with you?" he hissed, his words a venomous spit of disdain. "It's not hard. Just politely ask if they'd like a canapé, then leave. Maybe if you were a little smarter, you wouldn't still be a busboy deep into your thirties, huh?"

Noah's expression was unreadable, a mask of calm. Inside, however, he was calculating the myriad of ways he could dismantle this man, piece by piece, limb by limb, broken bone by broken bone. Of course, he wouldn't—not here, not now, not ever. But the thought of extending Brad's suffering over hours, testing the limits of his pain threshold to new, excruciating dimensions, flickered in his mind's eye for a fleeting, dark moment.

Brad, oblivious to the dangerous undercurrents, continued his tirade, poking a finger into Noah's chest. "Don't think you're irreplaceable. One more slip-up, and you can kiss your job goodbye," he threatened, unaware that to Noah, he was little more than a buzzing annoyance, one that could be silenced forever with the slightest of efforts.

"This is Wally." The voice in his comms was crisp with resolve. "I'm a go on the target."

Jenny's eyes darted to the room's corners, her voice a hushed whisper as she spoke into the glinting surface of her diamond watch where the receiver was. "Just hold back a moment, Wally," she instructed. "There's too many bodies around her. We don't want people seeing the drone if we can help it. This has to look as much like a heart attack as possible. If people see a bee sting her—or worse, a drone—then it'll really muddy the waters. Remember, Adrian was adamant it has to look like an accident. This is for Norah."

"Okay. Understood. Wally holding back," came the reply.

Meanwhile, Noah maintained his composure under Brad's withering glare. "You understand me, padre?" Brad hissed, his use of 'padre' a condescending jab rather than a term of endearment.

"Understood. It won't happen again," Noah

responded, his voice even, giving nothing away of the storm raging beneath his calm exterior.

"Good. Now refill that tray and get back among the guests," Brad ordered, turning away with a final scowl that suggested his displeasure ran deeper than it really should.

Noah moved to obey, his steps measured as he retreated to a service table laden with gastronomic creations. There, he replenished his tray, ensuring each appetizer was placed with precision, his movements fluid yet discreet. As he worked, he cast a surreptitious glance over his shoulder at Harmeet Singh.

She was in an animated conversation with an unlikely pair: a statuesque woman whose beauty was effortless, her every gesture the epitome of grace, and a man who was her opposite in stature and demeanor, short and somewhat rotund. The contrast was stark, yet there they were, absorbed in dialogue, the supermodel and the dumpy fellow, an allegory for the unevenly diverse tapestry of a gala such as this.

The security remained unrelenting, Curtis the bodyguard a looming presence at Harmeet's side, his broad frame and vigilant eyes constantly sweeping over those who dared to approach. He stood so close, so attentive, that to an outsider, he might have passed for her date rather than her protector—a sentinel disguised as a companion, ensuring that not even a shadow fell upon her without his notice.

"Wally, where's your position?" Noah's voice was low as he subtly adjusted the earpiece.

"I've had to change." Wally's voice came through the comms, static-free despite the buzz of conversations around him.

"Where are you now?"

"You see the bar to the target's right?"

"Uh-huh," Noah confirmed, eyes locked on the bar in question.

"I'm positioned on the rim of the large punchbowl," Wally relayed.

"It looks like the couple are about to leave her," Noah informed him discreetly. "That should mean the bodyguard will relax and there'll be fewer eyes. Are you ready?" Noah's gaze was fixed on Harmeet Singh's bodyguard, watching for the slightest change in his posture.

"Yes," came Wally's quick response.

"You see them now leaving?" Noah continued, watching as the supermodel and her companion excused themselves from Harmeet's side.

"Yes."

"The bodyguard now scanning the crowd?" Noah observed as Curtis' eyes began to sweep across the gathering, the subtle shift from protector to observer.

"Yes."

"Then go." Noah's instruction was a whisper, but it carried the weight of the mission.

In that heartbeat of a moment, Wally's finger hovered over the control. But just as the drone was about to take off from the punchbowl, a blur of motion caught Noah's eye. A bartender, moving with an urgency spurred by the sight of an insect at such an immaculate event, swung a ladle with lethal accuracy, smashing the drone into a glittering shower of tech and punch.

"What happened?" Wally's voice was tinged with

disbelief as his screen went dead inside the van he sat in about a block away from the venue.

Noah replied grimly, "A bartender just destroyed your drone. I take it you haven't got another."

"Not with a stinger," Wally groaned. "So not one able to administer the poison—and it's not exactly something we can just replace on the fly."

Noah understood the gravity of the moment; the mission hinged on subtlety and surprise, elements now lost. They had to adapt, and quickly.

"Okay," he said with a taut edge to his voice as he turned on his heel, the tray of hors d'oeuvres held securely in his grasp. He made his way to a service corridor that ran out of the ballroom. On the other side of the swing door, the sounds of the celebration became muffled, replaced by the clatter and clang of busy staff and the fluorescent hum of the lighting above.

Seeing a trash can, Noah briskly scraped the food from the tray into it, his movements precise, betraying none of the frustration boiling inside him. Clutching the now-empty tray under his arm, he slipped into a pantry, where rows and rows of pristine champagne flutes awaited their call to the party.

"Noah?" Neil's voice crackled through the comms, a note of urgency threading his words. "Where are you? What happened?"

"Wally's drone just got smashed. I'm going with my first idea," Noah replied, his voice a low murmur as he eyed the flutes before him.

Pulling a pair of thick black rubber gloves from his pocket, he snapped them on with a practiced motion. His hands then retrieved a small case from his pocket— his plan B. He flipped it open to reveal a vial set within a foam cutout, its contents deadly yet unassuming.

Taking a deep breath and holding it, he removed the vial with a steady hand, a drop of sweat beading on his forehead, unnoticed. With meticulous care, he smeared the vial's contents along the rim of a single champagne flute, ensuring an even, undetectable coat.

The gloves peeled off with a whisper, and Noah disposed of them and the vial with practiced discretion. He emerged back into the ballroom, a lone figure on the far side of the room, where a table adorned with a fleet of champagne flutes glinted under the lights. He filled the prepared glass with some of the golden fluid from the others, watching the bubbles ascend like tiny escapees to the surface.

With the flute now poised among its innocuous companions, Noah began his deliberate approach across the room toward Neil and Jenny, his expression the very picture of a diligent waiter, the tray a shield that hid the lethal secret it carried.

Reconvening with Neil and Jenny, Noah's expression was taut with the urgency of their improvised mission. "I need your help," he stated firmly, drawing them away from the clusters of mingling guests.

Neil, taken aback, replied with a furrowed brow, "What?"

"I need you two to get me to her," Noah explained, his gaze flicking to where Harmeet Singh stood, her laughter tinkling above the soft symphony of socialite chatter.

"How?" Neil's practical mind immediately sought a strategy.

"Go over and speak to her. Then I'll come along

and offer champagne. That's when her security will step in. I want you, Neil, to take two glasses from my tray. Specifically this one." Noah subtly gestured to the tainted flute. "You see which one?"

Neil nodded, his eyes locking on to the marked glass. "Yes."

"I want you to take one for yourself and give this one to Harmeet. You said she drinks, right?" Noah's voice was a low press.

"She does. We spent four days at her place in the Sierra Nevada. She has a vineyard there," Neil recounted.

"Oh. I forgot the vineyard," Jenny added, her voice laced with a hint of nostalgia. "Watching the sun go down while drinking pinot noir. Almost as good as the night skiing in Aspen."

A tense silence hung as Neil pondered, then, "I can't do it. I just can't. I mean, come on, Noah. I know her personally."

Jenny had no such qualms. "I'll do it," she said.

But just as she was about to reach for the glass, her phone chimed, and when she looked at it, her brows furrowed. "It's Max Shielding," she told Neil as she stepped away from them to answer the call.

"He's our head of cybersecurity," Neil explained to Noah.

"Jenny, we have a problem." Max's voice was tight with concern. "There's been a breach. Someone has broken into the system and gone through everything."

"What's everything?"

"Security cameras at the offices, call logs, bank histories, everything to do with you and Neil both personally and professionally."

Her eyes widened. "What? How serious is it?"

"We're still assessing, but they've had a good look around. They've even accessed all the security feeds at the Palo Alto mansion. Gone over everything. Like they were looking into what you and Neil have been doing for the last three months."

In the meantime, Noah's voice was persistent. "Neil, focus. This is our only shot. You have to take her the glass. It's now or never."

But before Neil could respond, the nasally tone of Brad the supervisor made Noah cringe. "You're not supposed to be serving champagne."

Noah turned, his expression one of barely veiled annoyance. Brad stood there, his posture rigid with self-importance. "Why are you serving champagne?" Brad continued, oblivious to the silent exchange of frustration between Noah and Neil.

It was then, as Brad went to escort Noah away from the scene, that Neil finally bit the bullet and put the mission first. His hand darted out, deftly securing the poisoned glass and another from the tray. With Noah otherwise detained and his wife busy on the phone to Max Shielding, it was now down to Neil. Tucking his discomfort beneath a mask of practiced charm, he approached Harmeet Singh.

"Harmeet, what a pleasure to see you here this evening," Neil greeted when he reached her and Curtis the bodyguard, who narrowed his eyes at him.

Harmeet turned to him, her smile bright. "Neil, I'm so glad to see you." Lowering her voice, she added, "I was beginning to think that there was no one interesting here."

Neil smiled, then offered the poisoned glass. "A drink?"

The bodyguard shifted to intercept, eyeing him with suspicion, his protective instincts coded into every fiber of his being. "Ms. Singh doesn't take drinks from…"

"It's okay, Curtis," Harmeet interrupted, accepting the glass from Neil. "It's Neil. I think we can trust Neil."

Trying to smile while feeling inwardly terrible, Neil raised his own glass, clinking it gently against hers. "To interesting people."

She smiled and echoed him. "To interesting people."

As they sipped, Neil watched discreetly as Harmeet Singh drank from the champagne glass he had so deftly delivered, unaware of the deadly payload it carried. He lingered for a moment, ensuring she drank, his eyes tracking every motion until she handed the empty glass off to a passing server. It was done. The poison was administered.

That was when he made his excuses and rejoined Jenny. She was just getting off the phone, her face a mask of composed urgency.

"We've had a security breach," she told him, her words quiet but sharp, her gaze piercing into Neil's.

Neil's eyes widened in alarm. "What do you mean?"

Jenny continued, her voice a hushed whisper in the opulent shadows. "Someone has accessed all cameras and email and phones. It's like they've gone over everything we've done in the last few months—every security camera we've been past, every call we've made. Even the cameras inside the G650."

Neil felt a chill despite the balmy evening. "How?

How did they get past our security?"

"They were thorough," Jenny admitted, a rare flicker of concern passing over her usually stoic features. "They even accessed security at the house —went over everything like they were looking for something."

Neil's mind went to the worst scenarios. "What are they looking for? What do they want?"

Jenny shook her head, her usual confidence tempered by the gravity of the breach. "I don't know. But whatever it is, they're digging deep. Max has placed the system on lockdown, but this… this is big, Neil. It must have something to do with Adrian and all of this stuff with Noah… But then, we're not even really involved in that."

Gazing across the ballroom at Harmeet Singh, Neil retorted, "Well, that's not really true anymore. Because we're certainly involved in it all now."

When he turned back to his wife, she was frowning.

"How do you mean?" Jenny asked.

"I mean that I just watched Harmeet Singh gulp champagne out of a poisoned flute."

Fixing her own eyes on the tech entrepreneur and her massive bodyguard, Jenny remarked, "Then that means all we have left is to wait."

***

As the evening unfurled its grandeur, a sudden shift in the atmosphere occurred. Harmeet Singh, the luminary of the tech world, began to falter. Her laughter tapered off into strained coughs, her hand fluttering to her chest as a look of discomfort crossed her polished features. The ambient noise of the gala dulled into the background as her condition visibly worsened.

The change in Harmeet did not go unnoticed. Her bodyguard, ever watchful, was the first to react, his previous stoicism unraveling into action. His eyes widened, and he stepped closer, his voice urgent as he asked, "Ms. Singh, are you all right?"

Harmeet, attempting to maintain her composure, managed only a weak nod before her knees buckled. The bodyguard's strong arms were there to catch her, his voice now raised, calling for help. Within moments, the area was abuzz with panic. The word "heart attack" rippled through the crowd, and a man, a doctor, or perhaps just a well-meaning guest, was shouting for someone to call an ambulance.

In the midst of the chaos, Noah, having momentarily slipped the ever-vigilant gaze of Brad, moved with purpose. His guise as a waiter gave him the invisibility he needed to weave through the gathering crowd. With a sleight of hand that had become second nature, he swooped in and secured the discarded glass —the vessel of their meticulously orchestrated plan, swiftly concealing it in a small, padded bag he had tucked in his jacket. The glass that had delivered the fatal dose was now evidence that needed to vanish.

With the bagged glass securely under his arm, Noah made his way to the service corridors, his exit from the building as inconspicuous as his entrance. As he slipped out into the cool night, the distant wail of approaching sirens filled the air. Harmeet's well-being, the ensuing investigation, the questions—it was all noise that faded into the background as Noah put distance between himself and the villa, his mission accomplished, the murder weapon in tow.

Minutes after his silent departure from the gala, he found himself across the street from Villa Montalvo, obscured in the shadow of a large oak tree that lined the serene Saratoga neighborhood. From this vantage point, he watched as the paramedics carefully loaded Harmeet Singh into the back of an ambulance, her figure limp and vulnerable on the stretcher. The giant bodyguard Curtis climbed in after her without hesitation. His large frame seemed to take up the entire space beside her, his hands clasped tightly, his vigilant eyes never leaving her face.

The ambulance doors closed with a definitive thud, and the vehicle sped off, sirens wailing into the night, cutting through the silence that had fallen over the area.

"You did well," came Schultz's sinister whisper of a voice, breaking the silence in Noah's earpiece. "Improvising like that when your little drone got squashed. I couldn't have done it better if I'd done it myself."

Noah's jaw clenched at the praise, a bitter taste in his mouth as he replied, "Then why didn't you do it yourself? Why all this work getting me to do it?"

Schultz's hiss was a sound of amused contempt. "It's better this way. Now stop asking questions. The second it's confirmed that she's dead, I'll give you the next name."

The line went dead, leaving Noah alone with the echo of Schultz's promises and the blaring echo of the ambulance as it disappeared into the distance. He stood motionless, a specter in the night, fully immersed in the gravity of his actions and their impending consequences.

Noah stood poised to melt away into the night, his senses still tuned to the dissipating wail of the ambulance siren, when a voice, unexpected and chillingly familiar, sliced through the quiet.

"You always did like to stay close to a kill, boss."

Noah spun sharply, his body tensed for conflict, to find Ralph emerging from the shadows. His eyes instinctively scanned the area for Marco, but he was conspicuously absent.

"Where's Marco?" Noah's voice was a low growl, his stance ready.

Ralph raised his palms in a gesture of peace, his face earnest. "I ain't with Marco," he assured him.

Noah's eyes narrowed, his every instinct on edge. "What is this?"

"Boss, we need to talk," Ralph insisted, his tone conveying a gravity that gave Noah pause.

"Does Marco even know you're here?" Noah questioned.

"No. He thinks I'm back at the hotel in my room. That's why we don't have much time." Ralph's voice was urgent, his gaze locked on to Noah's, pleading for trust in a situation where trust was the rarest commodity.

Noah, still wary, weighed his options. The night had already taken unexpected turns; one more could hardly surprise him. He gestured slightly, indicating for Ralph to speak, his body language open but guarded, ready for whatever revelation was about to come.

***

Ralph had a car nearby. They talked there. Inside the nondescript black sedan, Ralph produced his phone with the solemnity of a man about to reveal a truth that would unravel lies. He tapped the screen, and a grainy video illuminated the dim interior of the vehicle.

Noah's eyes didn't waver as the silent footage betrayed Marco engaging in a secretive exchange while sitting on a park bench. A second figure, enshrouded in the shadows of nearby trees, handed over a package with a sense of urgency that left no room for doubt—their actions were purposeful, sinister.

"It's the same guy Sarah saw Renée with," Noah said, his observation laced with a cold fury.

Ralph nodded solemnly, his features grim. "Yeah, Marco's been moonlighting on our missions. This was the second time he disappeared—the time I decided to follow. There's rot in the foundation, Noah."

"When was this?" Noah asked.

"Two days ago."

A frown etched deeper into Noah's brow. "And you kept this quiet because…?"

Ralph exhaled heavily, his defensiveness giving way to resignation. "I thought maybe he was in cahoots with you," he admitted. "But then Diana told me about Norah. Ever since then, I've been seeing things differently. I realized you didn't have a choice but to take out Allison and Molly. It got me thinking—someone inside E & E is playing a different game. That's when I started seeing the meeting between Marco and this guy in a whole new light."

Noah's eyes narrowed, absorbing the implications. "How'd you know I'd be here tonight?"

"I didn't buy Neil's line about not seeing you. And I knew something was up tonight... something big," Ralph explained, his voice gaining an edge. "When things started going down in there"—he nodded in the direction of the Villa Montalvo—"I figured you'd be out here, watching, waiting. I know how you operate, boss."

Noah reclined into the leather, his usual unreadable demeanor now pierced by concern. "I need to be less predictable," he conceded.

Ralph allowed himself a half-smile. "I know you, boss, like the back of my hand. Predictable or not, you have your tells."

Silence settled as the import of Ralph's words took hold. Noah's reflection in the rearview mirror gave nothing away as he said, "Thanks for this," his gratitude genuine.

With a quiet click, Noah opened the door, the night air rushing in to fill the space he vacated. He was about to close the door when Ralph asked, "What you gonna do, boss?"

Noah turned back to him. "About Marco?"

"Yeah."

"Nothing for now."

"And what do you want me to do?"

"Exactly what you have been. Keep chasing my shadow and keep watching Marco."

The door closed with a soft thud behind him, his silhouette blending into the night. As he disappeared, Noah's thoughts were already turning, considering each move in this perilous game where every single player held secrets close to their chest.

Every single one of them.

CHAPTER EIGHTEEN

Three hours after Harmeet Singh had been carried out of the Villa Montalvo on a stretcher, the members of Noah's makeshift team where all huddled in the dimly lit safe room. The atmosphere was thick with anticipation. Around a sturdy, unadorned table sat Noah, Neil, Jenny, and Wally. A lamp with a low-wattage bulb stood between them, more shadows than light playing across their faces as they waited for news.

Noah sat with his back against the wall, his posture relaxed but his eyes sharp and calculating. His gaze intermittently swept over his companions, an unspoken question in every glance. He hadn't breathed a word about the encounter with Ralph, the information on Marco sitting like a lead weight in his chest. The current situation was already a tangled web of uncertainty, and he was reluctant to weave further strands of doubt into the mix. His instincts screamed caution, especially around Neil and Jenny. Adrian's reach was far and their methods insidious. Noah couldn't afford the luxury of trust—not when betrayal might be seated at this very table with him. In the game of shadows and deception, Noah knew the fewer cards on the table, the better. For now, he would hold his newfound knowledge close, a hidden ace in a deck full of jokers.

Wally, his fingers drumming a silent rhythm on the wooden surface, appeared the most outwardly agitated. His mind was still replaying the demise of his drone, the plans that had gone awry, and the close call they'd all just survived. Nevertheless, despite the setback, there was a fire in his eyes—a spark that spoke of his readiness to dive back into the fray.

Neil was the picture of contemplation, his features set in a stern line as he held the screen of his phone in front of his eyes. He leaned forward, an elbow resting on the table, face lit up in the garish light of his social media feed.

As for Jenny, she sat looking bored, her chin resting on one hand, her eyes occasionally flickering to the screen of her husband's phone.

"It just broke," Neil muttered, his voice barely above a whisper. "Turn the TV on."

The faces around the table turned to the television screen mounted to the wall as Noah switched it on and set it to the news.

On the screen, a reporter stood outside the hospital, her expression somber, a crowd of onlookers and journalists behind her. The anchor's voice came through clear and composed. "We're now going live to Amanda Chen outside St. Clara's Medical Center. Amanda, what can you tell us about the situation?"

Amanda Chen looked directly into the camera, her professional calm belying the gravity of her report. "John, the tech world is reeling from the sudden death of Harmeet Singh, a giant in the field of artificial intelligence. She was rushed to the hospital after falling gravely ill at a charity gala earlier tonight."

The camera panned slightly to show the hospital's entrance, where the flashing lights of police cars cast a stark contrast to the quiet night. "Initial reports from the medical staff suggest that Singh suffered a major heart attack. Details are scarce at this moment, but the impact of this loss is already being felt across the tech community."

Back in the newsroom, John's solemn face filled the screen. "Amanda, given Singh's prominence, this must have caused quite the shock."

"It has indeed," Amanda responded. "Singh was not just a leader in her field but a philanthropist known for her generous contributions to global health initiatives. The gala tonight was in support of one such cause. The shock here is palpable, with many guests and colleagues in disbelief over her sudden passing. Especially when you consider that she was only thirty-five."

The anchor nodded gravely. "Yes, of course. Very tragic. Do we have any word on the family's response?"

Amanda shook her head. "No official statement has been made by the family as of yet. We expect more information to come to light in the following days as the medical examiner works to confirm the cause of death."

As the report continued, the four operatives in the hidden basement exchanged looks. The news was a public confirmation of their private knowledge, and with it came a new wave of tension. Each was acutely aware that the stakes had been raised, the game had changed, and in the shadows, unseen players moved their pieces into place.

As the CNN report faded into a low murmur, Noah's earpiece crackled to life with Schultz's unmistakable voice slithering into his consciousness. "Looks like you got her," Adrian hissed, a venomous satisfaction in his tone. "Well done. You're now one step closer to getting your daughter back alive. Here. I have a little treat for you."

There was a pause, a shuffle, and then a small, tremulous voice came through. "Daddy?"

Noah's heart constricted. "Norah, sweetie."

"Daddy, where are you? Where's Mommy?" Her voice was laced with the pure, uncomprehending distress of a four-year-old, her words a tiny fist squeezing his soul.

"I'm... I'm on a little trip, honey. But I'm going to be back really soon, I promise," Noah said, the words aching in his throat as he fought to keep his voice steady.

"I don't like it here, Daddy. The lady is nice, but it's not home." Norah's sniffles were audible, a soundtrack to Noah's spiraling desperation.

"I know, I know, and I'm so sorry, my brave girl. But I want you to remember that Daddy is doing everything to come get you. You're my superhero. You know that, right?" Noah tried to infuse his words with warmth and courage, despite the chill seeping into his bones.

"Am I really a superhero? Like in the stories?" Her innocence was a stark contrast to the dark world she was ensnared in.

"The best one. Superheroes are really brave, just like you. They have to be in strange places sometimes, but they're always strong because they know it's only for a little while. Can you be strong for me, Norah?" Noah whispered, each word a vow.

"I'll try, Daddy. But I miss you and Mommy lots and lots." Norah's voice wavered, a small sob breaking through.

"And we miss you more than there are stars in the sky, sweetheart. But I'm going to fix everything, and soon I'll read you your favorite bedtime story, okay? The one about the pig and the spider?"

"Okay, Daddy... I love you."

"I love you too, Norah. More than anything. And remember, every night when you look at the moon, I'm looking at the same moon, thinking of you."

The line went dead, leaving Noah in the silence of the safe room, his heart throbbing with a mix of sorrow and resolve. Each word from Norah had been a delicate thread, binding him to a promise he was determined to keep. He would do whatever it took to bring his daughter home.

Schultz's voice returned, sharp and clear, snapping Noah back to the grim reality of his situation. "Back to business," he said with cold authority. "Here's the next name. Roger Connelly, New York City. Like before, you have three days to get it done. However, unlike before, I want you to go noisy on this one. I want the world to know that Roger Connelly was murdered. And not only that. I want them to see it."

The line cut out abruptly, leaving a heavy silence in its wake. Noah's hand dropped to his side, the earpiece now a symbol of his tethered existence to a malevolent puppet master.

The others at the table watched him, their faces etched with concern and fatigue. Neil was first to break the silence, his voice tentative. "You okay, Noah?"

Jenny's response came sharp and protective. "Does he look okay, Neil?" she snapped, her eyes filled with a fierce empathy.

Noah felt the weight of their stares, the weight of his daughter's voice still reverberating in his ears, and the weight of the name Schultz had just given him. Roger Connelly. The name was a new burden, a new mission, another step in this treacherous journey.

Shaking the fog of emotions from his mind, Noah turned to face his team, his resolve hardening. "We need to go to New York," he declared, his voice carrying the unspoken urgency of their mission and the personal stakes that were driving him forward.

***

The night was still around Lake Temple, the moon casting its silvery glow over the water. Sarah sat at the edge of the jetty, her legs dangling over the side, the phone pressed against her ear as Noah's voice, a quiet murmur of strength and sorrow, reached her across the miles.

"Noah, tell me she was okay." Sarah's voice cracked. "Tell me our little girl was brave."

Noah's response was tender yet tinged with pain. "She was incredible, Sarah. You should have heard her— so strong, so sweet. She misses you."

Tears spilled over Sarah's cheeks, the droplets reflecting the moonlight as they fell. "I just want to be there with her, Noah. She needs her mom. I can't stand this."

"I know, baby, I know," Noah whispered through the line, his own voice heavy with unshed tears. "We're going to get her back. I promise you, this ends soon."

Sarah took a deep, shuddering breath, trying to compose herself. "I just... I feel so helpless."

"You're the strongest person I know," Noah reassured her. "Norah has your spirit. Hold on to that."

With a final goodbye, Sarah ended the call, her heart aching with a cocktail of fear and love. She rose to her feet, the wood of the jetty creaking softly under her weight.

At the other end, Diana stood, her presence a silent pillar of support. She walked over, her steps careful and soft. "Was that Noah?" she asked gently.

Sarah nodded, wiping away her tears. "Yes. He spoke to Norah."

Diana wrapped an arm around her, pulling her into a comforting embrace. "She's a remarkable little girl. She gets that from her mom."

Sarah leaned into the hug, the warmth a small comfort against the cold uncertainty. "I miss her so much, Diana. Every part of me just... aches."

"I know," Diana said softly. "But she's got Noah looking out for her, and soon, she'll be right back in your arms."

They stood together, the silence between them filled with unspoken understanding and shared concern.

Then Diana broached the topic neither of them wanted to discuss. "Has he killed the target yet?"

Sarah's voice was hollow as she replied, "Yes. He's on to the next name."

Diana's response was a whisper, a breath lost to the night breeze. "Oh my."

As Diana's words faded into the night, Sarah stood motionless, her eyes fixed on the dark waters of Lake Temple. The moon's reflection seemed to fragment with each gentle wave, like the pieces of her once whole family, now scattered by the relentless tide of their clandestine world.

Diana, sensing the depth of Sarah's turmoil, offered a quiet solidarity that was more felt than spoken. They remained there, two silhouettes against the vastness of the lake, bound by the silent strength of their shared resolve.

After a moment, Sarah broke the silence with a voice that carried the weight of her determination. "We can't let fear dictate us," she said, more to herself than to Diana. "Noah is fighting for us, for Norah. We must stand strong here."

Diana nodded, her gaze never leaving Sarah. "We will, Sarah. And when this is over, we'll help piece it all back together, for Norah, for all of us."

The night air was cool and still as they turned back toward the house, leaving the jetty behind. Each step they took was a testament to their courage, a silent vow that despite the darkness of their present, they would strive for a future where the light could find its way back to them.

CHAPTER NINETEEN

Noah and his team were on the move. In the quiet before dawn, the sleek silhouette of their Mercedes-Benz AMG GT 4-Door Coupe glided toward the east entrance of the Webster Street Tube on the edge of the Oakland Estuary. The hum of the engine was soft, almost meditative, as the city's pulse faded behind them, ushering them into the solitude of the tunnel. The car's headlights pierced the semi-darkness, casting elongated shadows that danced upon the curved walls.

Noah's hands were steady on the wheel. Beside him in the passenger seat, Wally sat with a watchful poise, his gaze occasionally flicking to the rearview mirror where Neil and Jenny were engaged in a hushed conversation on the back seat, their voices a low murmur against the thrum of the road.

As they were enveloped by the tunnel, the outside world fell away, leaving them in an encapsulated reality, the perfect setting for clandestine conversations. Noah reached up, pulling the earpiece from his ear with a practiced motion, and handed it to Wally without taking his eyes off the road.

Wally accepted the device, his fingers deftly

maneuvering his phone to scan it. "Okay. The signal is cut. He can't hear us under here," he confirmed, his voice a quiet rumble in the close confines of the car.

"What about the cameras?"

"Esmeralda has rerouted his feed to a doctored one in which we get caught in traffic."

"Good." Noah knew the importance of this confirmation—they could proceed with their plans without the lingering fear of Schultz's omniscient presence.

He glanced at Wally. "Did Esmeralda finish the *other* thing?" he asked, a note of urgency threading his otherwise calm demeanor.

"Only minutes ago," Wally responded, his attention now fully on Noah.

"And?" Noah prompted, the weight of the moment evident in the tightness of his grip on the steering wheel.

"They're clean," Wally stated, his words carrying the finality of a chapter closing. "They've had no contact with Adrian or anyone else, and their recent activity has been innocent."

"I thought so," Noah murmured, a mix of relief and resolve settling over his features. "Just had to be sure."

Neil and Jenny exchanged a confused look. "Sure about what?" Neil's voice broke the silence, innocent yet edged with a growing unease.

"Yeah," Jenny added. "Who's clean?"

"You and Neil," Noah revealed, his eyes meeting theirs in the rearview mirror for a fleeting moment before returning to the road ahead.

Jenny's brow furrowed. "What's that supposed to

mean?" Her tone demanded an explanation.

"It means that all yesterday Wally had Esmeralda going over all your data for the last few months."

"That was you?" Jenny's realization came sharp and quick. "The data breach was you?"

"Yes." Noah's affirmation was simple, unembellished. "I needed to be sure neither of you were the mole. You're not. That's why I can trust you with this next part."

"What next part?" Neil's voice was a mix of suspicion and intrigue.

Noah didn't answer immediately. Instead, he maneuvered the car to a gradual stop beside a nondescript service door within the tunnel's confines.

"Noah?" Neil said slowly, his tone suspicious. "What next part?"

"You'll see," Noah told him. "Now follow me."

He and Wally exited the vehicle, the car's interior lights briefly illuminating their determined faces before they shut the doors and plunged the space back into shadow. Neil and Jenny, after a moment's hesitation, followed suit, stepping out into the dimly lit tunnel, the overhead lights casting long, stark shadows as they gathered around Noah, ready to delve into the depths of the conspiracy that had entangled them all.

"What are we doing here?" Neil asked as Wally opened the service door built into the tunnel's wall.

"We're going to meet someone."

"Who?"

"You'll see," Noah said as he and Wally disappeared through the door.

The service corridor they entered was like the

bowels of a great beast, all concrete and steel, with pipes running along the ceiling like veins. It was narrow, utilitarian, with the walls painted a stark, uninviting gray that had long since started to peel in places. The air was cool and carried the musty scent of machinery oil and stale water. Their footsteps echoed off the hard surfaces, a steady cadence that punctuated the silence. Beyond the walls, the low rumble of traffic from the Tubes vibrated through the concrete and steel, a reminder of the world bustling unknowingly around them.

"Noah, please." Jenny's voice cut through the rhythmic thudding of their steps as they came to an abrupt halt. "What in the hell are we doing here?"

Before Noah could respond, the sound of approaching footsteps signaled the arrival of others. Two figures appeared at the far end of the corridor, their features obscured in the gloom, their silhouettes just shapes against the dimness. As the newcomers stepped into the harsh, sterile light of the overhead strip lighting, Neil and Jenny recoiled slightly, recognition dawning on their faces.

"Hello, 9," Noah greeted, his voice steady, betraying none of the shock that Neil and Jenny felt.

A dead woman stood before them, her posture as commanding as ever. "Hello, Noah," Allison Peterson replied, her voice carrying the weight of secrets kept and plans set in motion.

Next to her stood Molly.

"Dragon Lady? Molly?" Neil's astonishment was palpable, his words tumbling out. "You're alive!"

Allison and Molly, now fully visible under the unforgiving light, shared a look that was part resignation, part relief. They had played their roles in the shadows, and now they stepped back into the world of the living, where the real work would begin.

As the initial shock subsided, warm embraces were exchanged, a physical affirmation of relief and reconnection. Once the quiet celebration had passed, they all gathered around, the corridor now transformed into a makeshift conference room.

Allison stepped forward, her gaze encompassing Neil and Jenny Blessing. "Neither of you have ever heard of Protocol 9, right?"

They shook their heads.

"Then let me lay it out for you," Allison continued, her voice steady. "Protocol 9 is a failsafe at E & E. When an operative or an asset is compromised beyond salvage, we enact a death scenario. It's designed to be so convincing that even our own people would believe it."

"But how? How did you make it so believable?" Jenny asked, her brow creased with questions.

Allison glanced at Molly before answering. "Every detail was meticulously planned. For my 'death,' we used standard special effects and makeup to convince the watching Schultz. As I needed Molly's help behind the scenes, she had to 'die,' too. Then once our bodies were loaded into ambulances and away from Adrian's prying cameras, we escaped through pre-planned routes, leaving behind enough evidence to confirm our deaths without a doubt."

"And the deaths had to appear unsalvageable to our own people," Molly added. "That's the level of detail we needed to convince Adrian and whoever is financing him."

"But Harmeet Singh?" Neil interjected, still

grappling with the depth of his own deception regarding her death.

"Don't worry, Neil. You haven't killed her. She's still alive."

"How did you fake her death?" Jenny wanted to know.

Allison nodded to Noah. "Noah?"

Noah spoke up. "When Adrian assigned me Harmeet Singh as the next target, I covertly relayed the name to Allison. She and Molly, under cover, then met with Harmeet and her inner circle and laid out the entire plot and its implications for E & E. Ms. Singh was eager to cooperate after that."

Allison picked up the narrative thread. "The supposed poison was a carefully measured sedative. The 'ambulance' that arrived? That was Molly and me."

Noah went on, "With the media already tipped off, they could only watch as the ambulance arrived at the hospital. From there, Harmeet was moved to the top floor where there were no cameras—a precaution in case Adrian had eyes inside—and then whisked away to safety."

Allison's voice joined the chorus of explanations. "It was all to draw Adrian out. To make him think he's winning, to make him act without caution."

Noah concluded, "Now Schultz and his people believe they've eliminated key players. They're exposed, and we're ready to close the net. That's why we're here. That's why you're here. This was the trap, and he walked right into it."

The group absorbed the revelation, the pieces of a larger strategy falling into place. They were part of a grander scheme, a ploy designed to end Adrian's game once and for all.

"Who else is in on it?" Neil asked.

"Just Wally, and that's it," Noah replied, his gaze steady. "Even Sarah doesn't know. She still thinks I killed Allison and Molly."

A brief period of silence fell over them as they processed this. Then their attention shifted as Noah turned to Allison and Molly. "What did you get out of Harmeet?" he inquired.

Allison stepped forward, taking the lead in the explanation. "When Ms. Singh recovered from the induced symptoms, she confirmed our suspicions. She's the financial force behind the push to restore E & E's standing. I knew someone was financing it, but I'd not been aware exactly who. I thought there were a whole group of investors, but it seems it's mainly her."

Jenny's eyes widened. "So they're targeting E & E?"

"It seems so," Molly chimed in. "First they came for Allison, and then they aimed at our principal financier."

"Where's Harmeet Singh now?" Neil asked.

"Right now," Molly told him, "she's safe and secure at a location only a handful of people know about."

"Which is where Roger Connelly will be soon," Allison added with a decisive nod.

Neil, trying to keep pace with the rapidly unfolding plan, asked, "You've spoken with him?"

Allison answered, "Not yet. But we have arranged a meeting with him for later today at the Manhattan offices of the magazine he works for. I'm going as a potential backer for the magazine." Allison detailed her cover. "In the age of digital media, they're scrambling for investments. I'll be the wealthy heiress eager to funnel money into liberal media. Molly will accompany me as my assistant."

Noah interjected, "Plus, he might lead us one step closer to unraveling who's behind hiring Adrian."

"And to getting my goddaughter back," Allison said, her voice sharpening with a mixture of hope and resolve.

It was Wally who broke into their strategizing with a glance at his watch. "We should get moving," he urged. "If we're off Schultz's radar for too long, he'll start to suspect."

The group exchanged solemn nods, understanding the delicacy of their charade. "Good luck," Allison said, the sentiment echoed by nods around the group.

With a final farewell, they filed out of the service corridor the way they had come, each member of the team acutely aware of the stakes. As they dispersed, the echo of their footsteps in the tunnel seemed to affirm the gravity of their mission, a silent promise to tread carefully on the treacherous path ahead.

CHAPTER TWENTY

Seven hours after her clandestine meeting with Noah and his team, Allison Peterson strode through the faded doors of the Vanguard Voice's Manhattan offices, the heels of her designer shoes clicking authoritatively against the worn linoleum floor. Her coat, an ostentatious display of faux fur, bristled with every haughty step she took. As for Molly, Allison's 'assistant' scurried behind, a portfolio clutched against her chest, trying to keep pace with Allison's dramatic entrance.

"Keep up, girl!" Allison snapped without looking back, her voice dripping with manufactured impatience. Molly mumbled an apology, her eyes darting apologetically to the few magazine employees whose heads had peeked above their cubicles, curious about the commotion.

The editor, a man whose appearance was as worn and compact as the office he managed, greeted them at the entrance to his cluttered sanctum. He barely reached Allison's chest, and his glasses slid down the bridge of his nose as he wiped his forehead with a handkerchief that had seen better days. The sheen on his bald head caught the flickering light of the outdated fluorescent bulbs overhead.

"Miss Vanderbilt, a pleasure," he stammered as she

offered him a slender hand. For a moment, he stared at it, unsure what to do, his look of confusion reflecting off a large ruby she wore on her index finger. In the end, he went with kissing it—it seemed the thing to do.

After that, the editor guided them down a narrow hallway lined with framed but faded magazine covers. They arrived at a door with peeling paint that announced *Roger Connelly* in bold letters that barely clung to the wood. The editor rapped twice before pushing it open.

Connelly's office was a stark contrast to the outer chaos—a tiny sanctuary of organized clutter. Stacks of papers and books formed a miniature skyline on his desk. A lone window allowed a sliver of light to dance across the room, highlighting the dust motes hanging in the air.

Roger himself was an embodiment of his environment—unassuming yet intriguing. His almost white hair was a disheveled halo around a face etched with stories yet to be told. Despite the rounded edges of his frame and the tired sag of his cheeks, his eyes sparkled with what both women took for an indefatigable spirit. Approaching middle age, Roger Connelly was obviously a veteran of investigative journalism and the world it involves.

Once the editor withdrew, closing the door with a respectful click, Allison perused the room with a theatrical air of disgust. The walls, once vibrant, were now lined with yellowing wallpaper, and the carpet tiles told tales of a lifetime of spilled coffee and ink.

"I expected something more... professional," Allison said, her voice echoing slightly in the cramped space. She flung her heavy coat onto Molly, who nearly buckled under its weight as she carried it to a coat stand by the door.

Connelly's smile tightened, a mix of embarrassment and necessity. "We do our best with what we have," he replied, his voice betraying the strain of keeping the magazine afloat.

Allison took a seat, crossing her legs with a swish of expensive fabric. "Let's talk business," she declared, and the room seemed to hold its breath, waiting for the heiress to seal its fate.

Before the meeting got going, Connelly, with a nervous glance, inquired as to why Allison sought an audience with him in particular. Settling into a cracked leather chair that emitted a plaintive creak, Allison explained, "The exposé you did on Michael Sutherland's investment company a year ago."

"Oh yes," Connelly said with a smile. "One of the rare ones that got somewhere."

"Yes. Certainly. It got Sutherland in an orange jumpsuit for the rest of his life. You were very brave going after him. If it hadn't been for your exposé, the FBI would have never arrested him."

"You knew Jonathan Sutherland?" Connelly asked.

"Only through the scene. No, my late husband had had dealings with him in the past and always thought he was a crook. I was impressed that of all the people to take him down, it would be a little-known monthly magazine. It's rare to see such courage," she mused, "a David triumphing over Goliath."

Connelly was about to add something to this when Molly's peculiar behavior caught his eye. Since placing Allison's coat on the stand, she had gone to the windows and snapped the blinds shut with a swish. Now a small device appeared in her hand, and she was sweeping it methodically over the walls and furniture.

"What is she doing?" Connelly's voice trembled slightly, his gaze flicking between Allison and Molly.

"Don't you worry about my assistant," Allison reassured him smoothly, her voice a calm contrast to the tension growing in the room. "Tell me about the magazine's annual turnover."

His brow furrowed, Connelly's hands shuffled through the papers on his desk, seeking the financial reports with the numbers Allison requested. Meanwhile, Molly's device emitted a beep as she held it over a plant pot. Peering into it, her expression was unreadable as she noted something amidst the stones but left it undisturbed.

Connelly, still absorbed in his search for the required report, didn't notice Molly's discovery or her continued inspection—which led her to find something affixed under the surface of his desk.

"What is…?" he started, but Allison raised a finger to her lips, silencing him with a subtle yet clear command.

"Do try to find those figures," she prompted, maintaining the charade of a potential investor as Molly concluded her sweep of Connelly himself, finding nothing of note on his person.

"Look," Allison pressed, though her tone remained in character, "this office is rather stuffy, don't you think? Wouldn't you much rather continue this at a nice little hotel I know around the corner?"

Connelly, caught in Allison's firm gaze, could only nod. "Yes," he agreed, his voice a whisper, swept up in the current of her certainty.

***

Having taken Miss Vanderbilt's limousine across town, Allison, Molly, and Roger Connelly navigated the opulent corridors of The Pierre Hotel, their footsteps muffled by the plush carpeting that lined the floor. Staff members, recognizing the guise of the elderly heiress, nodded and bowed subtly in her wake, respecting the air of affluence she exuded in her haute couture fashion.

The grand hotel's decor was a testament to timeless elegance. Paneled walls adorned with intricate moldings and gilded accents reflected the soft glow of crystal chandeliers. Their private dining room, set at the back of the restaurant, was a secluded haven of luxury, enveloped in rich mahogany panels, and a grand chandelier overhead, casting a warm light over the antique furnishings and fine china laid out on the linen-covered table.

It was a world apart, a slice of the old-world charm that The Pierre was famed for, promising a dining experience as sumptuous as the setting.

But fine dining was the last of their concerns.

As soon as the private room's doors clicked shut and they were alone, Molly's hands were a blur, skillfully extracting Connelly's phone from his back pocket without his notice. She took it to the table and connected it to a waiting laptop, her fingers dancing over the keys with practiced ease.

Connelly, his confusion evident, turned to Allison, who, once again, calmly placed a finger to her lips—another silent command for patience.

Molly counted down with her fingers and flashed an 'okay' sign. "You can speak freely," she announced. "I'm running an audio file that'll cover our conversation."

Connelly's face creased with bewilderment. "W-what?"

Molly explained, "It's so that the person listening to the bug inside your phone thinks that we're having a normal meeting about finance. Using a sample of your voice lifted from your podcasts, I've made an audio file recreating a normal meeting inside this room between yourself and Mrs. Vanderbilt. It'll give us ten minutes."

"I'm sorry. Who's listening?"

"That's what we're hoping you can tell us," Allison replied.

Connelly's confusion only grew. "Who are you people?"

Allison's eyes met his with a steadying gaze. "We're your guardian angels, Roger," she said, a hint of mystery in her voice. "Now sit down. There's a lot to explain."

He cut his eyes at her. "So... you're not a rich investor?"

"No. So sit down."

With obvious apprehension, Roger Connelly took a seat opposite the women. Allison and Molly shared measured glances before turning their attention to him.

"We represent an organization," Allison began, her tone serious but vague, "that operates in conjunction with certain... government interests."

Connelly's eyes narrowed, absorbing the gravity of the situation. "Government interests? Like what?"

"Covert missions against America's enemies."

"And what—I'm in trouble?"

"Yes," Molly interjected. "You've managed to make

your way onto the kill list of a certain group of international assassins who go by the name of Adrian."

"I've never heard of them," Connelly scoffed, a hint of nervous laughter in his voice.

"We didn't think so," Allison replied smoothly. "Adrian and the man that heads them is a shadow. But we believe you're familiar with his mysterious employer. One my organization would like to know the identity of."

Connelly seemed to already gather what she meant. He leaned in, the gravity of the conversation pulling them closer. "It's got to be the Council," he said, the name leaving his lips like a curse. "It has to be."

Allison and Molly exchanged a knowing look. "The Council?" Allison probed.

"That's what they call themselves, but they have no official name," Connelly explained, his voice a mix of frustration and fear. "They're phantoms, hiding behind fronts."

"Fronts?" Allison queried. "Like who?"

"Like the Independent Armies of Revolution, the Ascension Council, the People's Revolutionary Army, United Jihad…"

Molly's response was quick. "We've encountered those groups before. Destroyed them."

Connelly's gaze sharpened. "Then that must mean you're E & E?"

Molly hesitated. "You've heard of us?"

"Only rumors," Connelly admitted. "A clandestine group protecting America's interests."

Allison, sensing the conversation drifting, steered them back. "Returning to the subject of the Council," she said. "Tell me about them."

Connelly leaned back, the shadows of the room seeming to edge closer with his words. "I've spent the last three years investigating them," he began, his voice low. "They're not just any group; they're the puppeteers of war, profiteers of global conflict."

Allison and Molly listened intently.

"They date back centuries," Connelly continued, "originally a series of elitist families, orchestrating chaos since the Middle Ages in Europe. They sowed discord there and then spread their machinations to the New World."

"And their goal?" Allison asked, going through the implications of such a group in her head.

Connelly's eyes went dark. "Profit. Control. They incite wars, fund both sides, and reap the benefits," he said, a bitter edge to his words. "This Council, they're merchants of death," he elaborated. "They don't just spark wars—they're the hidden hand guiding them, funding arms and fueling ideologies on either side. Divide and conquer. They profit from the very chaos and destruction they orchestrate."

Allison's expression was stony. "And they've been doing this undetected?"

"Under the guise of other entities, yes," Connelly affirmed. "Their reach is far and silent. They have roots in the old monarchies of Europe, leveraging wars to expand their wealth. Over time, they've morphed, modernized. Nowadays they're masters of social media. But the essence of their goals remains constant. They're a cancer on the world's peace, growing richer with every conflict they engineer." Connelly's voice dropped to a whisper, "But I've found one of them. A key player in the shadows."

Allison and Molly leaned in. "Who?" Allison's voice was barely audible.

"A French billionaire, Jacques Monnet," Connelly revealed. "He's a ghost in the public eye, but his wealth spreads through countless industries. Shipping empires, luxury brands, some of the biggest fashion houses of haute couture in the world. He's both old money and new."

Molly's brow furrowed. "How have we never..."

"He's smart, stays out of the limelight. His family rose from the ashes of the French aristocracy, kept their heads during the Revolution, then stayed afloat during Napoleon's reign by backing the right horse. When the monarchy was temporarily restored, they adapted before becoming once more republicans under the Third Republic, then the Fourth, the Fifth, thriving through every regime. The Monnets are survivors, chameleons."

Connelly's revelation came with a weight that filled the room. "I'm not alone in this, though," he admitted, his voice steady. "The CIA is involved."

Allison's eyes sharpened. "The CIA?"

"Yes." Connelly nodded. "For the past month, I've been working covertly with them, gathering evidence for a congressional committee that is due to open in one week. The Council aren't just a bunch of rich warmongers; they're fifth columnists orchestrating global instability from within."

Molly's hand went to her mouth in shock. "How deep does this go?"

"Very deep," Connelly said. "In Europe, they're propping up the Russian economy, perpetuating the conflict in Ukraine. In Asia, they funnel uranium into North Korea, destabilize the Chinese markets, have their agents within the Chinese Communist Party push authoritarian policies. And the Middle East? They're arming both Israel and Hamas."

Allison's face hardened. "So they're chaos merchants betting on every side."

"Exactly," Connelly affirmed. "They're nihilists who believe in nothing but themselves, pushing us toward a new world order they think they'll rule. In the past, E & E has been a thorn in their side. You've disrupted their plans without even knowing it."

Allison took in a deep breath as she thought about everything he had said so far. Then she leaned forward, her gaze locking on to his. "You need to disappear, Roger. Completely."

Connelly's eyes widened. "What do you mean?"

"You need to die. That way the Council will think that their plans are working. They'll think they're winning and will drop their guard."

"You mean fake my death?"

"It's the only way," Molly interjected, her tone serious.

"You're giving an interview on live television tomorrow morning, aren't you?" Allison put to him.

"Yes."

Molly explained the next part. "During the interview we would like to stage your assassination."

"You can make that happen?" Connelly asked, skepticism lacing his voice.

"We've done more with less," Allison assured him with a confident nod. "You'll just need to trust us."

Connelly took a deep breath, then extended a hand. "Let's do it."

They shook on it, a pact made in the quiet luxury of The Pierre Hotel.

***

Having just arrived in New York, a well-dressed Noah led his eclectic entourage through the revolving doors of The Plaza hotel, their entrance matching the opulence of the setting. Neil, clad in a faun-colored bespoke suit, nodded in appreciation at the grandeur, while Jenny's black Dior dress whispered elegance. Wally, ever the techie, looked slightly out of place with his hipster sports coat over Atari T-shirt combo, but his wide-eyed wonder was fitting for the occasion.

As they approached the reception, the concierge greeted them with a practiced smile. "Mr. Lightner," he said, "we've been expecting you. Please follow me to your penthouse suite."

The group was ushered into a private elevator, the brass buttons gleaming like the fixtures they'd soon find in their temporary home. Upstairs, the doors opened to a grand expanse that promised luxury in every detail, the cityscape framed perfectly by expansive windows that spread along the outer edges of the suite. Every room of the sprawling layout exuded a unique charm, from the master bedroom's plush king-sized bed to the marble-laden bathroom with its inviting soaking tub. Intricate details, such as the hand-painted ceilings and custom chandeliers, added to the sense of unparalleled luxury.

Noah was admiring the view of Central Park when the earpiece crackled to life and Schultz's voice, a wry amusement in his tone, came through. "You certainly like to travel in style, Mr. Wolf."

Noah's eyes didn't waver from the skyline as he responded, "Would you prefer we stayed at some dump in Queens that charged by the hour?"

"No. But you are a wanted man," Schultz retorted, a hint of a challenge in his voice.

"Only by a select few people," Noah shot back, his voice steady and confident. "You haven't seen my face on any wanted posters, right? My mugshot's not all over the news."

"You are correct. Only your former pals at E & E are after you."

"That's right. Because in order to keep E & E secret, there can't be any official fugitive status or warrant. No pictures on the news or sent to local law enforcement. That means I'm as likely to get caught here as I am in some underground establishment."

It was then that a subtle vibration in his left forearm caught Noah's attention. He glanced down discreetly to see a message scrolling across the implanted screen just beneath his skin: "9: Connelly onside." A knowing grin spread across his face, and he angled his forearm toward the team, sharing the silent but triumphant communication.

Schultz's voice, a blend of amusement and threat, filled Noah's ear. "Your time is ticking, Noah. Less than twenty-four hours to make Mr. Connelly disappear. Get it done."

The line went dead, but Noah's smile lingered. The hunt was on, but with Connelly now an ally, the game had changed. Noah's confidence was not misplaced; it was a beacon, drawing his team forward into the fray.

CHAPTER TWENTY-ONE

The next day was the day of Roger Connelly's assassination. The luxury suite was currently a picture of focused activity, each member absorbed in their role. The early morning light filtered through the thick curtains, casting a soft glow on the array of equipment laid out on the tables.

Noah stood in front of a dress mirror, adjusting the uniform of a studio technician. He checked each pocket of his work pants, ensuring he had everything he needed—tools that would blend in but serve a unique purpose.

Wally approached, holding a lanyard with a CBS Broadcast Center ID card attached. "It'll get you into any door in the building," he said, his voice a mix of pride and tension as he handed it over.

Noah took it, examining the ID with a critical eye. It bore his picture but another name, another identity. He slipped the lanyard over his head, feeling the weight of the persona he was about to adopt.

Turning to face the team, Noah surveyed the room. Jenny was double-checking her medical bag, her hands steady despite the gravity of their plan. Neil was quietly running through the checklist, ensuring that nothing had been overlooked. Wally was syncing the communication devices, a soft beep affirming their connection.

"You all ready?" Noah's voice cut through the quiet, commanding the attention of the room.

Jenny zipped her bag and nodded, her eyes meeting Noah's in the mirror. "Ready," she affirmed.

Neil looked up, his expression set in a determined line. "Ready," he echoed.

Wally gave a thumbs-up, his gaze locked on his tablet device. "All systems go."

Noah met each of their gazes in the mirror, a silent exchange of trust and readiness passing between them. He turned, taking in the room, the team, the mission ahead. This was it—the culmination of all their efforts.

***

A short while later, Noah's footsteps were muted against the plush carpet of the CBS Broadcast Center as he slipped through the maze of corridors. He kept his head down, a cap pulled low to shadow his face, the technician's uniform hugging his frame like a second skin. Around him, the air buzzed with the electric hum of nervous energy, the pre-show jitters palpable as staff scurried to and fro with clipboards and cables.

He kept his pace even, his eyes alert beneath the brim of the cap. The ID card swinging gently from his neck was his talisman, his golden ticket that Wally had assured would open any door.

A sudden "Hey!" rang out, causing Noah's muscles to tense. He turned, ready to face suspicion, ready to improvise his way out of being rumbled. But the man who had called out to him was holding out a microphone and headphones, his expression impatient.

"Take this to Mike on Camera Two, will ya? He's been hounding me for it," the man said, thrusting the items into Noah's hands without waiting for a reply.

Noah nodded, the tension releasing his shoulders as he took the equipment. "Sure thing," he murmured, and he continued on his way, seamlessly blending back into the orchestrated chaos.

On set, he handed off the items to Mike, receiving a curt nod of thanks. With his role momentarily fulfilled, Noah took a position at the edge of the stage, his presence just another part of the scenery.

In his dressing room, Roger Connelly, the man of the hour, sat nervously, his heart hammering in his chest. Not because of the interview ahead, but for the grand illusion about to unfold. His hands, usually steady and commanding, fluttered to his tie, adjusting it for the umpteenth time as he glanced at his reflection in the dressing room mirror. He was a seasoned speaker, a man who had faced cameras and crowds countless times before, but today was different. Today, he was not just the interviewee but also the star of a carefully choreographed act that would see him 'die' in front of a live audience.

As the makeup artist applied the final touches, Connelly took a deep breath. He rehearsed the plan in his mind one last time, the cues Allison had taught him to follow, the reactions he had to feign.

The call for 'places' came too soon, and Connelly stood, his legs firm despite the tremors that threatened to unsteady him. He walked to the set, each step a measured beat in the prelude to his televised 'demise.'

As he walked on stage, the studio lights were blinding, the cameras unblinking. Connelly took his seat, his eyes meeting the host's. As the red light on the camera blinked on, signaling the start of the live broadcast, Connelly's pulse raced, the investigative journalist on the precipice of the most dramatic moment of his life.

The studio lights cast a stark contrast of shadows across the set as Roger Connelly sat, his posture upright, exuding an air of composed determination. Across from him, the interviewer, a woman with sharp features and an even sharper intellect, gave him an encouraging nod. Her reputation for incisive questioning was well known; her blond bob haircut and piercing blue eyes had become a signature on screens across the nation.

"Mr. Connelly," she began, her voice steady and clear, "your investigations into global corruption have made you quite a few powerful enemies. Aren't you afraid?"

Connelly met her gaze, his voice firm. "Fear is a tool they use to keep the truth at bay. My fear is not for myself, but for a world that remains blind to the injustices that thrive in the shadows."

Off to the side, Noah stood with a pistol at the ready, hidden within his uniform. Schultz's voice slithered into his ear. "Remember, Noah, the world is watching."

Noah's grip on the weapon tightened, his hand sunk within a pocket of the work pants. "Just watch," he muttered under his breath.

The interviewer leaned in, her expression one of

concern laced with professional curiosity. "And what do you say to those who would have us believe your claims about global cabals are nothing more than you inciting panic to increase your magazine's revenue?"

Connelly's laugh was short and without humor. "Extreme times call for extreme measures. If I incite panic, it's only in those who have something to hide."

Roger Connelly sat poised and resolute under the hot studio lights, his gaze unwavering as he leaned into the microphone. The interviewer, a touch of awe in her eyes, gave him the floor. The camera zoomed in, capturing the intensity of the moment.

"And so," Connelly began, his voice resonant, broadcasting not just across the studio but to the millions tuning in, "we find ourselves at a crossroads. The institutions we trusted, the powers that be—they are enmeshed in the very fabric of the corruption they vowed to dismantle."

In the wings, Noah watched, the gun a cold presence in his hand. He waited for the cue, the prearranged signal that only he and Connelly knew.

"But there is hope," Connelly continued, his hands gesturing to underscore his conviction. "Hope that lies in the courage to speak out, to act against the tide of greed and…"

Noah moved, a silent shadow stepping into the light. His finger found the trigger just as Connelly's speech peaked.

"…to stand united for justice and for the good of all humanity instead of the vested interests of the—" Connelly's words were abruptly cut off by the sharp report of the gun. Then another report, a second shot supposedly hitting him in the chest. The studio gasped as his body jerked once and slumped forward, the special effects makeup bursting into a convincing display of blood and gore.

The interviewer recoiled, her professionalism crumbling into shock. Off-camera, the crew scrambled, a stampede of bodies heading for the doors.

Noah used the panic, retreating along with the crowd, his heart pounding a rapid tattoo against his ribs. The gun was tucked away, and he was once again just another crew member, his part played, his presence fading into the chaos he'd helped create.

As he slipped out of the studio, the clamor of the broadcast room was muffled by the closing door. The corridor beyond was the complete opposite—empty, silent, the calm after the storm. Noah's departure went unnoticed, his presence evaporating like smoke, leaving behind only the resonance of his actions. He moved swiftly through the empty corridors, his footsteps now a rhythmic whisper against the carpet. He discarded the technician's uniform in a maintenance closet, swapping it for the quantum cloak and jeans he had stashed earlier. His baseball cap still pulled low, he blended into the sea of panicked employees and visitors milling around the CBS Broadcast Center.

He made his way to the service exit, avoiding the main thoroughfares that would now be buzzing with frantic activity. His knowledge of the building's layout, meticulously studied and memorized, paid off as he navigated through less frequented paths.

Emerging into the bustling streets of New York, Noah's senses were assaulted by the cacophony of city life. Horns blared, people chattered, and the city breathed around him, oblivious to the drama that had just unfolded within the walls of the CBS Broadcast Center. He paused for a moment, taking in the cold air, letting it cleanse the adrenaline that still surged through his veins.

With a quick glance to ensure he wasn't being followed, Noah then melded into the crowd with ease, his pace relaxed but purposeful. Around him, life in New York City continued unabated.

***

The studio had erupted into pandemonium. Police had already locked down the building, still searching for the active shooter. It was less than ten minutes later that Jenny and Neil made their entrance to the studios and were rushed straight to the set. Dressed in the unmistakable uniforms of paramedics, they moved through the studio with the confident haste of seasoned professionals responding to an emergency.

Neil's hands were steady as he deployed the gurney, his eyes scanning the set with feigned concern as they approached the "body" of Roger Connelly. Jenny, with a medical bag slung over her shoulder, joined him. They worked in tandem, assessing the "wound" to his chest and securing Connelly on the gurney with swift, calculated movements.

As they locked the wheels and prepared to move, the reporter found her footing again, her journalistic instincts overtaking her initial shock. Her voice, though quivering with the aftershocks of the event, was clear as she began to narrate the unfolding events. "Ladies and gentlemen, please stay with us," she implored, her gaze locked on to the camera. "We've just witnessed a shocking development during our live interview with

Mr. Roger Connelly..."

The camera followed Jenny and Neil as they navigated the gurney through the studio, capturing every tense moment as they edged closer to the exit. The carefully rehearsed urgency in their steps was convincing, each movement choreographed to sustain the elaborate ruse.

***

Noah was at least two blocks away when the emergency vehicles started bombing past in the other direction. He hoped Neil and Jenny were already there.

As he quickened his pace, the voice in his ear crackled to life. "Impressive work, Mr. Wolf." Schultz's voice was smooth, almost appreciative.

Noah's body tightened at the sound of his enemy. "Glad you enjoyed the show," he shot back.

Schultz's chuckle was a dark rumble in Noah's ear. "Oh, I did. But remember, the finale is what the audience really stays for. And our finale is yet to come."

Noah's eyes flicked to the reflections in the shop windows as he walked, half-expecting to see Henrik Schultz's silhouette lurking behind him. "I'm not one for cliffhangers," he said. "Let's just bring the curtain down."

"Patience." Schultz's tone was a warning wrapped in a promise. "All in due time. But for now, take a bow, Mr. Wolf. This round is yours."

The conversation ended there, leaving Noah with his rage as the city swallowed him, just another pedestrian on the crowded streets, his face one among many, his heartbeat slowly returning to normal as he disappeared into the throng.

CHAPTER TWENTY-TWO

The emergency room was a blur of motion and stark white light as Neil and Jenny charged through the double doors, their burden heavy between them. On the gurney lay Roger Connelly, his face pale beneath the artful makeup of feigned death, his chest barely rising.

"He's still got a faint pulse," Jenny cried out, her voice high with orchestrated panic, as they approached the nurses' station.

A nurse looked up, her eyes sharp with professionalism. It was Molly, her role as critical as any actor on a stage. "Bring him through, quickly now!" she commanded, her hands reaching for the gurney.

Wally, wearing the scrubs of a surgeon, appeared at Molly's side, his movements precise and practiced. Together, they wheeled Connelly toward the elevator, the urgency of their actions leaving no room for doubt or questions. The doors closed on them, cutting off the curious glances of the ER staff—all of whom had never seen these strange people before.

Inside the elevator, the tension that had been wound tight began to unravel as they ascended. Molly checked the corridor cameras, a small nod indicating they were clear. Wally pressed the button for the top floor, where the final act of their plan would unfold.

The doors opened, and they moved with renewed haste, pushing Connelly into the operating theater. The room was prepped, sterile and silent. They worked quickly to clean Connelly, removing the blood packs and special effects makeup that had so convincingly mimicked a gunshot wound.

As they cleaned him up, Neil was already on his phone, his fingers tapping rapidly. His social media company, a powerhouse in the digital space, was now a weapon as effective as any gun. "You've just been announced as dead," he informed Connelly, a wry smile on his lips. "Congratulations."

Connelly, his color returning now that the ruse was nearly complete, let out a breath he'd been holding. "Hell of a thing, being dead," he quipped, the tension easing from his shoulders.

After that, they snuck him out of the hospital and drove him away. The following journey to the safe house was shrouded in secrecy, the roads less traveled unfurling before Allison's armor-plated Mercedes as it whisked away its precious cargo. Inside, Roger Connelly sat in contemplative silence, flanked by Allison and Molly, the tension of the day's events still clinging to them like a persistent fog.

They drove through the night, the moon a silent watcher in the sky, until the car finally slowed, turning onto a secluded driveway. The house that awaited them was a fortress masquerading as a beachfront retreat, its security as unassuming as it was impenetrable.

As they approached the front door, a soft chime greeted them, followed by a warm, synthetic voice. "Welcome back, Allison," the AI, Esmeralda, announced, its tone friendly yet devoid of true emotion. "And greetings to our new guests."

Allison led the way inside. "Esmeralda, ensure full privacy mode," she instructed, and the AI promptly acknowledged with a quiet beep.

Connelly took in his surroundings, the opulence of the safe house a far cry from the cold studio floor where he'd played his part hours earlier. "Impressive," he murmured, his eyes tracing the lines of modern furniture and high-tech amenities.

The sound of footsteps drew their attention as Harmeet Singh and her bodyguard Curtis, a mountain of a man with watchful eyes, entered the room. Harmeet's gaze was sharp, her intellect apparent in the quick assessment she made of Connelly.

"Allison has told me much about you, Mr. Connelly," the tech billionaire began, extending a hand in greeting. "Your work in uncovering corporate corruption has been... inspirational."

Connelly took her hand, the grip firm and assured. "And your courage in standing with us, knowing the risks, is commendable," he replied, a mutual respect settling between them.

The bodyguard remained silent, his presence a clear statement of the seriousness of the situation they all found themselves in.

With the group gathered in the living room, the ocean's roar became a backdrop to their strategic discussions. They were a collection of individuals bound by a common cause, each a piece in a much larger game—a game they were determined to win.

***

The message "9: All safe" glowed on Noah's forearm, a beacon of reassurance as he stood in the luxury suite at The Plaza. Then, as if on cue, the earpiece crackled to life, Schultz's voice slithering through. "Time for a little chat, Mr. Wolf," he drawled, every syllable dripping with malice.

Before Noah could respond, another voice came through—a small, trembling voice that cut through him sharper than any blade. "Daddy?" It was Norah, her voice laced with tears. "You said you'd come. You promised."

Noah's heart clenched. "I know, sweetie, I know. Daddy's doing everything he can. You've got to be brave for me, okay?"

"Why aren't you here yet?" Norah's voice broke, a sob hitching her breath. "You and Mommy need to come. I want to go home."

"Soon, baby, I promise," Noah whispered, his throat tight, the promise feeling like ash on his tongue. "I love you. Remember that. Mommy and I love you so much."

The line was silent for a moment, and then Norah was gone, whisked away, leaving Noah with a silence that was louder than any explosion. Then Schultz was back.

"I really will kill you after all of this," Noah hissed into the earpiece, his voice a low growl of barely contained fury.

Schultz's laugh was a sound Noah thought could curdle blood. "That day may be sooner than you think."

"What's that supposed to mean?"

"It means that there's only one name left on the list, Mr. Wolf. Does that make you feel better?"

"Just tell me who it is," Noah demanded, his hands clenching into fists.

"No, not yet. This one doesn't need to be done for another week," Adrian said, his tone mockingly casual.

"A week?!" Noah exploded, his composure shattering. "You're going to hold my daughter for another week?!"

"She's being treated fairly. Think of it as... her being on a little vacation. She'll be right as rain when you're done." Schultz's voice was infuriatingly calm. "Like before, I'll give you the last name three days before the job. So do try to stay out of trouble until then."

The line went dead, Adrian's presence retreating but leaving a trail of ice in its wake.

Noah, his jaw set, pressed the device Wally had rigged up—a cuff-like contraption sitting just above the ear. A click, and his voice, along with any nearby, was cloaked from the earpiece's prying microphone.

Noah turned to face Wally, their eyes meeting across the room. "We have a week," he said, his voice a quiet storm of resolve.

"Good," Wally replied, his fingers already dancing over a tablet. "It shouldn't take that long to find him."

CHAPTER TWENTY-THREE

In the dim light of next morning, Sarah and Diana sat in a nondescript sedan that blended seamlessly with the others parked along the bustling street. They'd decided to ditch the Durango and use a rental car from now on, just in case Renée was beginning to notice the SUV.

With their gazes fixed on the sleek façade of the E & E offices, they had only moments ago watched her enter the building. The day was still young, but the air in the car was already tense, thick with unspoken questions and suspicions.

As they watched, Sarah fiddled with a pair of binoculars, her gaze occasionally darting to the office building's entrance, waiting for their target to emerge. Diana, ever the voice of reason, kept her focus on their surroundings, aware of the delicate nature of the mission.

"Do you think it was Adrian she was meeting with at the diner?" Diana finally broke the silence, her voice low and contemplative.

"It was probably just one of his people, not actually him," Sarah replied, her eyes still scanning the area.

Their conversation was cut short as Renée emerged

from the building, her stride purposeful and swift as she got in her car and entered the morning traffic. Without a word, Sarah started the car, and they began to follow at a safe distance.

The chase led them to a secluded gun range nestled in the hills outside the city. Parking their car on an adjoining hillside, they observed Renée through the binoculars, watching as she let off steam at the range. The sound of gunfire was distant but clear, each shot echoing through the valley.

"Do you think Noah will kill him?" Diana asked, her eyes not leaving the figure of Renée, who was now methodically reloading her weapon.

"Who? Henrik Schultz?"

"Yes."

"If I know Noah like I think I do," Sarah responded, her voice firm and unwavering, "he'll do everything he can to kill whoever has harmed our daughter. Whether that's Adrian, Schultz, or the people behind them. He'll make sure they pay. All of them."

As the sun hung in the bare sky, casting a golden hue over the landscape, Renée packed up and left the range. Sarah and Diana watched her get back in her car and drive toward Kirtland's main gate.

"Looks like she's leaving town again," Sarah observed, starting the car. They had more questions than answers, but one thing was clear: The chase was far from over. The road ahead was uncertain, but they were determined to uncover the truth, whatever it might be.

***

The cool embrace of the New York air was a stark contrast to the sterile environment of the Gulfstream G650's cabin from which Marco and Ralph emerged. The sprawling tarmac of Kennedy Airport was abuzz with the distant roar of jet engines, but E & E's private hangar stood silently at the edge, a secretive monument amidst the chaos.

Waiting for them was Frank Mazzarri, E & E's chief presence in New York. With a reputation for loyalty as unyielding as the steel structures of the city and a proficiency in the art of clandestine operations, Mazzarri's expertise in covert surveillance was unmatched. His face, etched with the marks of a seasoned operative, was stoic as he briefed them. "Gentlemen," he began, his voice betraying no emotion. "Knowing Wolf's propensity for luxurious accommodation, my sources have been successful in locating him."

"Where?" Marco practically snapped.

"He and his team have taken up residence at The Plaza."

As they slid into the Mercedes sedan waiting to whisk them away, Mazzarri continued, "I have a pair of operatives in the lobby as we speak."

Marco, unimpressed, arched an eyebrow. "Only two?"

Frank Mazzarri glanced at him through the rearview mirror, the city's shadow dancing across his stern features. "We're stretched thin in the city. And the directive from Doc Parker was explicit. This operation is to remain clandestine. Too many bodies, and we risk exposure."

The car pulled away, merging with the New York traffic as Frank spoke with a finality that closed any argument. "If the government catches even a whiff of E & E's involvement in an internal assassination, we'll be dismantled before we can mount a defense." The weight of the situation settled in the car like a fourth passenger, silent, unseen, but definitely there.

***

At the same time as Ralph, Marco, and Noah were on a collision course in New York, almost two thousand miles southwest, the gravel was crunching under the rental's tires as Sarah and Diana rolled to a stop at the edge of a quarry pit. It was the destination Renée had led them to.

They sat in silence, the car's engine ticking as it cooled. The frozen quarry lay sprawled before them like a giant, dormant beast. Its steep, rocky walls, striated with layers of sediment and ice, reflected the stark midday sun. Patches of snow clung to the crags and crevices, contrasting sharply with the dark, rugged stone. Below, the quarry floor was a tapestry of frozen puddles and scattered debris, remnants of past excavations now abandoned.

"What the hell is she doing here?" Diana's voice broke the quiet, her eyes fixed on Renée's car a short distance away.

Sarah's gaze was steely, her hands tight on the steering wheel. "I think we should go and find out," she replied, her voice laced with a determination that had carried her through ever since Norah's disappearance.

They watched as Renée stepped out of her vehicle, her movements deliberate as she approached the quarry gate. With methodical precision, she unlocked the chain, opened it, and slipped through.

Diana's hand found the door handle, but she hesitated, looking to Sarah for the final nod. Sarah, already reaching for her own handle, met Diana's eyes. "Let's go."

The two women moved with practiced stealth, their footsteps muffled by the icy dirt as they trailed Renée from a safe distance. The sun hung high above, casting a bright light over the quarry's concentric circles. As Renée's figure descended toward the bottom of the pit, Sarah and Diana took cover behind a mound of earth, their eyes never leaving her. Renée's lone figure seemed to merge with the shadows as she approached a mineshaft, the entrance dark and foreboding despite the daylight.

"Come on," Sarah said abruptly, her voice a harsh whisper as she rose from the dirt, her eyes reflecting the intense sunlight like a predator's. "It could be where they're keeping Norah."

Diana nodded, and they set off again, their bodies low, moving from cover to cover. The quarry loomed around them, a silent witness to their pursuit.

Renée reached the mineshaft and paused, her head turning as if she sensed she was not alone. But when she didn't spot her pursuers, she continued on, disappearing into the mouth of the tunnel.

Having ducked behind a dormant bulldozer, Sarah and Diana exchanged a glance, a silent agreement passing between them. This was it. The moment they had been waiting for. They hurried after Renée, their hearts pounding not just with the exertion but with the fear and hope of what they might find within the dark.

**

The Plaza's ornate lobby was a hubbub of opulence, but Marco and Ralph didn't care. They moved through it with a single purpose. Frank Mazzarri followed close behind, his eyes scanning for unseen threats. They split up, Marco and Ralph making a beeline for the main elevator while Mazzarri entered a back door in order to take up a strategic position near the service elevator.

"Cover the exits," Marco instructed the two men stationed in the lobby as he and Ralph marched past. His voice was calm, belying the adrenaline that surged through his veins. The men nodded, their hands subtly adjusting the cut of their jackets where pistols lay concealed.

The elevator took both men to the penthouse. Upstairs, Marco produced a skeleton card that instantly unlocked the door of the penthouse suite. There was a soft beep, and the door clicked open. Ralph drew his pistol, his other hand pushing the door open as they burst into the suite.

Ralph stepped forward, his gun leading the way. That's when he saw him—Noah Wolf, standing serenely in the center of the room. Noah's hands were clasped behind his back, his posture relaxed as if welcoming old friends rather than armed intruders.

"Hello, Ralph," Noah greeted, his voice a calm oasis in the tension-filled room. His eyes then shifted past Ralph to Marco, who seemed oddly composed given the circumstances. "You can close the door, Marco."

Confusion clouded Ralph's features. Marco holstered his pistol, not with the swift motion of a threat but with the carelessness of routine, and did as instructed. The door shut with a soft click, sealing the room in a silence that was almost tangible.

Marco walked past Ralph, taking a seat on the couch beside Neil and Jenny, who looked on with expressions that were hard to read.

Ralph's eyes darted around the room, seeking an explanation, a threat—anything that made sense of this bizarre scene he was now witnessing. That's when Wally emerged, as if from nowhere. He had a device in his hand that he swept over Ralph.

"What the hell's going on, Noah?" Ralph's voice was a mix of betrayal and demand, his gun still outstretched though its purpose now uncertain.

Noah's expression remained unfazed, the air thick with unspoken revelations.

***

The beam from Sarah's phone cut through the oppressive darkness of the mineshaft, its light a solid entity in the pitch-black tunnel. Diana's flashlight trailed alongside, casting eerie shadows against the jagged walls. They moved cautiously, the silence of the mine broken only by the crunch of their footsteps on the gravel and the distant, hollow drip of water.

It was then, at the end of the rocks, that they found it—an incongruous door set into the stone, as if guarding the earth's own secrets.

"She must have gone through there," Sarah said, walking right up to it.

Without another word, she reached for the handle, her hand steady despite the unknown that lay beyond.

"I'm not sure about this, Sarah," Diana suddenly

said.

Turning to her from over her shoulder, Sarah replied, "We have to know."

The door groaned open to reveal a room awash with harsh, artificial light. Diana squinted against the brightness, her eyes struggling to adjust. There was movement, shapes and shadows converging on her, and before she could react, hands were upon her.

"Sarah?" she cried out, her voice tinged with panic as she was ushered forcefully into a chair. The straps came next, binding her arms and legs with an efficiency that spoke of practice.

The lights dimmed to a more bearable level, and as her vision cleared, Diana's heart plummeted into her stomach. Renée was there, standing alongside Sarah, both looking down at her with an unreadable expression.

"Sarah?" The name came out softer this time, a plea for understanding from the woman she thought she knew.

Sarah's face was a mask of solemn resolve. "I'm sorry, Diana," she said, her voice devoid of the warmth Diana had come to associate with her friend. "We had to be sure."

The finality in Sarah's tone was a cold hand around Diana's heart, the reality of her situation settling in like the chill of the stone that surrounded them.

CHAPTER TWENTY-FOUR

The penthouse suite at The Plaza was a scene of tense drama, with Ralph standing rigid, his gun still pointed at Noah. Wally was holding his device close to Ralph's left ear. The light on it flickered and then steadied to a solid red. Wally gave a nod to Noah, confirming their privacy.

"It's okay, Ralph." Noah's voice was calm, a stark contrast to the tension in the room. "You can speak freely here. Wally and Esmeralda have developed a frequency jammer that blocks out the earpiece's signal."

Noah then theatrically took out his own earpiece. "Henrik? Henrik Schultz, are you there?" He spoke into the device, his voice laced with a mocking tone. There was no reply, just the silent affirmation of their secured privacy. Noah placed the earpiece on the table, his eyes locking with Ralph's.

"You can stop aiming that gun at me. I know it's you and Diana who are the moles," Noah said, his declaration left hanging in the air.

"W-what?" Ralph's voice wavered, his weapon trembling in his grasp as he turned to look at the others in the room, searching for an ally or perhaps an escape.

"Seeing you at Kirtland the day of Allison's and Molly's murders was the first clue. How you happened to be there in the perfect place to spot me," Noah began to recount, his gaze never leaving Ralph. "Then when Schultz was so blasé about me being spotted, despite his orders for discretion, my suspicions doubled."

Ralph's expression was a mix of shock and fear as Noah continued, "Schultz wanted me seen. He wanted me to go on the run. For all of E & E to know I'm the killer. That's why he sent you."

Ralph just stared at him.

"And Diana's sudden involvement with Sarah?" Noah went on. "That only made me suspect you more. And it became too obvious when you tried to seed doubts about Marco. That was when the puzzle was complete."

"But the guy Renée is meeting?" Ralph's protest was weak, the gun in his hand now lowering slightly.

"One of Adrian's pawns, reaching out to her with concocted intelligence about the murders. He's making it look like she's the mole to deflect suspicion from you and Diana while you spy on us," Noah explained, his voice now a shade colder. "But all of that doesn't matter now. The only thing that does, Ralph, is why?"

The question hung in the air, a challenge and a plea all at once. Ralph's arm dropped to his side, the gun now hanging uselessly as the weight of his betrayal settled upon him.

***

Diana's heart raced as she struggled against the restraints, the cold metal of the chair pressing into her.

Suddenly, she spotted that there was a fourth person inside the room with them. Across from her sat a man—battered, bruised, and bound just like her. Recognition sparked as she realized he was the stranger from the diner.

"You recognize him?" Renée's voice was like a blade, sharp and direct.

Diana's mouth had gone dry, her words coming out in a stutter. "No... What is this? Please... Sarah." She turned desperately to her friend.

Sarah's face was a mask of ice. "You do know him," she replied, her voice devoid of any warmth they once shared. "Now answer her question."

"I've never seen him before in my life," Diana insisted, her gaze flickering between Sarah and Renée, searching for some semblance of reason.

"You may never have seen him before the diner," Renée said, "but you know who he is."

Diana's silence was her answer, her wide-eyed stare betraying the fear and confusion swirling within.

Renée continued, her tone a mix of disgust and resolve. "This man is one of Adrian's goons. He contacted me with supposed intel on Molly's and Allison's assassinations. The evidence he handed me in the diner was fake—doctored media and a sophisticated listening device hidden in the hard drive so he could listen in on me."

Sarah's eyes bore into Diana. "The same type that was found in your car. And the same type you planted in my home," she accused. "Now tell me, Diana. Where's my daughter?"

Diana's response was immediate and passionate. "I would never hurt Norah," she exclaimed. "I saved her life, Sarah. Remember that? Whatever this is, it's a misunderstanding."

"No, it's not," Sarah said, her voice steady and unyielding. "You see, Noah and I had our suspicions from the start. That's why we never discussed you openly with Adrian listening."

The room felt colder, the air heavier. Diana's resolve faltered, her staunch demeanor dissolving into a cascade of fear and regret. Her shoulders slumped, and she let out a tremulous breath that seemed to carry the weight of her world. Her eyes, once defiant, brimmed with tears as the truth clawed its way out.

"I... I can't keep this up," she whimpered, her voice barely above a whisper, quivering with each word. "It's been... too much."

Sarah, her arms folded, watched the transformation, her expression unreadable. "Diana, what are you talking about?" she asked, her voice steady but not unkind.

Diana lifted her head, her eyes locking with Sarah's. "He's listening," she pleaded.

"Not in here, he's not," Renée assured her. "You can talk freely."

Diana's wet eyes quivered. "Adrian," she gasped between sobs. "A month ago, when Ralph and I were in Prague, they... they took me. Adrian's men." She clutched at the arms of the chair, her knuckles white.

Renée leaned in, her face a mix of concern and suspicion. "What did they do, Diana?" she pressed.

With a shuddering breath, Diana's words tumbled out in a rush. "They put something inside me, a device..."

"What type of device?"

"A bomb… A tiny bomb inside my skull."

Sarah's eyes widened in horror. "A bomb?"

Diana nodded, tears streaming down her cheeks. "Yes. And if I don't follow his orders, if I step out of line or if Ralph does… Adrian will detonate it. They gave us earpieces to wear. He's always there, listening, a constant threat. I'm… I'm so scared."

The room fell silent, the gravity of Diana's confession hanging heavy in the air. Sarah stepped forward, the anger that had etched her features softening into something akin to empathy. She crouched in front of Diana, her hand reaching out to gently touch her arm.

"Diana, look at me," Sarah said, her voice a soothing balm.

Diana's tear-streaked face lifted, her eyes meeting Sarah's. There, in the depths of Sarah's gaze, she found not the anger or betrayal she expected, but a compassionate resolve.

"We can help you. But you have to trust us. You have to help us stop Adrian," Sarah implored, her voice imbued with a quiet strength that resonated in the stillness of the quarry room.

"I… I want to," Diana stammered. "I want this to end."

Renée stepped back, a silent observer to the unfolding alliance. Sarah's gaze never wavered from Diana's face. "Then let's end it," she said firmly. "Together."

***

In the opulent confines of The Plaza penthouse, Ralph stood opposite Noah, the weight of his betrayal heavy in the air between them, his eyes downcast, his voice low and laced with regret.

"I love her so much, boss. She's the one truly good thing I have. Without her, I'd be... I'd be dead inside." Ralph's words were thick with emotion. "You can understand that, can't you?"

Noah's expression was hard to read, his arms still folded across his chest as he regarded the man who had been both friend and traitor. "I can understand love, Ralph. What I can't understand is silence. You should have come straight to me."

Ralph met Noah's gaze, a desperate plea etched on to his face. "I was scared, boss. Not for me, but for Diana. Adrian's reach is long, and his retribution... you've seen what he's capable of."

"You think I haven't been scared too?" Noah shot back, his voice sharpening. "Every minute since this began, I've been terrified—for Norah, for Sarah, for all of us. But I chose to trust my team. You chose to trust Adrian."

Ralph's jaw clenched, and he took a step forward. "It wasn't a choice. It was a gun to our heads. You know I'm not a coward, boss."

Noah's stance softened slightly. "No, you're not a coward, Ralph. You've been cornered. I can accept there's a difference."

Silence stretched out as they stood there, two men entangled in an impossible situation. Finally, Noah broke the quiet. "So what now? You stay Adrian's lapdog until he's done using you? Or you make this right?"

"How can I make this right?" Ralph's voice was almost a whisper, a mix of defiance and despair.

"Come back to us, Ralph. Help us take down Schultz, Adrian, and anyone else that's sitting in the shadows. For Diana. For Norah. And for all the Dianas and Norahs he's holding over us," Noah implored.

Ralph's resolve flickered in his eyes, a battle raging within. "And if I do, what then? How can we stop a man who's always one step ahead?"

Noah stepped closer, his voice a fierce whisper. "We do it by being *two* steps ahead. You know Schultz's tactics, his plans. You could be the edge we need."

Ralph stood motionless, the offer hanging before him like a lifeline in a stormy sea. Finally, he nodded, a decision made. "All right, boss. I'm with you. Let's take this bastard down."

Noah extended a hand to Ralph, a gesture of truce and renewed alliance as they prepared to face the darkness together.

***

The day had taken on a colder edge as Diana and Sarah emerged from the quarry's gaping mouth under a clear, brisk January sky. The air tasted of dust and betrayal, and Diana's thoughts churned with the revelations that had unfolded in the shadows below.

"Can you believe Renée?" Sarah's voice was a mix of exasperation and anger, cutting through the chilly air. "All those theatrics, just to lose us in the tunnels. She's playing games. I'm convinced of it now."

Diana's response was a murmur, her mind elsewhere. She felt the weight of the device in her head with every step, a silent, deadly companion that had marked her every move for the past month. And in her ear, almost like a caress, she could hear Schultz's breath —a reminder that she was never truly alone.

"Yeah, games," Diana echoed hollowly, her voice barely carrying over the crunch of gravel underfoot, now partially frozen in the winter chill.

Now that she had chosen to go against him, she could feel Schultz's presence not just in her ear but all around her—his network, his power, his eyes seemingly on her at all times. The soft, rhythmic sound of his breathing was a leash keeping her tethered to a reality she desperately wanted to escape.

Sarah glanced at her, a furrow of concern forming between her brows against the stark winter light. Now she knew the weight that had been placed on Diana's and Ralph's shoulders, she knew that they had had little choice but to comply with Adrian's demands.

"Where'd you think Renée went?" she asked, playing the game while giving her friend a sympathetic look.

Diana forced a smile, a brittle thing that didn't reach her eyes. "I don't know," she said. "Maybe she was meeting that guy again."

They walked on, the quarry receding behind them, its secrets now hidden not in darkness but in the harsh daylight. But for Diana, there was no leaving the darkness behind. It lived within her, right inside her head. Adrian's device was an ever-present shadow that whispered death with every breath she heard in her ear, even under the cold January sun.

***

The towering opulence of The Plaza faded into the background as Ralph, Marco, and Frank Mazzarri made their way out of the hotel. Under the watchful eyes of the many security cameras, they walked with the weariness of men who had been chasing ghosts.

"It's like he vanished into thin air," Ralph grumbled, his voice a low rumble of discontent easily picked up by Adrian's earpiece. "We had him cornered, but he's nowhere to be seen."

"You know what," Marco said, his stomach grumbling louder than Ralph's complaints as he glanced across the lobby and caught sight of a hotdog stand just beyond the entrance, "all this chasing our tails has made me hungry. I'm gonna grab a bite. You want anything?"

"Nah," Ralph replied. "I'm good. I'll wait here."

"What about you?" Marco asked Frank Mazzarri.

Mazzarri, ever the professional, nodded toward his two men stationed in the lobby. "I've already had lunch. You go right ahead. I'll debrief with these two. Make sure our exit is as discreet as our entrance was supposed to be."

"Suit yourselves," Marco said, heading out into the street.

Left to his own devices, Ralph felt a chill that had nothing to do with the cold January air. Since leaving the suite, the earpiece had been silent. Now its low hiss abruptly broke the silence, Schultz's voice sneering in his ear. "What happened? I lost you."

Ralph tensed. Then he answered, "Frank used some type of device when we got to the floor. It blocked any signals in case Wolf was monitoring the hallway.

Must've worked on your earpiece, too."

There was a pause, a moment that stretched out as Schultz appeared to process this information. After a few agonizing seconds, he said, "I take it Wolf wasn't there."

"No," Ralph confirmed, tinging his voice with bitterness for effect.

"You disappoint me, Ralph." Adrian's voice oozed with menace. "I told you where he was. You were supposed to catch him before letting him go, having convinced him to kill your pal Marco. That was the plan, wasn't it?"

Ralph's throat tightened, the words struggling to find their way out. "It wasn't my fault, Henrik. He must've—"

Schultz cut him off sharply. "Excuses are like prayers in an empty church, Ralph. Pointless. Remember, your actions have consequences. Not for you, but for dear Diana."

A cold sweat broke out on Ralph's brow. "Please, Henrik, we missed him once. That's all. We know he's in New York. He has to be. Otherwise, how's he gonna get to Connelly? It's just a matter of time before we find him."

"But time is running out. I need all the players in their places, and Wolf isn't in his. Perhaps I should lose a pawn. How about dear little Diana?"

"Please, Henrik," Ralph said, deflated, gazing out of the door with a look of despair on his face as Marco stood out there spreading mustard along his hotdog. "She has nothing to do with me missing Wolf," he added, practically pleading. "That's on me."

Schultz chuckled, a dry sound devoid of any humor.

"But that's where you're wrong. She has everything to do with this. You both chose your sides when you took my deal. And we both know what that deal entails. Your actions have consequences, Ralph. Consequences on *her*."

Ralph could feel the walls closing in, the grandeur of The Plaza's lobby turning into a gilded cage. "What do you want me to do?" he asked, his voice barely above a whisper.

Schultz's response was as cold as the marble beneath Ralph's feet. "Find him, Ralph, and enact the plan. I want his and E & E's ruin. Otherwise, the next time you see Diana, it will be through a glass pane at the morgue."

The earpiece went dead, leaving Ralph with Schultz's threat ringing in his ears. He stood motionless for a moment, looking around the luxurious lobby of The Plaza. Its beauty now seemed to mock him, a stark contrast to the darkness that clouded his mind. He felt trapped, caught in a game much bigger than he had anticipated, with stakes far higher than he could afford.

Outside, the bustle of New York continued unabated, oblivious to the turmoil unfolding within the walls of the grand hotel. Ralph watched Marco devour his hotdog with an enviable simplicity, free from the tangled web of deceit and danger that had ensnared himself.

CHAPTER TWENTY-FIVE

The next few days blurred together for Noah, each one marked by the oppressive awareness of Schultz's continued surveillance. He stayed out of sight, his movements limited to New York, conversations with Sarah his only respite. She, along with Diana, maintained their ruse, tailing Renée with convincing dedication.

To any outside observer, their pursuit was relentless, a game of shadows and deception. But beyond Adrian's eyes and ears, they were working against him. The day after Diana's agreement to aid them, they had shadowed Renée to R&D. Once inside the building's signal-proof walls, they severed Adrian's auditory thread, allowing them to delve into the technology that held Diana in bondage.

The device they'd placed inside her head was a masterpiece of malignant engineering. Implanted at the base of Diana's skull, it was made of a polymer composite that was as strong as steel but invisible to metal detectors. It housed a micro explosive, no larger than a grain of rice but capable of causing catastrophic damage. It was designed to rupture a blood vessel in the brain, simulating the effects of a natural embolism—lethal and leaving no trace of foul play.

The R&D team, a group of experts with furrowed brows and somber expressions, analyzed the device while Diana lay in an MRI scanner. They employed advanced imaging techniques and consulted with neurosurgeons, but the conclusion was unanimous: the risk of detonation was too high. Removal was off the table. It was a bitter pill for Diana. The death sentence hanging over her head by the thinnest of threads would continue. For now at least.

Meanwhile, Neil, Jenny, and Wally were entrenched in a digital war room, screens aglow with streams of data and maps dotted with potential locations as they triangulated the signals from the three earpieces they now at access to, using an array of receivers, cross-referencing times, signal strength, and patterns. Every intercepted transmission was a piece of the puzzle, a breadcrumb leading them closer to Schultz and Adrian.

Their breakthrough came on the fourth day. Wally, his eyes red-rimmed from hours of scrutiny, sat up straighter, a line of code catching his attention. "Here," he muttered, fingers flying across the keyboard. "This is it."

Jenny leaned over his shoulder, watching as the digital map zoomed in on a warehouse on the edge of Albany. "Contact Noah," Wally said, his voice steady despite the excitement that sparked in his eyes.

"Why?" Jenny's question was automatic, her focus split between the potential lead and the work still at hand.

"I think I may have found him," Wally said, the implication of his words charging the air with a new energy.

**

The New York subway was a living, breathing entity, its veins pulsing with the rush of commuters, its heartbeat the rhythm of ceaseless trains roaring on the tracks. In this subterranean world, Noah and the other members of his team were in the midst of orchestrating a deception, a calculated performance aimed at misdirecting Adrian's ever-watchful eye away from those coming for him.

"Keep your eyes sharp," Marco murmured, his words barely audible over the noise of the subway. His gaze darted among the faces, searching for the familiar one that would signal the resumption of their faux pursuit.

Ralph nodded. "He's here," he replied, his tone laden with a mix of duty and dread.

Above them, hidden in the anonymity of the crowd, Noah watched discreetly like a hawk stalking its prey. The game had to look real, so they were playing it like it was real.

They were skilled, Marco and Ralph, trained in the art of covert operations. But Noah Wolf was the ghost, unseen amidst the throngs, a master of evasion. His senses attuned to the rhythm of the chase, his body coiled and ready to move on a moment's notice, he descended down the escalator onto the subway platform.

Marco and Ralph were just ahead of him, weaving through the crowd and moving away. Noah got close, so close that he could almost reach out and tap their shoulders. But he held back, his discipline ironclad.

A brief pause, a tilt of Ralph's head. He sensed something amiss. But when he twisted around, there were nothing but the faces of strangers.

Noah had stepped away just in time, swallowed in the wake of the heaving rush hour crowd. The sea of people was a perfect camouflage, and Noah remained unseen, a shadow among shadows.

As Marco and Ralph turned their attention to an arriving train, Noah took his cue. He blended into the surge of bodies heading for the train on the other side of the platform, a silent predator among a sea of unsuspecting prey. The subway car's doors slid open, and he slipped inside, just another commuter in the city that never sleeps.

With the train pulling away from the station, the lights of the cars blurring into the tunnel's darkness, Noah was gone, a specter in the city's underbelly, leaving Marco and Ralph to ponder the emptiness of their hunt.

As he leaned back in his seat, the faint buzz of his forearm signaled an incoming message, drawing his gaze.

The soft light of the letters illuminated the dim carriage as the words scrolled across his skin: "W: we've found him."

A slow smile spread across Noah's face, a stark contrast to the rapid drumming of his heart. He touched the forearm, acknowledging the message, and the light faded away as quickly as it had appeared.

"Gotcha," Noah whispered to the heaving carriage, a vow and a victory all at once. He knew the next steps would be a delicate dance of danger and opportunity, but for the first time in what felt like an eternity, the endgame was in sight.

With renewed vigor, Noah pushed off the wall and stepped back into the night. The message from Wally was a beacon, a signal that the tide was turning in their favor.

CHAPTER TWENTY-SIX

They worked fast, wasting no time. Within minutes of pinpointing Schultz's location, Neil and Jenny were in the air, aboard an MH-6 Little Bird that was being piloted by Wally. With Noah under Adrian's relentless surveillance, it fell to the rest of the team to execute this critical phase of the operation.

Their destination, nestled in upstate New York, was ominously close. The three earpieces, functioning as modern-day compasses, had led them to their target. Adrian's stronghold, a location they hoped Schultz was using to house Norah, was a seemingly abandoned warehouse. Concealed behind a façade of disuse and owned by a labyrinthine network of shell companies, it was an obvious deception.

As dusk cloaked the sky in shades of twilight, Wally expertly set the chopper down in a secluded field nearby. Under the protective cloak of the encroaching night, Neil and Jenny made their stealthy approach toward the outskirts of the warehouse. The building stood forlornly amidst its crumbling counterparts, a forgotten relic in an area left behind by the relentless march of time and economic progress. Its unassuming appearance was a strategic guise, however, meant to deflect attention and breed underestimation.

Guided by Wally's hushed, digitalized directives through their communication devices, they moved with calculated precision. "This is it." Wally's voice crackled through the earpieces. "The place Schultz has been coordinating his communications from. It's the center of the spider's web, and you two are about to step right into it."

With methodical precision, Neil and Jenny approached the chain-link barrier surrounding the building. The fence, crowned with coils of barbed wire, posed little challenge to their specialized equipment. Using silent cutters, they snipped through the metal with discreet efficiency, slipping through the breach like shadows blending into the darkness.

Beside the building, the flattened grass and disturbed earth told a story. Kneeling beside a patch of black oil, Jenny whispered into her comms, "Looks like there was a chopper here recently."

Standing, she made a few discreet hand signals to her husband, and the two of them placed their eyes back to the scopes of their weapons. They were armed with silenced MK18s, compact rifles favored for their close-quarter engagements. These weapons, equipped with advanced scopes for precision aiming, were ideal for stealth operations.

They came to a stop in front of a nondescript door, the final barrier to their objective. Jenny leaned close to her comms, her voice a hushed whisper. "Okay, Wally. Cut the power." As her words dissipated into the night, a blanket of darkness enveloped the area. Streetlights winked out, building illuminations ceased, and the sliver of light seeping from beneath the door before them vanished into oblivion.

Neil and Jenny snapped down the ocular lens assembly of their NVGs. Then, with precise efficiency, Jenny aimed her silenced MK18 at the door's lock. A muffled burst of gunfire shattered the stillness, the lock splintering apart under the force of her shots. Neil, acting swiftly, drove the sole of his boot beside the remnants of the lock, sending the door crashing inward with a muted thud.

The two of them surged forward into the darkness, the green of their NVGs burning through the blackness like a flaming torch. The interior of the warehouse was a stark contrast to its crumbling façade. Pristine and almost surgically clean, it bore the resemblance of a high-tech military installation. The walls were lined with dormant high-tech equipment and control panels, flanked by empty weapon racks and secured storage lockers, all meticulously organized in a silent, orderly fashion.

As they moved methodically through the building, signs of a hasty evacuation were evident everywhere. A half-smoked cigarette was still warm in an ashtray. "They were just here," she whispered, a mix of frustration and anticipation lacing her voice.

In one of the rooms, they found a haunting sight. Unlike the rest of the place, this room was delicately decorated, filled with children's toys and soft colors. It was a stark anomaly, a room that looked like it had recently housed a little girl: Norah. She had been right here, right in this room. The cheerful decor and the presence of toys seemed to mock them.

"They must have known we were coming," Jenny

hissed into the dark.

Neil surveyed the room. One thing was out of place: a laptop that sat on the end of the bed. When he picked it up, the device was still warm. Flipping it open, the screen illuminated with six separate body-cam feeds.

Wally's voice, strained with tension, crackled through their earpieces. "What do you see, Neil?"

Neil, his attention fixed on the screen, slowly pieced together the pattern of movements, the interplay of shadows and light. A realization dawned on him, clear and unsettling. "I see..." he began, his voice trailing off as the full implications of what lay before him unfolded in his mind.

The grainy, green-tinged footage from the body-cams painted a picture that was all too clear. On a couple of the cameras it was obvious that two operatives, clad in tactical gear and armed with carbines, were disembarking from an inflatable boat onto a deserted beach.

As a large beachfront mansion came into view, Neil furrowed his brow, a terrible dread washing over him. "That looks like Allison's place in the Hamptons, doesn't it?"

Jenny's hand came over her mouth, stifling the gasp that threatened to escape. Her eyes widened, reflecting the horror on the screen. "We need to let them know," she whispered, a plea, a prayer, a curse—all carried in a single breath.

Wally's panicked voice filled their ears. "I'm already on it. But the lines are all dead. Something is blocking the signals."

Jenny turned to her husband. "Noah."

Neil was already in motion, his phone pressed

against his ear, his other hand clenched into a fist. The ringtone seemed to echo in the void of inaction, urging Noah to answer, to hear, to understand that instead of being the ones making the play, they were being played.

The call went to voicemail. "Noah, they're at the safe house," Neil snapped the second the beep sounded. "Adrian's men—they're in the Hamptons."

The laptop showed the six operatives fanning out, their discipline a stark contrast to the serene backdrop of the coastal retreat. Each step they took was a moment closer to their sinister goal, each second that ticked by a countdown to a confrontation they were trained to win.

***

Noah sat inside the subway car surrounded by the hustle of the commuters when the earpiece vibrated with life. Schultz's voice, a harbinger of dread, slithered into his ear. "You've been busy, Mr. Wolf. A commendable performance, but it's all been for naught."

The world seemed to pause, the din of the subway fading into a distant hum. Noah's hand instinctively moved to his side, fingertips grazing the outline of his concealed pistol. "What are you talking about, Henrik?"

Schultz's chuckle was a sound devoid of warmth. "On the contrary, what are you talking about? Did you really think I wouldn't notice your little game of hide and seek?"

The subway car, a capsule of anonymity, suddenly became a cage. Noah felt the walls closing in, the faces around him morphing into potential threats. "I don't understand—"

"Knock it off!" Schultz cut in, real anger in his voice

for once. "You almost got me, you know that? But now it is you who has been gotten."

"Henrik, if you harm—"

Schultz interrupted with a cold laugh, devoid of any trace of humor. "Oh, Mr. Wolf, 'harm' is such a gentle word for what's about to happen. My men have just arrived at your little sanctuary in the Hamptons. I do believe that's where you're keeping dead people these days. A Mr. Connelly, Ms. Singh and Mrs. Peterson, I believe. Isn't that right?"

Each word was a dagger, and Noah felt them pierce the armor he had carefully constructed. The world shrank and bore down on him, squeezing Noah. "I swear to you, Henrik—"

The reply was merciless. "Swear all you want, but it changes nothing. Your move in Albany, my move in the Hamptons. We're playing chess, Noah, and I'm always two steps ahead. Remember?"

At that moment, the subway car emerged into the nighttime streets, and his phone's signal came back. It chimed with Neil's message, and soon his urgent voice broke through, a desperate message that overlapped Henrik Schultz's taunting. "Noah, they're at the safe house. Adrian's men—they're in the Hamptons."

The train car blurred into a mirage of abstract shapes and colors as Noah grappled with the reality of the situation. Schultz's move was clear, a counterstrike that put everything Noah held dear at risk.

CHAPTER TWENTY-SEVEN

In the serene embrace of Allison Peterson's Hamptons beachside mansion, a game of Monopoly was the chosen distraction from the weighty concerns that lingered like shadows at the edge of the room's warmth.

"Park Avenue, again, Roger? You're bleeding me dry here," Allison chided with a wry smile as she handed over the mock currency to the investigative journalist.

Afterwards, she glanced at her phone beside the pile of colorful banknotes, its screen dark, no new calls or messages alerting her to trouble. With a small, reassuring nod to herself, she returned to the game.

Roger Connelly's chuckle resonated in the room. "It's all about location, Allison," he retorted, his eyes twinkling with humor.

Harmeet Singh placed her miniature top hat on the coveted space with a gentle tap. "Your empire is growing, Roger. But remember, empires can fall," she mused.

Beside her, Curtis the bodyguard remained an unmoving presence, his eyes occasionally flicking to the windows, to the shadows that danced with the moonlight. His voice, when he finally spoke, was soft yet carried the weight of their collective vigilance. "It's quiet out there... too quiet."

Molly glanced up from her position, her hand resting casually near the concealed firearm under the coffee table. "Quiet is good. Quiet means we're still safe," she replied, though her eyes betrayed her readiness for anything but.

The serenity of the house, however, was nothing more than a thin veil. One that was soon to be torn apart. Outside, darkness enveloped the team of six—ghosts clad in tactical gear, their forms obscured by the night. They communicated without words, their intentions clear in the silent choreography of their disciplined approach. Night vision goggles rendered the world in shades of green, painting the environment in a spectral light.

The team leader, his gaze fixed on the sprawling mansion, raised a hand, halting their advance.

"Tech, confirm our signal jam," he whispered into the comm, his voice barely a breath.

The tech operative, hunched over a device that blinked with a constellation of lights, nodded. "All comms are dead in the water. They're isolated. Wolf's calls won't reach them, not with us catching all phone signals," he confirmed.

Assured, the team leader signaled the advance.

The operatives moved with the precision of a well-oiled machine. Two of them, having only seconds ago emerged from the cold embrace of the Atlantic, moved across the beach with the stealth of marine predators. Their bodies, wet and glistening, left faint trails on the sand as they melded back into the shadows.

Elsewhere, another pair dropped from the branches

of the gnarled trees that lined the property, their descent as silent as the fall of leaves. They landed with the grace of cats, their presence betrayed by nothing more than the brief disturbance of the foliage.

The darkness of the night was their ally, the silence their pact. Laser pointers, affixed to their weapons, flickered on and off, a coded language of danger that directed their formation. Each beam of light, visible only through their NVGs, was a sinister marker that heralded the impending storm.

The kill squad, a shadow team sculpted by darkness and armed with the tools of their lethal trade, moved with calculated stealth toward the beachside safe house. In their hands, they carried a device that was the key to their silent invasion—a sophisticated piece of hardware no larger than a hardcover book yet one that contained the digital equivalent of a master key.

This was no ordinary hacking device; it was a custom-engineered marvel of technology, designed to interface seamlessly with the most advanced security systems in the world. Its matte black casing was nondescript, but inside, it thrummed with the potential to disarm, to disrupt, to deceive.

One of the operatives, his fingers gloved against the night's chill, connected a slim cable from the device to an access panel discreetly placed at the side of the safe house. The device came to life, its screen a lattice of code that scrolled with purpose. He navigated through the menus with the confidence of one who had done this many times before, selecting the option marked *Infiltrate*.

The device initiated a sequence, sending a surge of encrypted signals into the heart of the house's security.

Esmeralda was a formidable opponent—her algorithms state-of-the-art, designed to repel and alert. But the device carried a weapon tailored for this very encounter —a virus, coded to slip through her defenses like a whispered secret.

As the digital assault commenced, Esmeralda's virtual senses were bombarded. She attempted to reroute, to shut down access points, but each move was anticipated. The virus was a chameleon in her system, adapting, hiding, attacking. Lines of code cascaded across the device's screen, a visual representation of the cyber battle being waged.

The operative watched as the progress bar inched forward. The virus was insidious, wrapping around Esmeralda's core like a serpent, squeezing, constricting, until with a final surge, it uploaded completely. The AI's defenses faltered, her digital consciousness succumbing to the intruder's commands.

"Esmeralda is down," the operative murmured into his mic, his voice barely above a whisper.

In the silence that followed, the security systems lay dormant, the alarms silenced, the locks disengaged. The wolves had breached the gates, and the hunt was about to begin, the operatives poised on the threshold, ready to transform the safe house into a battleground.

All the while, the lambs remained unfazed. Laughter echoed within the walls of the living room, a stark contrast to the silent menace that loomed outside. The Monopoly board lay sprawled between Allison, Molly, Roger Connelly, Harmeet Singh, and her bodyguard—an image of false normalcy.

"Boardwalk, again? That's going to cost you," Roger quipped, a mock frown on his face as he reached for the dice.

"Only if you think you can bankrupt me," Harmeet replied with a smirk, tossing a handful of colorful bills his way.

Molly's eyes danced with mirth as she moved her piece, the thimble, next. "Don't count your hotels before they're built," she teased, the lightness in her voice belying the hand that hovered near her concealed sidearm.

Curtis, the bear-sized bodyguard, chuckled, though he kept his gaze fixed on the window, where the night pressed close, a shroud waiting to fall.

And then it did. Fall.

Without warning, the room plunged into darkness. The dice halted mid-roll, the laughter abruptly ceased. "They've cut the power," Allison stated, her voice steady, as she stood, her instincts kicking in.

"Positions," the bodyguard commanded, his earlier levity gone, replaced by the precision of his training.

Allison, Molly, and Curtis swiftly drew their pistols in smooth, practiced motions. Harmeet stayed close to Curtis, her eyes wide with the sudden shift in the atmosphere, relying on her bodyguard's expertise to keep her safe. Meanwhile, Roger Connelly found himself under the protective watch of Molly and Allison, their experience as operatives evident in their calm, focused demeanors.

Allison's whisper broke the tense silence. "We need to move."

The group did so, silently, communicating in glances and subtle gestures, as they began to navigate through the house. The carefree banter that had filled the living room seconds before seemed like a very long time ago now, the board game pieces frozen in time, a reminder of the calm before the storm. Each step through the vast house was taken with deliberate care, mindful of any noise that could give away their position or intentions.

Outside, the dark night seemed to press heavily against the windows, silently observing the drama as it unfolded. As they progressed, the house felt eerily still, the only sound being their short, trembling breaths. Then, from above, a distinct noise shattered the quietude—the unmistakable sound of a floorboard groaning as someone moved across the room directly overhead.

Just as they were processing the noise from above, a sudden, jarring sound came from the nearby utility room, heightening the tension. The unmistakable sound of the door being quietly opened, followed by soft, cautious footsteps, indicated another person was entering the house.

The realization that the intruders were entering from multiple points set in, heightening their alertness. Every sense was tuned to the slightest sound, every shadow scrutinized for movement. Allison, Molly, and Curtis tightened their grips on their pistols, ready for the confrontation that seemed inevitable.

"Contact front!" Curtis suddenly shouted.

The laser sight from one of the operative's weapons pierced the blackness, casting an ominous red dot that danced across the hallway they'd just entered.

An asterisk of muzzle flash lit up the room. Molly rolled to cover, her weapon drawn in a fluid motion. "Targets inbound!" she called out, both words punctuated by the bark of her gun.

Allison overturned a thick oak table, then shoved Roger Connelly behind it. "Stay there!" she shouted.

A second operative joined the fray, entering from another doorway.

"Contact left!" Allison called out.

Curtis pushed Harmeet behind a couch as he aimed his pistol, the room erupting with the sound of gunfire.

***

Noah had gotten straight out of the subway and into his car. It was now tearing through the night, a missile of steel and determination hurtling down the darkened roads that led along Long Island from New York. The engine's roar was a primal scream, echoing the turmoil within him as he pushed the Dodge Charger to its limits, the needle on the speedometer creeping higher with every passing second.

Henrik Schultz's voice was a venomous whisper in his ear, the earpiece transmitting not just his words but the smug certainty behind them. "You won't reach them in time, Noah. Soon, they'll all be dead."

The taunt was a blade to Noah's gut, twisting with the knowledge that each moment lost was a moment closer to catastrophe. His grip on the steering wheel tightened, knuckles white as the pale moon that shone down from above.

"I will stop you," Noah snarled, the words torn from the depth of his soul. He swerved around a slower car, the tires screeching in protest, the sound a siren call to the forces of fate.

Schultz's laughter was a sound devoid of humanity. "By all means, try. But we both know how this ends.

You're racing toward a conclusion already written."

The car's headlights cut swathes through the darkness, twin beacons seeking out the destination that seemed to recede before him. Noah's jaw was set, a silent vow that he would defy Schultz's prophecy.

As Noah's car disappeared into the night, he was a lone warrior against the odds, his resolve an unspoken promise to those he raced to save. Schultz's voice, still lingering in his ear, was the countdown to an unknown fate.

***

The safe house had become a war zone, its walls reverberating with a cacophony of gunfire and the sharp cries of combat. The acrid scent of gunshots filled the air, stinging the nostrils as flashes from the muzzles of firearms cast stark, fleeting shadows across the walls and furniture.

In the midst of the madness, two of the operatives lay still, their part in the assault over. But the price had been steep. Roger Connelly, the seasoned journalist, was gravely wounded, a dark stain spreading across his abdomen, his breaths coming in ragged gasps as Curtis hauled him along.

"Keep moving!" the bodyguard bellowed, half-dragging, half-carrying Connelly, his voice a mix of command and desperation.

Stopping, they tried to stem the tide of blood that left a gruesome trail on the polished floors as they moved. While Curtis saw to Connelly, Molly and Allison provided cover, their weapons barking back at the shadows that advanced with relentless intent.

"I'm gonna die, aren't I?" Connelly asked Curtis,

sitting with his back to the wall, pale, shaking all over, and quite clearly already in shock.

"Just hold on," the bodyguard replied as he tightened a tablecloth he'd taken from one of the rooms to use as a tourniquet. It oozed with blood as he secured the knot, the bullets having ripped a pretty big hole in Connelly's stomach.

They began moving again, backward along a corridor, a retreat marked by the sharp crack of their guns and the thud of bullets embedding into the walls and furniture.

Harmeet Singh's face was ghostly pale, her body trembling uncontrollably—not from cold, but from the chill touch of fear. She flinched with every gunshot, often becoming rooted to the spot, her mind struggling to process the violent unraveling of her world.

"Harmeet?!" Curtis' shout snapped her from her paralysis. "You need to get behind me now!" His command cut through the fog of her shock, compelling her legs to move.

"The safe room is just a little farther," Allison shouted, her voice the thread they all clung to. "We just need to get there. It's impenetrable and has medical facilities."

***

The interior of the Charger was lit only by the glow of the dashboard and the occasional flash of a streetlight as he weaved through the night at breakneck speed. The phone was on speaker, Neil's and Jenny's voices punctuating the roar of the engine.

"Noah, we just got off with Doc Parker." Neil's voice was tense, strained over the line. "He's got a team inbound, but they're at least thirty minutes out."

Noah's eyes remained fixed on the winding road ahead, the car's headlights cutting through the darkness as he navigated the treacherous turns along the Hamptons coastline. "It's too long," he growled, downshifting as he took a sharp curve. "I'll be there in ten."

Jenny's voice came through, filled with worry and resolve. "Be careful, Noah. You won't do anyone any good if you wrap yourself around a tree."

A humorless laugh escaped him, short and sharp. "Worry about those at the house, Jenny. I'm not the one surrounded by Adrian's goons."

The sound of the ocean waves crashing against the shore reached him through the car's open window, a reminder of the natural beauty that was now the backdrop for something horrific.

"Harmeet, Connelly, Allison, Molly... they're sitting ducks until I get there," Noah's grip on the steering wheel tightened, the leather creaking under the pressure. "And Schultz is just... playing with us."

Neil's voice was steady, attempting to pierce through the panic that threatened to cloud Noah's focus. "You've got the best chance of getting there first. Just... make sure you do get there, Noah."

"I will," Noah affirmed, his voice like steel. "Keep me updated. Anything changes, I need to know—immediately."

The phone line crackled with Jenny's affirmation, and Noah dropped the call, his full attention returning to the perilous drive.

***

After what felt like hours but was in fact not much short of two minutes, they stumbled into the basement. The safe room loomed before them, a promise of sanctuary against the siege. But as they approached, the reality of their situation set in with cruel clarity—the air-sealed door that should have been their salvation remained shut.

Panic edged into Allison's voice as she punched in the code to the safe room a second time, her fingers moving with desperate speed. "Come on, come on," she muttered under her breath, the red light on the keypad blinking mockingly with each failed attempt.

The air-sealed door remained stubbornly closed, the electronic lock unresponsive. Allison's brow furrowed in concentration and frustration. "It's not accepting the code or my fingerprints," she announced, her voice laced with a mix of anger and dread. "Their virus must have spread to it."

Curtis, standing guard with his pistol trained on the stairway, cast a quick glance over his shoulder. "Can you override it?" he asked, his voice steady despite the tension that crackled in the air.

Allison shook her head, her eyes never leaving the keypad. "The virus has locked us out. It's controlling everything." Her fingers danced over the keypad in another futile attempt.

Molly, standing close to Roger and Harmeet, clenched her jaw. "We need a plan B," she stated, her eyes scanning the room for any other means of escape or defense.

The sound of boots at the top of the stairs grew louder, a relentless approach that echoed in the confined space of the basement—each step a countdown to an inevitable confrontation.

"Is there another way out of here?" Harmeet asked, looking around the basement, which felt more like a trap than ever.

Allison's hands stilled on the keypad. She turned, her back to the unyielding door, facing the small group. "There's no other way out. We stand our ground here," she declared, her tone resolute despite the grimness of their situation.

Curtis nodded, his expression grim. "Then we make our stand. Back to back, watch each angle," he instructed, positioning himself so he could cover the stairway.

Molly and Allison positioned themselves back to back with him, the three of them forming a small circle of defense, their weapons at the ready. Harmeet, meanwhile, took a position at the back of the room with the badly wounded Connelly. They were cornered, the basement a cul-de-sac from which there was no escape. The bodyguard, his charges huddled behind him, turned to face the approaching threat.

And then, a silence fell—a silence that was louder than any gunshot. Connelly's struggles had abruptly ceased, his life slipping away on the cold, hard floor of the basement. Harmeet Singh looked up at the others, her eyes meeting theirs in a moment laden with unspeakable grief. "He's dead," she declared, the finality in her voice a sharp counterpoint to the footsteps that crept ever closer.

With the operatives' shadows inching down the basement steps, a slow march of death appeared to be underway as the survivors braced for what was to come.

The end, it seemed, was nigh, and their fortress had become their tomb.

***

The night air was sharp against Noah's face as he sped along the secluded roads leading to Allison Peterson's Hamptons beachside mansion. Each passing second was a race against time, his car hugging the curves of the coastal road, the tires occasionally skidding on loose gravel.

The ocean's rhythmic roar was now a constant companion, its waves crashing in the darkness, a natural symphony underscored by the car's growling engine. Noah's mind was a whirlwind of scenarios, each more dire than the last. He imagined the faces of Allison and Molly, their lives hanging in the balance, the threat of Schultz's shadowy operatives all too real.

His hand moved to the glove compartment, flipping it open to reveal a Sig Sauer P320, its matte black surface a familiar comfort. He checked the magazine—full—and then placed the pistol on the passenger seat beside him, ready for what lay ahead.

The mansion was just minutes away now, its location marked by the faint glow of lights against the night sky. Noah's heart pounded in his chest, adrenaline coursing through his veins. He knew the risks, the danger of going in alone, but waiting was not an option. Every second counted.

***

In the aftermath of the onslaught, the basement had transformed into a mausoleum of the fallen. Allison sat slumped against the impregnable door of the safe room, her breaths coming in ragged gasps as blood seeped from a wound just above her hip. Her pistol, the last vestige of defiance, hung limply in her hand.

Around her, the stillness was punctuated by the grim sight of the dead. Connelly lay sprawled on his back, his once vibrant eyes staring blankly at the ceiling, a dark halo of blood around his torso. Harmeet's body was crumpled against the wall, several bullet holes in her chest, her face frozen in a final expression of shock. The echoes of her last breath still haunted the air. Her bodyguard Curtis lay face down, his protective stance immortalized in death.

Molly, motionless, was draped across the stairs, her own wounds hidden beneath her. To Allison's grief-stricken eyes, she too was gone, taken by the night's cruel deeds.

Three more of the operatives who had stormed their sanctuary were also silent. Two of them lay at odd angles on the stairs, the life bled from them, their mission ended. Another was upstairs, sitting with his back against the wall, a blood-coated hand on his stomach, his blank eyes staring ahead.

A click from Allison's pistol broke the hush, the sound as hollow as her empty chamber. "Shit," she groaned, the noise a whisper of frustration and defeat.

The final operative descended carefully, his steps measured, his rifle pressed against his shoulder at the ready. He surveyed the carnage with clinical detachment, confirming the deaths of Connelly and Harmeet with a cursory glance, ignoring the others who were not his concern.

"Site secure, sir," he reported into his radio. "Only Peterson is still alive." He waited, his posture one of disciplined patience, as instructions crackled through his earpiece. "Okay, sir. I await your presence."

Moments later, footsteps announced another's arrival. A figure appeared at the top of the stairs. When he began descending with an air of triumph that did not touch his cold eyes, Allison knew she was face to face with none other than the man they were hunting.

Her gaze narrowed, her voice dripping with contempt. "Henrik Schultz."

His lips curled into a smirk. "You recognize me, even after all the work I've had done. I am flattered."

"No matter how many times you visit the plastic surgeon, Schultz, you'll always have that ugly look in your eyes," Allison spat back.

Schultz chuckled, unfazed. "I must admit, I've always admired you, Allison. Running something as big and powerful as E & E. But there are bigger players in this game now, ready to swallow you whole."

"And what's in it for you?"

"Why, Allison, isn't it obvious? Power. I am being offered a place at the table, a chance to join the Council. All I need do is destroy E & E."

Allison's retort was sharp, cutting. "All that power won't make up for your little dick, Henrik."

A flicker of irritation crossed Schultz's face before he motioned to the operative, who obediently handed him an iPad. With a swipe of his finger, Schultz initiated a video call, the screen illuminating his features in a ghoulish glow.

The call connected, revealing an elderly Frenchman with an air of aristocratic disdain. His sharp, hawk-like features were accentuated by a neatly trimmed white beard and a pair of piercing blue eyes.

"I have the targets, Jacques," Schultz announced.

"Show me," Jacques Monnet commanded, his English thick with an accent of entitlement and contempt.

The iPad's camera panned over to Harmeet Singh's lifeless form. "Ah, Ms. Singh," Monnet remarked. "The bitch who refused the Council, then tried to resurrect those bastard dogs E & E. Look where it got you, putain."

Next, Schultz focused the iPad's attention on Connelly. "Ah," Monnet sneered. "The meddler, now silenced. And your men have his evidence?"

"Yes, Jacques," Schultz replied dutifully. "It's all secured, and our viruses are already purging any traces from the CIA's database."

"Good. The world isn't ready to see behind the mask just yet. Now show me the dragon bitch."

Allison stared hard at the old man on the screen, her eyes defiant even in the face of death. Jacques Monnet stared back with a nonchalant expression of disdain.

"You've been quite the thorn in our side, Madame Peterson. But it's time for the dragon to be slain."

"Go to hell, Frenchie," Allison hissed, her spirit unbroken.

The elderly billionaire's mouth twisted into a cruel smile. "A pleasure, but you first, chérie."

The operative, a mere executor of another's will, raised his weapon, and Allison Peterson, the Dragon Lady, stared right back at it. "Bring it on," she snarled as the operative's finger settled on the trigger.

CHAPTER TWENTY-EIGHT

Noah's Charger raced down the long gravel driveway of the Hamptons mansion, tires spitting stones in their wake as he approached the looming house. The night was eerily silent, the only sound the roar of the engine and the crunch of gravel beneath the wheels. As he neared the house, his focus entirely on the task ahead, an unexpected shadow surged from behind the mansion, startling him.

A helicopter rose like a phantom, its rotors slicing through the night sky. The sudden appearance of the aircraft caught Noah off guard, its silhouette stark against the moonlit backdrop. The high beams of his car, still blazing, threw a harsh light on the chopper as it ascended.

Reacting swiftly, Noah slammed the brakes, bringing the car to a skidding halt just short of the mansion's entrance. He grabbed the Sig Sauer off the passenger seat. In his grip, it felt like ice, its metal surface a conduit for the rage that surged through his veins. The Charger's door flew open, and he leaped out, the door slamming shut with a resounding thud that was drowned out by the overwhelming noise of the helicopter overhead.

Using the car as cover, he held the aim of his pistol on the chopper, his eyes tracking its ascent, a mix of fury and calculation in his gaze as he assessed this new development.

Realizing it was too far to do any damage with the 9mm, he watched, helpless, as the aircraft gained altitude, its form becoming one with the shadowy clouds above. The thudding blades were like a sinister drumroll, punctuating the night with the reality of Henrik Schultz's master play.

Then, just as the chopper seemed to meld into the darkness, a figure emerged from the side of it, hanging perilously out of the aircraft. The figure raised a rocket-propelled grenade launcher, its shape unmistakable even in the dim light. With a chilling sense of dread, Noah realized their intention. A fiery trail cut through the night as the grenade was launched, heading straight for the mansion with devastating precision. It arced through the air, a deadly comet trailing fire. Noah watched in horror as it struck the side of the sprawling Hamptons mansion, the impact point erupting in a violent explosion. Flames instantly burst forth, greedily licking the elegant façade of the house.

The mansion, a symbol of luxury and tranquility, was now a scene of chaos and devastation. The grenade had hit a central part of the house with precision, its explosive payload igniting an inferno. The fire spread rapidly, fueled by the mansion's opulent furnishings and the dry timber of its construction. It was clear that the grenade was no ordinary explosive; it was an incendiary device specifically engineered to create a raging inferno.

Tongues of flame leaped from window to window, the heat so intense it caused the glass to shatter and burst, sending shards flying like deadly confetti. Thick, acrid smoke billowed into the night sky, forming a dark cloud above the once majestic residence.

Noah felt a surge of helplessness and fury as he witnessed the destruction of the mansion. The fire roared, a beast unchained, consuming everything in its path, its bright orange glow stark against the dark Hamptons night. The elegant structure, which had once stood as a testament to wealth and beauty, was now being devoured by an unstoppable inferno, its grandeur crumbling under the assault of the relentless flames.

Noah's hand tightened on the gun as he watched the helicopter disappear into the expanse of the night, the sound of the helicopter's rotors fading into the distance, leaving behind the roar of the fire and the crackling of the burning mansion. It was obvious that the blaze would attract attention, and with it, more danger. But for a moment, all Noah could do was watch in stunned silence as the fire raged, a bright, searing reminder of the violence that had been unleashed upon this once peaceful retreat.

He had to act fast.

Noah burst through the burning door of the house, the heat and smoke immediately assaulting his senses. As he navigated through the smoldering wreckage, his heart pounded in his chest, each beat a frantic search for survivors. The basement door loomed ahead, the flames licking its edges, the heat intensifying with every step he took.

Checking the tracker app on his phone, Noah located the signals of Molly and Allison in the basement, where the fire was rapidly encroaching. With urgency propelling him forward, he descended the stairs, the heat and smoke growing thicker, the air almost unbreathable as he stepped over the dead bodies of operatives.

The basement was already a furnace, the flames having found their way inside, creating an inferno that threatened to consume everything. Amidst the chaos, Noah spotted a figure collapsed on at the bottom of the steps. It was Molly, her body barely moving, each breath a faint struggle against the overwhelming heat.

He rushed to her side, his heart pounding with a mix of fear and hope. Gently, he checked for signs of life, scarcely daring to believe she could have survived the bullet wound to her upper chest. But to his amazement and relief, a faint whimper escaped her lips as he touched her, a fragile thread of life amidst the devastation. "Molly?" he whispered, his voice thick with emotion.

Her response was barely audible, a soft murmur of consciousness that filled him with a surge of urgency. "I've got you, Molly," he assured her, his voice a blend of determination and deep concern. With utmost care, he lifted her over his shoulder, her body light yet precious in his grasp.

As he turned to leave, his gaze swept over the fiery chaos of the basement. The outlines of the others were barely visible through the leaping flames, an eerie, haunting sight that seared into his memory. The fire had made it impossible to reach them, each figure a tragic silhouette swallowed by the blaze.

With Molly secure, Noah made his way out of the inferno, the heat and smoke assaulting his senses, the crackling flames roaring around them, a relentless enemy closing in. Each step a battle against the searing heat and blinding smoke, Noah picked his way out of the safe house.

The promise of vengeance for the fallen echoed in his heart as he carried Molly into the cool embrace of the night, laying her carefully in the passenger seat of his car. "Press this against the wound," he instructed, placing a cloth in her hands.

Her fingers, pale and slick with blood, complied weakly.

As he ignited the engine, Noah could hear the sound of sirens growing louder, an ominous crescendo that promised complications he couldn't afford. With a sideways glance at Molly, who was fighting the encroaching darkness with every shred of will, Noah floored the accelerator.

The Charger burst forward, tearing away from the burning safe house and the nightmare that had unfolded within its walls. As they raced down the driveway, the rearview mirror reflected the churning flames of the sanctuary-turned-graveyard.

The second they veered onto the highway, the lights of the police cruisers were a kaleidoscope of urgency in the rearview mirror. Noah's hands were steady on the wheel, each maneuver calculated with the precision of a man who had evaded capture more times than he could count.

As he crossed a junction, two more police cruisers came swinging out of the road to his left, the sharp crackle of a bullhorn tearing through the night. "Pull over! Pull over!" But Noah was a ghost as he hit the coastal roads. His only response to their demands was his engine's roar as he pushed the Charger faster.

The pursuit was fierce, the police cruisers like hounds on the scent, their engines howling in a mad chorus behind him. Noah's eyes flicked to Molly, her breaths shallow but determined, her hand gripping the makeshift bandage with a tenacity that mirrored his own.

A police helicopter emerged from the darkness above, a predatory bird with its searchlight casting a blinding eye upon Noah's car. The light felt almost solid, boxing him in, a spotlight on a stage he never wanted to share.

He swerved, tires screeching against the asphalt as he took the turns along the Hamptons coastline, the searchlight trailing him like a relentless hawk. The coastal roads were treacherous allies, their curves a test of skill and nerve. As for the police cruisers, his superior skill had already put distance between them. Just not the chopper.

He ducked into a side road, a narrow path barely visible in the night, his heart pounding against his ribs. Behind him, the police were losing ground in the chase, their cruisers ill-suited for the serpentine twists that Noah's Charger devoured with predatory eagerness. Its powerful engine roaring, he skillfully drifted around each sharp corner, and with each calculated turn, he widened the gap between himself and his pursuers. As he navigated the winding road, the flashing lights grew dimmer and dimmer in his rearview mirror.

A sharp turn took them through a canopy of trees, their branches clawing at the chopper's searchlight, breaking its beam into fractured shards of light that floated along the dark little road. Noah switched the headlights off. He felt the car slide, a controlled dance with physics as he drifted around a tight bend, gravel flying like shrapnel.

For a moment, they were out of the helicopter's sight, a fleeting ghost in the coastal woodland. Noah seized the opportunity, his eyes scanning for an escape, a path back to anonymity.

There! An old service road, overgrown and forgotten, a relic of a time when this part of the Hamptons was less traveled. He swung the car onto the path, branches scratching against the metal like the fingers of the night trying to hold him back.

The helicopter swept past, its scarchlight a moment too late, its gaze piercing the main road where Noah no longer was. A short while later, the police cruisers sped by, their sirens a fading cry as Noah drove deeper into the shadows, until he parked amongst a cluster of trees.

In the quiet that followed, only the car's hot, ticking engine and Molly's soft moans filled the air. They were alone now, the chase behind them, the road ahead uncertain.

***

Even after everything he had already done to them, Henrik Schultz wasn't done with them yet. The night was still young for the master puppeteer, and he had one more move to make.

In New York, Marco's phone rang with a sudden urgency that cut through the hum of the car's engine. The gruff voice of Doc Parker emerged from the speaker, terse and heavy with unspoken gravity. "I need everyone back at base," he said, his voice a command more than a request.

"What's happened?" Marco pressed, his hands tightening on the wheel.

"Something very bad. I'll brief you when you're back at Kirtland. Parker out." The line went dead before Marco could ask any further questions, leaving a void filled with ominous silence.

In the passenger seat beside him, Ralph shifted uncomfortably, a foreboding sense settling over them. Their confusion was short-lived, however, as Schultz's voice slithered into Ralph's earpiece. "You almost led them to me, you know," he hissed, a serpent's whisper of betrayal and accusation.

Ralph's heart skipped a beat, his mind racing. "No, Henrik. You've got it wrong," he stammered, though a cold realization was dawning on him.

Schultz's reply was a death knell. "Only through you and that bitch wife of yours giving over your earpieces could they have found us. My plans were nearly destroyed because of you and her."

The words were a punch to Ralph's gut, the truth undeniable and cruel. "No, Henrik, please…"

"But don't worry. I'm a man of my word," Schultz continued, his voice smooth as poisoned honey. "I'll give you one minute to call dear Diana and say goodbye."

The line cut off abruptly, leaving Ralph with a churning pit of despair. Hands shaking, he could do nothing more than hurriedly dial his wife's number on his cell phone, each ring reverberating in the hollow of his chest.

Diana picked up, her voice a balm to his panicked state. "Ralph?"

"Baby... baby," came barreling out of his mouth.

"Ralph, what's wrong?"

One and a half thousand miles southeast in Kirtland, sitting inside their rental, Sarah eyed Diana, sensing the change in her tone. "Diana? What is it?"

Back in New York, Ralph was torn, a tempest of emotion warring within him. "Diana, I... I love you so much, baby," he began, the words a floodgate of all the things left unsaid, all the moments they'd had and all those they would never have.

In Kirtland, Diana's expression softened, her eyes locking with Sarah's, an unspoken question there. "I love you too, Ralph. You're scaring me. What's going on?"

Ralph's voice broke as he spoke, each word heavy with the weight of finality. "I've always loved you, from the moment I first—"

And then, without warning, a silent explosion erupted within Diana's head. She dropped the phone, and her body jerked violently, her eyes going blank as she slumped forward in the passenger seat.

"Diana? Diana? Diana!" Ralph's voice was a desperate plea, the world shrinking to the sound of his own voice echoing uselessly through the phone.

Sarah, horror-stricken, caught Diana as she fell. "Diana!" she screamed, her hands searching for a pulse that was no longer there, a bead of blood falling from one ear.

In New York, Ralph could only listen, his heart shattering into a million pieces. The minute was up. Diana was gone. And with her, a part of Ralph that he knew he'd never get back.

CHAPTER TWENTY-NINE

Noah's Long Island safe house emerged from the shadows like a sentinel, its fortified exterior a silent promise of temporary respite from the chaos that had engulfed him. Parking inside the garage, he got out of the car and rushed around to the passenger side as the automatic doors closed them off from the world. With Molly's unconscious form cradled in his arms, he hurried into the house, the weight of her life literally in his hands.

The interior was spartan, utilitarian, every item and fixture designed for efficiency. He moved through the dimly lit corridors, his footsteps resolute, the soft moans from Molly a counterpoint to the sterile silence that enveloped them.

Reaching a backroom, he gently laid her onto a medical chair that stood like an altar in the center—a stark, stainless steel promise of either salvation or finality. His hands worked with methodical precision as he prepared the space, the clink of surgical tools on a metal tray providing a metallic chorus to the procedure ahead.

Water splashed as Noah scrubbed up, stripping

away the grime and horror of the night's events, the acrid stench of the fire still strong in his nostrils. He donned a surgical mask, his face hardening with focus, every line and crease set in determination.

Molly's murmurs cut through the clinical atmosphere, her pleas for Allison a haunting refrain. "Ali… Ali…" Her words were a delirious loop.

With a steady hand, Noah administered a sedative, watching as Molly's restless movements slowed, her voice trailing off into a land of uneasy dreams. He worked quickly, his movements those of a man well-versed in emergency field medicine, his mind partitioned between the task at hand and the lingering loss of the night.

She was lucky. The bullet had not reached her lung and was merely lodged in her mammary. But it was also stubborn, a piece of leaden death trapped within Molly's flesh. Noah's tools were precise, his hands unwavering as he extracted the foreign object, the room filled with the sound of his controlled breathing and the occasional clink of metal whenever his tweezers dropped another piece of the shattered bullet into a kidney dish.

Blood welled, but he was ready, staunching the flow with practiced ease, the wound now clean, the threat of the bullet no more than a nightmarish memory. He worked to close the incision, sutures threading through skin, sealing the breach.

As he finished, Noah allowed himself a moment to look at Molly's face, her features slack with sedation, her spirit fighting a battle beyond the reach of his surgical skills. He whispered a vow into the quiet of the room, a promise to the unconscious and the departed. "I will make this right."

Noah cleaned Molly's wound, the precision of his actions giving nothing away of the turmoil that roiled within him. He dressed the wound with methodical care, each layer of gauze a barrier against the world's cruelty.

Once the dressing was secure, he retrieved a bag of blood from the medical fridge, Molly's type, just in case. He started the transfusion, watching as the crimson liquid made its way through the line, a steady drip that was a marker of hope.

She'd lost a lot tonight, the bullet having grazed several blood vessels. She lay still, her breathing shallow but even, the rise and fall of her chest a silent rhythm that filled the room. Noah allowed himself the faintest sigh of relief—she was out of immediate danger.

That's when Henrik Schultz's voice invaded the space, a smug intrusion that curled around Noah like a python. "I can't believe you almost made it," he hissed. "You should have seen my face when I saw your car arriving at the gate seconds after we had gotten into the chopper."

"Where's my daughter?" Noah demanded, the words a snarl of barely contained fury.

"She should be dead. That was the deal, wasn't it?" Schultz's tone was taunting, a cat playing with a cornered mouse.

"Where is she?" Noah's voice was a blade, honed and deadly.

"Still alive and well. But for how long is entirely up to you. No more games, Noah Wolf. Now you complete the kill list for real. As my other targets are now dead, I can forgive you your former deceit. But believe me when

I tell you it will be the last of my mercy."

Noah's mind reeled. "How did you find them?" he pressed, grappling for some understanding. "It can't have been Ralph or Diana."

"Does it matter at this stage?" Schultz's dismissal was a cold slap. "Now if you want to ever see your little girl again, you must complete the list."

Clenching his eyelids closed, Noah growled, "Who's next?"

"The last name is Jackson T. Whitmore."

Noah's eyes opened sharply. "I'm sorry. Did you say who I think you did?"

"Yes. I did. The last name on the list is the newly elected president of the United States of America. And like with Connelly, I want you to go loud. I want you to do it in a way that everyone gets to see. That's why you're going to do it in three days' time at his inauguration ceremony with the whole world watching."

The words landed with the weight of a tombstone. The president. The shock of it reverberated through Noah, a physical blow that left him reeling. His clenched fist struck the wall, the sound a hollow echo in the room.

The president of the United States. The final name on a list that had brought nothing but death and despair. Noah's mind reeled with the impossibility of it all, the enormity of Schultz's demand hanging in the air like a guillotine poised to fall.

***

An hour later, under the cloak of twilight, Neil and

Jenny approached the Long Island safe house, their car gliding along the road with the stealth of a shadow. The day's traumas seemed to hang in the air around them, an invisible yet very real presence. Inside the car, the radio hummed quietly, the media space dominated by the news of the Hamptons explosion. Reporters' voices, tinged with urgency and disbelief, recounted the event, their words interspersed with snippets of interviews with local residents, many of which had to be evacuated.

As they turned into the garage of the safe house, the car's headlights briefly illuminated the stark concrete walls before they were extinguished, plunging the space back into semi-darkness. Neil killed the engine, and for a moment, they sat in silence, each lost in their thoughts about the day's harrowing events and the uncertain road ahead.

With a collective deep breath, they stepped out of the car, their movements synchronized and purposeful. The garage was quiet. The only sound was their footsteps echoing slightly as they moved toward the interior door of the house. Jenny reached out to open it, her hand steady despite the adrenaline that still coursed through her veins.

As the door swung open, they were greeted by the familiar but now deeply somber face of Noah.

"We took every back road and blind turn," Neil whispered to him, his voice a hollow murmur. "No one followed."

Inside, the dim light threw their elongated shadows against the bare walls and sparse furniture of the safe house, a somber trio united by a common sorrow. "You heard about Diana, right?" Neil asked, his words seeping out slowly, as though each syllable was a burden too heavy to lift.

Noah, standing rigid against the kitchen counter, nodded, his reply a guttural affirmation from deep within. "Yeah, I spoke to Sarah not long ago. She filled me in."

Jenny hovered at the edge of the conversation, her hands wringing together in a ballet of anxiety and despair. "How is she holding up?" Her inquiry was gentle, the kind of tone you use when the news expected is nothing but dire.

"Not good," Noah said, his voice barely above the sound of a breaking heart. "She had to watch one of her best friends die in her arms. Now she thinks her daughter is next." His eyes met theirs, and in that shared gaze, they found a bleak solidarity.

In the safe house's sparsely furnished back room, Noah guided Neil and Jenny to Molly's side. She lay still, her chest rising and falling with the labored breath of the sedated, her face a canvas of pain and peace intertwined. Jenny reached out, her fingers brushing Molly's cheek in a silent promise of comfort. The gentleness of her touch was such a stark contrast to the violence that had marred their lives tonight.

The moment was fleeting, however; time was a luxury they could not afford. Neil's phone came to life in his hand, the screen flickering with the grim news that had already spread across the airwaves. "It's everywhere," he murmured, the artificial light throwing ghostly shadows across their faces.

From the phone, the news anchor's voice spun the tale of a high-stakes police chase and a brutal massacre at a Hampton's residence. "Multiple dead bodies found... speculation of a high-level gang war... a beachside residence, typically silent, now screams of untold secrets..."

Neil's thumb paused over the screen, freezing the image as the anchor continued, "Witnesses report a vehicle fleeing the scene, the identity of the driver still unknown..."

Noah's gaze was steel, his mind churning with the implications. "It was you who called the cops, wasn't it?" he growled into the earpiece, his voice a controlled tempest aimed at Henrik Schultz, who he knew was listening.

The answer slithered back, a serpent's hiss of affirmation. "Yes. I didn't want you lingering around."

Noah's eyes flickered with a dangerous light. "And you wanted me exposed, too," he accused, his voice a tight coil of anger.

Schultz's chuckle was a sound devoid of humor. "Perhaps. But what does it matter when I have your daughter?"

The words were like a physical blow, each syllable a hammer against Noah's resolve. "You've wanted me exposed since Kirtland," he snarled, piecing together the treacherous puzzle Schultz and his people at Adrian had crafted.

"Yes, it makes your fall from grace all the more spectacular," Schultz purred. "The great Noah Wolf, a traitor and a murderer."

Noah's fury simmered at the edge of eruption. "If you hurt her—"

But before the threat could fully form, a small, frightened voice cut through the tension. "Daddy, Daddy..."

Norah's voice, laced with terror, was a knife to Noah's heart. "I was so scared, Daddy... We had to go in a helicopter... The man says you have to come. There are bad people here. Please, Daddy..."

Each word was a strike to Noah's core, a daughter's plea that resonated with his primal instinct to protect. His hands shook with the effort of containment, a visual tremor that betrayed his internal storm.

The silence that followed was deafening, filled only by the ragged edges of Norah's sobs and Noah's heavy breathing. Then, Schultz's voice slunk through, a vile whisper that sought to dominate. "Finish the list. Get your girl back. Then get on with whatever is left of your life."

***

The remnants of Noah's team congregated in the dim light of the safe house's main room. Molly, still weak but conscious, lay on a makeshift bed, her eyes reflecting the gravity of their situation. Wally's entrance was quiet, but the news he carried landed with the weight of an anvil.

"I had to take Esmeralda offline," he announced, his voice laced with frustration. "She's been hit with something advanced, something... invasive. I've never seen anything like it."

The team exchanged uneasy glances, the unspoken question hanging heavy in the air—how could something they thought was impenetrable have been breached? Wally's admission that he'd never seen anything like it only deepened the mystery, casting a long shadow of doubt over their defenses.

"How long has the virus been there?" Noah's

question cut to the heart of their vulnerability.

Wally shook his head, the gesture one of both apology and concern. "That's the thing; I don't know. It could have been lying dormant, waiting to be triggered, or it might have been a recent infiltration."

"It must be how they found the safe house," Jenny mentioned.

The room fell into a tense silence, the implications of Wally's news settling around them like a fog. It was Neil who broke the stillness, his voice steady as he asserted, "We can't focus on the breach now. We have one objective—to save Norah."

Jenny nodded in agreement, the strategist within her rising to the surface. "Then the president's assassination is our only play. It's a Hail Mary, but it's all we have."

"We'll need an inside man," Molly interjected behind them, her voice firm despite her pallor. "I might have a contact. Someone who owes me a favor, deep within the Secret Service. I can contact them under the guise that there's a threat that E & E is dealing with. That way they won't ask too many questions."

Noah's eyes met each of theirs in turn, a silent call to arms. "We do this," he said firmly, "we do it right. No half-measures. If we're going to kill the most protected man in the world, we need to be flawless."

CHAPTER THIRTY

In the bowels of the safe house, the team stood together, the pieces of their plan beginning to form a whole. They hadn't slept for a very long time, and though the sun had risen outside, they were unaware of its existence on the other side of the safe house's closed blinds.

"Take a look at this," Wally informed them as he held out the screen of a tablet.

The team huddled closer, their minds coalescing around their audacious plan. Wally meticulously laid out the schematics of the Capitol's west front, the site of the upcoming presidential inauguration. The detailed blueprint sprawled across the screen, each section and landmark clearly marked.

"Here's the layout of the inauguration site," Wally began, his fingers tracing the digital map. "The president will be sworn in here"—he pointed to a spot on the map—"on the central platform. This area is going to be heavily guarded, with layers of security."

He zoomed in on the platform area. "Secret Service will be everywhere, both visible and undercover. Snipers on rooftops, agents in the crowd. The president's personal detail will be especially tight during the swearing-in."

Moving to another part of the schematic, Wally

highlighted the audience area. "The public will be here, along with VIPs. It's a controlled space, but it's also the most vulnerable due to the sheer number of people."

He then focused on the escape routes. "In case of an emergency, like an attack, there are several pre-planned evacuation routes. The primary one is through the Capitol, into a secure underground tunnel that leads to a designated safe location."

Wally shifted the image to show the surrounding streets. "These roads will be blocked off, but in case of a high-level threat, they can quickly become escape routes for tactical teams."

He then pointed to a few discreet locations on the map. "Snipers and surveillance will be set up here, here, and here, covering all angles of the platform. In the event of an attack, their first reaction will be to shield the president and evacuate him from the site."

Wally paused, allowing the team to absorb the information. "The Secret Service's response to a shooting will be immediate and overwhelming. They'll lock down the entire area and move POTUS to a secure location at lightning speed. Any aggressor will face the full force of their counter-attack."

He looked up from the tablet, meeting the team's eyes. "This is going to be a fortress on Inauguration Day. Penetrating it without being detected will be extremely difficult, and the window for action will be incredibly small. The quantum cloak will be key," Wally stated. "It'll take away the Secret Service's eyes, giving Noah the chance to take the shot and vanish with the fleeing crowd."

Neil leaned over the layout, his finger tracing the path through the crowd. "We'll need to get you into position here"—he pointed to a spot near the front —"just outside the view of the nearby sniper nests on top of these buildings. It's a blind spot we've identified."

Molly, her face drawn from pain but eyes sharp, interjected, "What about extraction? The Secret Service will lock the place down within seconds."

"That's where the parametric speaker comes in," Noah replied, his voice a low rumble of confidence. "The sounds of several more gunshots, decoy shots, fired remotely at the same time from a different angle. It'll draw attention away from my position."

The team nodded, their faces a mix of determination and the weight of the burden they were about to shoulder. Noah continued, laying out the finer points of the plan. "Once the shot is fired, I'll slip under the stage using the maintenance tunnels here." His finger tapped a concealed entrance on the map. "On the other side of which will be my getaway vehicle."

"And the weapon?" Neil asked, his mind already running through scenarios.

"A high-precision rifle," Noah detailed. "A Remington 700 Spectre. It's been shortened for concealment and will rest in a custom harness under the quantum cloak. Perfect for the job."

"What about the metal detectors at the gates?" Jenny asked.

"Easy," Wally answered for Noah. "The rifle is an R&D special. Crafted from advanced non-metallic materials, undetectable and silent."

As they digested these final details, Henrik Schultz's voice crackled through the earpiece, breaking the tense silence. "Well done, Mr. Wolf," he said in a tone of cold amusement. "Your plan, especially the part with

the speakers—ingenious. It's the perfect vanishing act."
There was a brief pause, before he added, "But of course,
there'll be no disappearing after this. Not for you or E &
E."

The team exchanged glances, the intrusion of
Schultz's voice a jarring reminder of the dangerous
game they were playing.

"Cheer up, Mr. Wolf," Schultz continued, his tone
laced with a sinister edge. "Soon you will write yourself
into the history books."

The line went dead, leaving a chill in the room that
went beyond the air conditioning. Noah turned to the
others, a resolute look on his face. "Pack light, move
fast," he said. "We're on a tight schedule." His voice was
a mix of leadership and urgency, a clear call to action.

***

It took them less than three hours to reach the capital.
Their Washington safe house was now awash with
tension as the team gathered for their final meeting
before they committed the hit to end all hits. The air
was thick with unspoken fears and the heavy burden
of what was to come. Ralph had joined them, insistent
that he had a part to play in the game they were playing.

He moved among them, his presence a quiet storm
of guilt and resolve, his recent loss hanging about him
like a shroud. But within it, he sought redemption.

"We can't afford any mistakes," Noah stated, his
gaze piercing each member of the team. "Not today."

Ralph nodded, the shadow of Diana's absence a
constant reminder of the stakes at hand. "I'm ready,"
he said, his voice gravelly with determination. "Let's do
this—for Diana, for Norah, for all of us."

The team's eyes met, a silent pact forming in the space between them. They would see this through, each playing their part in a mission that had grown beyond them, a mission that was now for the world.

As they dispersed, each to their assigned roles, Ralph pulled Noah aside. "I owe you. I owe her," he said, his eyes haunted but burning with a fervor that had been absent before.

Noah clapped a firm hand on Ralph's shoulder. "Today, we set things right."

***

A few hours later and the world outside was already bustling with the inauguration's pomp, but within the safe house's walls, Noah's reality narrowed to the voice on the phone. "I love you." Sarah's voice came as a tremulous whisper through the line, the complete opposite of the rambling cacophony of the day's events. "Please bring our little girl back."

Noah's response was a soft murmur, the ferocity of his warrior's heart tempered by the tenderness of her words. "I will," he vowed, the simplicity of the promise belying the labyrinth of danger that lay before him.

Their call was a delicate dance of hope and heartache, each word a step closer to the precipice of action upon which Noah stood. "Be safe," she added, the three words heavy with unspoken prayers.

The line went silent, but the echo of Sarah's love lingered, bolstering Noah with the strength of shared conviction. In that moment, he was more than a soldier; he was a father and a husband, bound by love's unyielding chain.

CHAPTER THIRTY-ONE

Inauguration Day dawned with the fanfare of a nation's ceremonial passage, the air electric with anticipation and patriotism. The streets of Washington swelled with crowds, a sea of faces adorned with stars and stripes, the atmosphere a blend of celebration and solemnity.

Since Ronald Reagan's 1981 ceremony, the inaugural stage has been set against the grandeur of the Capitol's west front, a tradition that continued to symbolize a nation's enduring commitment to democracy. This hallowed ground, with its sweeping views of the National Mall, the Washington Monument, and the Lincoln Memorial, has been a witness to the peaceful transition of power for decades.

Over the past twenty-four hours Noah and his team had pored over the layout of the site, noting its historical significance and architectural nuances. The expansive space, designed for public gatherings and ceremonial pomp, offered them a canvas on which to enact their plan. The Capitol's west front, a symbol of transparency and openness, ironically provided the perfect cover for their operation. With the eyes of the world fixed upon the podium, Noah's quantum cloak would allow him to blend into the crowd, away from the eyes of the cameras watching meticulously, and there, in the shadows, he would raise his weapon, the echoes of gunshot reverberating through the annuls of history.

Noah and his team emerged into a river of American spectacle, each member acutely aware of the weight they carried. They were dressed plainly, the quantum cloak looking like any old coat, Noah's presence on the cameras as invisible as the breaths they took. Equally well hidden was the Remington 700 Spectre, the modified rifle so neatly tucked under the cloak that it revealed nothing—not in the way he walked nor in his body shape.

The throng teemed with life; children on their parents' shoulders waved tiny flags, Uncle Sams on stilts loomed above, their laughter mingling with the chatter of the crowd. Patriots, clad in the nation's colors, shared smiles and stories, oblivious to the undercurrent that ran beneath the day's joyous façade.

As they approached a security checkpoint, the atmosphere tensed imperceptibly. Metal detectors loomed ahead, manned by alert Secret Service agents. Noah walked through the archway of one, his heart rate steady, his face an unreadable mask. The detector remained silent, betraying no hint of the concealed high-tech weaponry he carried. The non-metallic nature of the Remington 700 Spectre ensured that his passage was smooth, its advanced composite materials undetectable by the standard security measures.

On the other side, Noah let out a quiet breath, a small victory in their high-stakes play. The members of his team, now indistinguishable from any of the other patriots, slipped through the security checkpoints, their movements deliberate, their preparations indiscernible to the watchful men and women of the Secret Service.

Jenny and Neil found their spots, blending seamlessly with the onlookers, their eyes communicating in the silent language of their shared mission. Wally, stationed at a vantage point, his equipment at the ready, surveyed the scene through a pair of field glasses.

As Noah activated the quantum cloak, a hush fell over his world. He moved through the crowd, unseen by the innumerable cameras watching the day, drawing ever closer to the stage where destiny awaited.

As Noah wove through the sea of people, the faint hiss of the earpiece broke through the hum of the inauguration's fervor. Schultz's voice slithered through the connection, a poisonous reassurance. "Your daughter is safe, for now, Mr. Wolf. Complete your mission, and I will leave her at a nearby park for her daddy to come pick her up. Now hurry. History awaits."

The finality of the line going dead was a harsh reminder of the knife's edge he was walking upon, the weight of Schultz's words settling like barbed wire around his heart.

As the nation's anthem swelled to the heavens, echoing off the marble monuments and grand façades, the team found their places amid the throngs of spectators. They were invisible actors on the world's most watched stage.

Neil's voice was first to break the static of the radio. "Neil in position." His vantage afforded him a clear view of the dais, the weight of his responsibility grounding him.

"Jenny in position," came the soft, determined affirmation, her eyes scanning the crowd, a sentinel among the unsuspecting masses.

Ralph's transmission was tinged with a somber resolve. "Ralph in position." His post, a high balcony, gave him oversight of the entire scene, a strategic advantage for their intricate play.

"Marco in position" sounded next, clear and concise, from the fringes of the crowd where the final member of Camelot could act quickly if the need arose. The Cajun had insisted on joining them upon arriving at the Washington safe house an hour before they were due to leave.

Then, finally, Noah's voice, calm and resolute, signaled the culmination of their meticulous planning. "Noah in position."

Each confirmation was a silent thunderclap, signifying the moment of truth was at hand.

***

In the sterile opulence of his own Washington, DC safe house, Henrik Schultz, the man at the head of Adrian, settled into a leather armchair with the ease of one used to command. On the large screen before him, the pomp of the inauguration unfolded, a scene he intended to mar with a spectacle of his own design.

A hush fell as Norah was ushered in by one of Schultz's many assistants, her small form dwarfed by the grandeur of the room. "Come, sweetie. Come watch this with me," Henrik coaxed, patting the chair beside him, his voice a velvet veneer over the steel of his intentions.

Norah hesitated, her eyes wide and glistening with unshed tears. "Why?" she asked, her voice a tremulous whisper, betraying the confusion and fear she felt.

"To see a moment of history," Schultz replied smoothly, masking the venom of his plan with a grandfatherly smile. "Your daddy will be there too."

Her small body tensed, a rabbit poised to flee, but she took a step forward, driven by the innate desire to see her father, to find some solace in the chaos that had become her world.

As she settled into a chair positioned beside Schultz's much larger one, her gaze locked on to the screen. All the time, Schultz watched her, a predator in the guise of a protector.

***

The atmosphere at the inauguration was a powder keg of anticipation. Crowds filled the National Mall, their eyes fixated on the grand stage where history was about to be made. The solemn oath was moments away.

"Are you ready?" Jenny whispered into the comms, her voice barely audible over the hum of the crowd.

Wally, his fingers poised above the control panel inside his van, responded with a terse, "Ready."

On stage, Jackson Whitmore stood with dignity, his hand raised as he prepared to take the oath. "I, Jackson T. Whitmore, do solemnly swear that I will faithfully execute the office of president of the United States, and will to the best of my ability preserve, protect, and defend the Constitution of the United States," he intoned, his voice resonant and clear.

Noah, hidden within the crowd, felt the weight

of the Remington 700 Spectre beneath his cloak. His heart pounded in his chest, the gravity of the moment pressing down on him. The ceremony continued, interlaced with the team's final preparations, building to a climax no one would ever forget.

"And so help me God," Whitmore concluded, turning to face the crowd, a symbol of the nation's enduring values.

"Now!" Jenny's voice crackled through the comms.

In one fluid motion, Noah drew the customized Remington from beneath the quantum cloak. His finger hovered over the trigger, the crowd oblivious to its sudden presence, all eyes on the stage as he aimed the rifle directly at the newly sworn-in president.

Simultaneously, Wally pressed a button, activating the parametric speaker. A sharp crack, indistinguishable from a sniper's shot, sliced through the air. The sound, focused and precise, erupted in the path of the president.

Whitmore clutched his chest, stumbling back. Secret Service agents swarmed the stage with choreographed precision, enveloping the president in a protective cocoon. The crowd's breath hitched as a single, collective entity, their momentary silence erupting into a tidal wave of shock that swept over the National Mall. Faces painted in stark whites and deep shadows under the harsh January sun became a living mosaic, each tile a human countenance frozen in disbelief and burgeoning panic.

Noah, in the eye of this storm, threw down the rifle and went with the flow of bodies like a leaf on a river, his form a ghost amidst the rising chaos. As he slipped away, his departure was the silent slink of an apparition fleeing the break of day, his form merging with and then evaporating into the tapestry of frenzy and fear. On the camera feeds, now being diligently poured over, he was nothing but a smudge, ignored and unseen as he snuck from the site underneath part of the staging at the back.

Out on the street with the first of the fleeing masses, he quickly reached a stashed motorcycle that came alive under his command. Its engine's growl was a feral snarl, heralding the onset of an impending storm.

Waiting for him was Ralph, astride another black Ducati. With a decisive twist of the throttle, the pair catapulted forward, their bikes leaping into action like beasts unleashed, twin engines merging into a singular, formidable force racing against time.

Leading the way, Noah tore through the side streets of Washington, the clamor of the city a distant echo to the thunderous beat of his racing heart. Each pulse was a drumbeat spurring him on to the final, inevitable showdown.

***

In the secure room of Henrik Schultz's Washington stronghold, the inauguration played out on the large television screen, the president's fallen figure prominent at the podium, a Secret Service agent kneeling over him performing CPR. Norah sat beside the assassin, her small frame dwarfed by the leather chair, her eyes wide with a mix of fear and confusion.

"Look what your daddy did!" Schultz said gleefully, pointing at the screen where chaos had erupted. He offered a bowl of popcorn to Norah, who took it hesitantly, her gaze never leaving the screen.

As the scene unfolded, Schultz's face lit up with a victorious grin, convinced that his plan had reached its deadly conclusion. "Brilliant," he muttered to himself. "Absolutely brilliant."

***

Noah and Ralph cut through the crisp January air, the growl of their Ducatis a low purr against the city's raging dissonance. The grandeur of Schultz's stronghold emerged from the shadows, veiled behind the quaint façade of an old Washington manor, its wrought-iron gates and stone walls hiding the strategist within.

Ralph, carrying the weight of his recent past and a resolve sharpened by grief, rode with purpose. "I've been here before," he said, his voice barely carrying over the wind, "with Schultz. I know the place."

They dismounted with the synchronicity of seasoned operatives, stowing the bikes in the cover of overgrown ivy that clung to the manor's perimeter walls. Noah and Ralph then approached the manor with practiced stealth, their movements as silent as the frigid January day that enveloped them. Ralph led the way, his familiarity with the stronghold guiding them.

The old Washington manor, a façade of grandeur and history, concealed a nest of danger within its walls. Its imposing structure, adorned with ornate stonework and towering columns, stood as a testament to bygone opulence, casting a long, foreboding shadow in the evening light. As they neared the building, they could sense the presence of Schultz's men—highly skilled operatives, loyal and deadly.

"Four men," Ralph whispered, his eyes scanning the

interior through the darkened windows. "Trained by Schultz himself. We need to be quick and silent."

Noah nodded, his hand instinctively reaching for the suppressed P320 at his side. The two men split up, each taking a different route toward the manor, blending into the shadows like wraiths.

Noah moved through the underbrush, his steps light and calculated. He reached a back entrance, a door barely visible beneath the overgrowth. Silently, he picked the lock and slipped inside, the shadows of the manor swallowing him whole.

Inside, the air was still. Noah's senses heightened, every sound and movement was amplified in the quiet. He moved through the corridors, his footsteps muffled by the plush carpeting.

In the main hall, he encountered the first of Schultz's men, a shadowy figure patrolling the area. With the precision of a predator, Noah advanced when the man's back was turned, his movements fluid and soundless as he came swiftly up behind him. Before the man could react, Noah had him in a chokehold, swiftly and silently incapacitating him.

Meanwhile, Ralph, entering from the other side, encountered two operatives in a dimly lit room. Years of training kicked in as he engaged them, his movements a blur of efficiency as he fired two suppressed shots. In moments, the two men lay motionless on the floor, taken down with swift precision. It was clear to him that the men weren't expecting this attack.

Regrouping, Noah and Ralph moved deeper into the manor with a singular focus. The dimly lit corridors of the house were silent except for the soft echo of their movements. As they rounded a corner, they were abruptly confronted by the fourth operative, a hulking figure emerging from the shadows like a wraith— his hair the same dim strawberry-blond of all Adrian operatives, his face that same blank canvas.

The guy was quick, his movements honed by rigorous training, but Noah and Ralph were quicker, their reactions a product of necessity and survival. Ralph lunged first, his attack a feint designed to distract. The operative parried, turning his attention to Ralph, which provided Noah with the opening he needed.

In a fluid motion, Noah closed the distance, his hand striking with precision at the operative's exposed side. He targeted a vulnerable point, a nerve cluster that instantly weakened the man's stance. As the operative reeled from the strike, Ralph capitalized on his disorientation, delivering a powerful, upward elbow strike to the man's chin, snapping his head back.

The operative staggered, his training insufficient against the relentless assault. Noah then executed a swift, well-placed heel kick to the operative's knee, hyperextending the joint and sending a jolt of pain that buckled the man's leg. As he fell to one knee, Ralph finished the encounter with a controlled, powerful strike to the back of the operative's neck, a move designed to incapacitate without fatality.

The guy slumped silently against the wall, effectively neutralized, his fall soft, almost soundless. Noah and Ralph exchanged a quick, wordless glance, acknowledging the necessity of their actions, before a sudden muzzle flash cut through the darkness—a stark, deadly beacon.

Ralph's instincts were honed from years in the field;

he lunged, pushing Noah aside. The gunshot—a muted roar in the confined space—echoed off the walls as Ralph's body thudded to the ground.

"Noah…" His voice was a choked whisper as blood blossomed across his shirt. "Finish it… for her…"

Ralph had pushed Noah into another room. He stood with his back pressed against the cool wall, his breath steady and controlled. In his hand, he gripped the P320. Its weight was a familiar comfort in the mist of uncertainty. He could hear the measured steps of Henrik Schultz in the corridor outside, each footfall a reminder of the razor's edge upon which they stood. They were hunters, each aware of the other's presence, engaged in a deadly dance of intellect and will that was now reaching its end.

Schultz paused not far from the doorway. "Mr. Wolf," he hissed, his voice a blend of admiration and challenge, "I must admit, I didn't expect you to find me here. How did you manage it?"

From his concealed position, Noah's voice was calm, betraying none of the adrenaline coursing through his veins. "It was your virus, Henrik. The one your people used to infect Esmeralda. We found out it was phoning home—sending data back to a source."

A hint of surprise flickered in Schultz's tone. "You reverse-engineered my virus?"

"Exactly," Noah replied, his eyes fixed on the sliver of light from the corridor, anticipating Schultz's next move. "We broke down its code piece by piece, uncovered its communication protocol. It was designed to blend in, but we caught it. Every time it transmitted data, it revealed a bit more about its destination."

Schultz's shadow loomed larger at the doorway, his

presence an ominous threat. "And you traced it back to me…"

Noah's grip on the pistol tightened, ready for any eventuality. "We monitored the transmissions, followed the digital trail straight to your server. It wasn't easy. We had to get through layers of encryption, but it led us here, to you. And imagine my surprise to find out that, like me, you always like to stay close to the kill. It took us less than five minutes to ride here."

There was a moment of quiet acknowledgment from Schultz, a respect for his adversary's cunning. "Impressive. I didn't think you had it in you to play such a good game, Wolf."

Noah's voice was steady, imbued with a resolve born of countless battles. "I'm Camelot. We play every game, Henrik. And we play to win."

A moment of silence followed, only the men's breathing filling the space. The standoff in the corridor was a taut thread, poised to snap at the slightest provocation.

"So I take it," Schultz began, breaking the brief quiet, "the president isn't dead?"

Noah smiled. "No," he said with a smirk. "The president is alive and well. I just needed long enough to reach you. That was all. I knew that you'd want to watch it on the live CCTV feeds all around the Capitol. That you'd hack into the system to get a better view of it all. This was what gave us our final piece to locate you. You see, we're playing chess, Henrik, and I'm always two steps ahead. Remember?"

Schultz didn't say anything, not right away. But what Noah said must've burned because he flew into a rage. The tense silence in the corridor was shattered when, with a swift and practiced motion, the assassin lobbed a flash grenade into the room where Noah was concealed. The device spun through the air, its arc a brief, fatal dance. Noah, realizing Schultz's intent, squeezed his eyes shut and turned away, but not before the grenade erupted in a blinding flash and a deafening bang, disorienting him with its concussive force, throwing him against the wall.

Taking advantage of the momentary chaos, Schultz burst into the room, his assault rifle at the ready. The air thick with the stench of the grenade's discharge, specks of debris floated in the shafts of light that pierced the smoky air.

Noah, stunned but rapidly regaining his senses, reacted instinctively. He lunged toward Schultz, closing the distance before the latter could properly aim the rifle. The two men clashed, the sound of metal and grunts of effort filling the room.

In the scuffle, Noah managed to grip Schultz's rifle, pushing it upward as shots rang out, the spray of bullets harmlessly embedding themselves into the ceiling. Schultz, taken aback by Noah's ferocity, struggled to maintain control of his weapon. As did Noah with his own. Amid the tussle, his P320 was knocked from his grasp, clattering to the floor and skidding away. Simultaneously, with a forceful twist, Noah wrested the rifle from Schultz's hands, losing grip of it himself so that it clattered against the far wall, out of reach for both men.

Unarmed, the two stood face to face, their breathing heavy, bodies coiled into fighting stances. Noah's eyes, mirrors of the storm within, locked with Schultz's. Words were superfluous now. They circled, two primal forces. The atmosphere bristled with raw, unspoken fury as both men, now stripped of everything but their resolve, prepared to settle their fates with bare hands and bared souls.

The two men exploded into violence, slamming into one another with the force of colliding storms. Their fight was a blur of motion, an eruption of pent-up fury, desperation, and years of training. Schultz, embodying the raw power of Muay Thai, launched a barrage of elbows and knees, each strike a thunderous declaration of his intent. Noah, countering with the calculated precision of Krav Maga, deflected and parried, turning Schultz's own momentum against him.

Their movements were a tempest, Schultz's powerful roundhouse kicks slicing through the air, only to be met by Noah's swift Jiu-Jitsu takedowns. The rooms of the house became a chessboard of struggle, each fighter anticipating and countering the other's moves in a dance as old as combat itself.

In the thick of the battle, the world outside faded away, leaving only the sound of ragged breaths and the sharp impacts of flesh against flesh.

Noah's uppercut tore through the air with deadly intent, but Schultz, rooted in Judo's principles, seized the motion to flip his adversary. Noah, his body honed by Sambo's versatility, contorted mid-fall, landing with the grace of a predatory feline.

The battle raged on, an exchange of shattering Muay Thai elbows and Taekwondo kicks slicing the space between them, a maelstrom of martial prowess. Then, in a flash of steel, Schultz revealed yet another trick—a hidden blade that shot out and extended from his elbow. Noah's response was instinctual, a sidestep that whispered with mortality, the lethal glint passing just millimeters from his skin.

In that brief moment of evasion, Schultz capitalized on Noah's shifted focus. Like a serpent striking, he lunged forward, his arms wrapping around Noah's neck in a vise-like chokehold. The move was swift and precise, locking Noah in a desperate grasp that threatened to strangle the life from him. With a calculated maneuver, Schultz shifted his weight, using his body as a lever to bring Noah to his knees.

As they descended to the floor, Schultz's breath came in ragged gasps, yet his grip never wavered. "You know," he hissed close to Noah's ear, the exertion evident in his voice, "this is my preferred method of killing. Manual strangulation." The words dripped with a cold glee. "There's something… intimately final about watching the life fade from their eyes."

Nearby, an oval mirror hung on the wall, a silent observer to the deadly struggle. In its reflection, Schultz's eyes locked on to Noah's fading figure, a brutal scene framed in glass. Noah's struggle was mirrored back at them, his face contorted in a desperate fight for life, while Schultz's eyes gleamed with a cold, predatory satisfaction.

In the relentless crush of Schultz's grip, every sinew in Noah's body strained against the inexorable march toward oblivion, his breaths coming in short, ragged gasps. The room spun as oxygen became a scarce commodity, his vision starting to blur at the edges. His adversary's strength was a relentless tide, and Noah, caught in its deadly pull, felt his resistance ebbing away. Schultz's eyes bore into him from the mirror, a look of triumph just moments from fulfillment.

But destiny had not forsaken Noah yet. From the edge of death, a wounded Ralph emerged—a silent avenger, a ghost wrought from pain and purpose. He moved with the last vestiges of his strength, his approach unseen, his timing impeccable. As Schultz's arms constricted around Noah's throat with the promise of victory, Ralph struck. A blur of motion, a rush of air, and suddenly, the balance shifted.

The sharp edge of retribution, once poised to claim Noah's life, now turned its cruel kiss to Schultz as Ralph brought the tip of his hunting knife level with Schultz's right ear, his deathlike image just outside of the mirror's view. With the fury of an avenging angel, Ralph drove the blade of his knife home, and in that single, pivotal moment, Schultz's features slackened abruptly from ruthless intent to stunned disbelief, the handle of the knife sticking out of one side of his head.

As Schultz fell sideways, a lifeless puppet with strings abruptly cut, Ralph's battered form slumped beside him. Noah, meanwhile, spent a few seconds getting his breath back, as well as his eyesight. When he'd managed to gather himself, he quickly realized why he was still alive and made his way to Ralph, dropping to his knees beside him.

The chaos of battle had now faded into a solemn hush around them. Ralph's breaths were shallow, his voice a rasp. "I got… the bastard."

Noah's hand found Ralph's, a firm grip in the sea of fading light. "You did good, Ralph. You saved us all," he assured him, the past transgressions dissolving in the gravity of redemptive sacrifice.

A weak chuckle escaped Ralph's lips. "Guess… I'm forgiven?"

"Always," Noah confirmed, his voice thick.

As Ralph's light dimmed and then went out, Noah gently closed his eyes, a silent vow passing between them. A terrible despair filled him, cold and hollow, but then, suddenly, it was broken by the sound of a tender voice piercing the gloom.

"Daddy!" Norah's voice, small and powerful, filled the hallway. Noah turned, his heart lurching with relief and love as his daughter ran to him.

"Daddy, you came!" Her small arms encircled him, his world righted in that embrace.

"I promised, didn't I?" Noah's words were a whisper as he lifted her, cradling her against his chest, her safety his sworn duty.

"You did. You did," the little girl sobbed.

"Let's go home, sweetie."

Together, they left the house, stepping into the new dawn and leaving the shadows of the past behind.

***

In the aftermath of the staged assassination, Neil, Jenny, Marco, and Wally found themselves in the unique position of escorting the president to a secure location. As they drove through the city's quiet streets, the tension of the day slowly began to dissipate.

"You played your part perfectly, Mr. President," Marco remarked, glancing at the president through the rearview mirror.

Jackson Whitmore, looking more relieved than anyone in the vehicle, gave a weary but genuine smile. "Thank you, son. It was quite the performance, wasn't it?"

Neil and Jenny exchanged a look, a silent communication of their shared relief and disbelief. Wally, ever the tech expert, was already on his phone, ensuring their route remained secure and untracked.

As they navigated the darkening streets, Neil's phone buzzed, breaking the silence. It was Noah. "I've got good news and bad," he started, his voice heavy with the weight of the day. "Norah's safe. She's with me."

A collective sigh of relief filled the car, smiles breaking through the tension. But Noah wasn't finished. "Ralph… he didn't make it. He saved my life, stopped Schultz. But he's dead."

"What about Adrian?" Jenny asked.

"Schultz and all of Adrian's network, they're gone."

The car fell silent, a somber mood settling over its occupants. The president, overhearing the conversation, spoke up. "Your sacrifices will not go in vain. Our great nation owes you more than we can ever repay." His words were a solemn vow, a recognition of the gravity of their actions and the cost of their victory.

CHAPTER THIRTY-TWO

It was a day later when Jacques Monnet sat alone in his vast study, his silhouette barely distinguishable against the opulent backdrop of dark wood and ancient books. The room, usually a haven of tranquility and power, now felt like a gilded cage. Outside the latticed windows of his chateau, his sprawling estate stretched into the dusk, but the beauty of it was lost on him. He was a prisoner of his own making, a pawn in a game far beyond his understanding—and now far beyond his control.

The glass of cognac in his hand, a liquid gold that spoke of wealth and success, seemed a bitter mockery of his current predicament. The Cuban cigar, once a symbol of his indulgence and status, now hung listlessly between his fingers. His eyes, usually sharp and calculating, were clouded with fear as he stared out the window, lost in thoughts of impending doom.

Jacques was a low-ranking member of the Council. He had always known the risks, but the lure of power and the thrill of being part of something greater than himself had blinded him to the true nature of the game he was playing.

The secure line of his phone rang, shattering the eerie silence of the room. Jacques' heart skipped a beat as he reached for the receiver, his hand trembling uncontrollably. "Number Thirty-Four," a cold, disembodied voice greeted him. "This is Number Four."

"Bonjour, Number Four," Jacques managed to reply, his voice barely above a whisper.

"Your bringing the assassin into the fold has been a failure. Your attempts to destroy E & E and to hide your own identity, and thus the identity of the Council, have failed."

Each word was like a nail in Jacques' coffin.

"But the assassin did succeed in cutting off the head," Jacques pleaded desperately, clinging to any semblance of success. "He got us Allison Peterson, didn't he?"

"But not its best man. Noah Wolf is still alive, and so too is E & E," the voice retorted, as cold and unyielding as a razor blade.

Jacques felt a chill run down his spine. He knew the implications all too well. Failure was not tolerated within the Council, and the consequences were always dire.

"There will be other days to fight Noah Wolf and E & E," Jacques tried to reason, but his voice lacked conviction.

"But not for you, Number Thirty-Four," Number Four replied, his tone final.

Jacque's face drained of color. He knew what was coming, yet he couldn't help but plead, "But the assassin got to Connelly. The evidence was destroyed by his men."

"But your name is still known. Noah Wolf knows it. He will come for you," Number Four stated matter-of-factly.

"Then I will hide," Jacques said, a faint glimmer of hope in his voice.

"No. It has already been decided. The Council has decided. I am now going to hand you over to Number One for sentencing."

The line crackled with static as the call was transferred, and then an elderly man with a cold, cruel tone spoke. "Judgment has passed. You are to be a martyr, Number Thirty-Four. You understand?"

Shaking uncontrollably, Jacques answered in a half whisper, "Yes, sir. I understand."

The call ended abruptly, leaving Jacques in a deafening silence. He swallowed the cognac in one bitter gulp and pulled open a drawer of his desk. Inside lay the tools of his imminent martyrdom, a final testament to the consequences of failure within the ruthless world of the Council.

As he gazed out into the twilight, Jacques Monnet, once a man of power and influence, realized the tragic irony of his fate. In his pursuit of control, he had become the most controlled of all.

***

In the tranquil setting of Temple Lake, the final chapter of Noah's harrowing journey unfolded. Arriving at the farmhouse in the Charger, Noah and Norah were greeted by the shimmering waters of the lake that had once felt like a distant dream. As the car came to a stop, Norah's excited voice cut through the air from the passenger seat. "Mommy, Mommy!"

Sarah emerged from the house, her eyes widening with a mix of hope and disbelief. The moment she saw Norah clambering out of the car, tears streamed down her face. "My baby, you're safe!"

The family embraced, a tangle of arms, relief, and unspoken promises. "I thought I'd lost you both," Sarah sobbed, clinging to them.

"We're here, we're together," Noah reassured her, his voice thick with emotion as he wrapped his arms around his family. "That's all that matters now."

As the sun dipped below the horizon, its rays bathed the lake in a golden light, encapsulating the family in its warm embrace. In this moment, their love shone like a steadfast beacon, illuminating a path forward from the shadows that had once ensnared them.

As the family settled into the comforting embrace of the lake house, Noah's phone rang. It was Molly, her voice a mix of shock and relief. "French special forces just stormed Jacques Monnet's mansion in the Alps," she said. "They found him dead, a self-inflicted gunshot."

The news hung in the air, a final, somber note to their tumultuous symphony. Noah looked out over the lake, the ripples catching the last rays of the setting sun. "It's not over," he whispered, more to himself than to anyone else. The chapter of fear and shadow had closed, giving way to a night of peace and the promise of a new dawn.

EPILOGUE

In the grand and storied chamber of the Senate, with its soaring ceilings and stately columns, President Jackson T. Whitmore stood before the assembly, a commanding presence under the watchful gaze of history.

"Ladies and Gentlemen of the Senate," he began, his voice resonating through the hallowed hall. "Today we face enemies not at our borders but within the very fabric of our nation. Shadows that operate in silence, seeking to unravel the democracy we hold dear."

He paced his speech slowly, each word measured. "These hidden adversaries, these architects of deceit, they believe they can weaken us, divide us. But let me remind them—America was forged in the fires of resistance against tyranny, against those who sought to control us."

The room hung on his every word, the air charged with an unspoken urgency. "We expelled the British crown to build a nation of the people, by the people, for the people. And we will stand against any force, any entity that dares to threaten that foundation."

His voice rose, a crescendo of conviction. "This nation, our great America, will not yield to shadowy threats. We will arm ourselves with truth, with unity, and with the unyielding resolve that has defined us since our inception. We are a nation birthed from the courage to dream, to fight, and to achieve the unthinkable. Let this be a clarion call to every corner of our nation: that we shall not be undone by fear nor fractured by division. Instead, we shall rise, as we have always risen, united and indomitable in our pursuit of liberty and justice for all. Together, as one nation, indivisible, we will not only endure; we will prevail, and ensure that the lamp of freedom burns brightly for generations to come. Onward, to a future forged by our collective will, determination, and the unwavering belief in the enduring promise of America."

The Senate erupted in applause, Senators rising to their feet, moved by the president's words—a stirring call to action against the unseen enemies of their cherished republic.

As the chamber continued to reverberate with the echoes of applause, one senator slipped away unnoticed, his expression a mask of indifference. In the dimly lit back corridors of the Capitol, he dialed a number with a practiced hand.

"Yeah, they're lapping it up," he reported, his voice a low murmur.

The response was calm and calculated. "Don't worry, Number Eighteen. We merely regroup and lick our wounds. Like we always have throughout the centuries. You see, we have always played the long game. And we always win in the end. Noah Wolf or no Noah Wolf." The call ended, leaving the senator alone in the shadows, the weight of the conversation heavy in the air.

***

At the joint funeral of Allison Peterson, Diana, and Ralph, the mood was somber, the air thick with grief and remembrance. The team, a family forged in adversity, gathered to pay their respects.

Noah stood stoic, his eyes a deep well of unshed tears. Sarah was beside him, her hand a comforting presence on his back. Little Norah, dressed in a black dress that seemed too solemn for her youth, clutched her father's hand tightly.

Neil, usually not one for emotion, found himself overwhelmed, tears slipping down his cheeks. Jenny, his wife and pillar of strength, wrapped an arm around him.

Wally stood quietly, head bowed, lost in his thoughts and the memories of fallen comrades.

Doc Parker, a mentor and guide to many, looked on with a face etched in sorrow, his eyes reflecting the loss of not just colleagues but family.

As the priest's eulogy flowed, a tribute to the bravery and sacrifice of the departed, each member of the team was caught in their own reflections, united in their grief and their determination to honor the legacy left behind by their fallen friends.

***

Back at the serene lake house, the mood was a blend of somber reflection and a quiet resolve. Sarah, ever the gracious host, brought out coffee and freshly baked Danishes, setting them on the table with a gentle smile. Norah played quietly in a corner, her innocence a stark contrast to the gravity that hung over the adults.

Outside, overlooking the tranquil expanse of

Temple Lake, Noah, Neil, and Jenny stood together. It was here they made their pact, fueled by a need for justice and a deep-seated desire for revenge. "We'll find them all," Neil said, his voice firm. "Every last one of the Council's leaders."

Jenny nodded, her eyes hard. "The president has given us his word. Unlimited resources. We'll tear them down, piece by piece."

As they stood in silent agreement, Noah's gaze was distant, thoughtful. "There's something else," he finally said.

The others turned to him. "What is it?" Jenny asked.

"I'm pretty certain," Noah said, his words heavy, "that Diana and Ralph weren't the only moles in E & E. There's at least another one, still hidden. And I intend to root them out."

The declaration hung in the air, a new mission, a new purpose. As the sun set over Temple Lake, casting a golden hue over its calm waters, the trio stood resolute, their pact sealed. Team Camelot faced a future fraught with danger and uncertainty, but their determination was unshakable. With the promise of retribution against the Council and the hidden enemy within E & E, their journey was far from over. But in that moment, as the day gave way to night, they found strength in their unity.

ALSO BY DAVID ARCHER
& VINCE VOGEL

To see what else we have to offer, please
visit our respective websites.

www.davidarcherbooks.com
www.vincevogel.com

Thank you once again for reading our work!

Printed in Great Britain
by Amazon

38498319R00192